Love in Tennessee

For Nora,
A new great friend
who made my evening
et Cornelia St Cafe,
NYC   Warmest regards,
            John

john.bowers76@gmail.com

Also by John Bowers

The Colony
No More Reunions
Helene
The Golden Bowers
In the Land of Nyx
Stonewall Jackson
Chickamauga/Chattanooga

The Remembrance of Things Present (A Play)

Love in Tennessee

JOHN BOWERS

 RED HEN PRESS | *Los Angeles, CA*

Love in Tennessee
Copyright © 2009 by John Bowers
All rights reserved

Book layout by Sydney Nichols

Library of Congress Cataloging-in-Publication Data

Bowers, John, 1928-
 Love in Tennessee / by John Bowers. — 1st ed.
   p. cm.
 ISBN 978-1-59709-456-6
 1. Tennessee—Fiction. 2. New York (N.Y.)—Fiction. I. Title.
 PS3552.O873L68 2009
 813'.54—dc22
                    2009027652

The Annenberg Foundation, the James Irvine Foundation, the Los
Angeles County Arts Commission, and the National Endowment for
the Arts partially support Red Hen Press.

First Edition

Published by Red Hen Press
Los Angeles, CA
www.redhen.org

To our wonderful group who helped more than I can say and who made this book possible: Laura Shaine Cunningham, Ron Nyswaner, Nina Shengold, Zach Sklar, Mary Louise Wilson, and Da Chen.

For Lale

Contents

Part III

The Tennessee Waltz

Will it come like a change in the weather?
Will its greeting be courteous or rough?
Will it alter my life altogether?
O tell me the truth about love.

—W.H. Auden

Like Tennessee, New York is as much a state of mind as a place. I saw Manhattan for the first time when my father, mother, and I came by train to visit my big brother who was stationed in the army in nearby Brooklyn. It was shortly before the Second World War, and my father was a telegrapher for the Southern Railway. We came on passes. On the trip we ate meals of country fried chicken and deviled eggs my mother had prepared and stored in a former Christmas fruitcake tin, never imagining going to the dining car or buying sandwiches from the hawkers who passed. We came from a small town in East Tennessee and the Great Depression was still with us.

When the train pulled into Penn Station and we alighted, a whole new breathtaking world opened. I was eight and I became smitten. New York was something. The place was big. Can you imagine its size to someone whose main drag back home was one block long? Can you imagine the sight of double-decker buses going up and down Fifth Avenue to someone used to wagons carrying hay and watermelons?

High up in a hotel on Times Square, our windows opened onto grit, the klaxons of taxis, and muffled shrieks far down below. You pulled a chain from a box up above the toilet and water cascaded down. I kept doing that, time after time. We went to real live restaurants, the picnic fare in the fruitcake tin long gone. Waiters wore tuxedoes or aprons around their middles, sharper than anyone I ever met in Tennessee. I got to go to the Automat where I almost fainted in ecstasy. You got to watch a sandwich whirl into view. Then after wiggling a coin or two into a slot, you could open a tiny door and pull one out. It was magic.

We went to the Aquarium in Coney Island and I got to look an octopus in the eye. My mother who used to teach school got to go to the Main Public Library. My father, whose county back home was "dry," got to go to a saloon. We journeyed down to Union Square to watch men in short sleeves make wild speeches atop wooden boxes. My tall strong father hoisted me up in his arms so I could see better; my mother was young and pretty. My father told my brother, who was in uniform, not to say anything because he might set off an anarchist. The danger almost thrilled me to death. There was no place like New York. I made up my mind right then to return.

Part I

On the Road to Eros

the secrets of the barn

The barn sat out back from our house. In the middle of the night you could hear its planks groan and the tin roof rattle. The hard packed ground inside had a strand or two of straw from bygone days and there were a few rotting boards up on high where a hay loft had been and down below stalls for long-gone horses.

I learned the trick of climbing inside and outside the barn, wiggling through a loft window, then straddling the high peaked roof. It took a lot of maneuvers and toeholds and swinging by my hands, but I could do it in my sleep. An ancient apple tree that produced nuggets the size of golf balls shaded the peaked roof. Up on the roof it felt dangerous, and the thrill was enlarged because I had been told, over and over, not to climb up there. I couldn't help it. From up there I could see the home of Miss Mary Louise Luster who taught mathematics in high school. I sat there and imagined her lifting her skirt up. Her uncle, a man who walked around town with one shoulder lower than the other and with the nub of a wet cigar always sticking out the side of his mouth, once talked a couple of my chums and me into the barn to watch him flail away at himself. He said what came out was buttermilk, but we knew that wasn't so. We didn't know exactly what was going on, but we knew never to look him in the eye on the street or get alone with him again. We knew not to tell our parents or anyone else about it.

We didn't even mention it to each other later. But whatever he had stirred up I easily transferred over to his niece, Miss Mary Louise Luster. She had watery blue eyes, which I took as a sure sign that she was caught up in some outlawed practices herself. Any number of things might be going on with her. Up on the roof, all alone, I liked to think of Miss Luster coaxing me into her house, gazing at me with those watery blue eyes, and then doing all sorts of shadowy things. For variety's sake, I liked to conjure up Miss Josephine Pouter, our librarian, and the fact that I had once glimpsed white flesh above her rolled stocking. I sat on the peaked roof and thought of that and grew faint.

Up on the roof you could think your thoughts. But the outside kept encroaching. First, the cows. Mr. Burstein, our neighbor, got the idea to have cows, and he was fearless in the pursuit of an idea. Mr. Burstein wore glasses that worked their way down his nose, and he was always on the move. My father had a weakness for Mr. Burstein. Generally my father didn't like businessmen, certainly no one in the Republican Party, but he clicked with Mr. Burstein. They complemented each other. My father was often out of work. Mr. Burstein was always working; he couldn't work enough. The trouble was, all of Mr. Burstein's ventures, try as he might, went bankrupt. They were curious about each other, but wary. My father was a loner and few came to visit him, and he seldom ventured to other people's houses. He and Mr. Burstein conferred in our side yard or on the street.

My father told Mr. Burstein stories that always ended with a chortle. My father had grown up on a farm with eleven brothers and sisters. Chance had brought him to this town, married with two sons, and now he worked for the railroad. He seemed unhappy in any line work, amused the rest of the time or brooding. Mr. Burstein was there in town with two sons much older than me, married to a woman with the biggest tits I'd ever seen. He liked to poke around town looking for opportunities. He had somehow ended up in East Tennessee from Eastern Europe. When, why, or how he never brought up. No one wondered much about how anyone had got there. Mr. Burstein and family just had got there—like the rest of us. From somewhere else. One of Mr. Burstein's sons later went on to Harvard and came back with what passed as an English accent.

Mr. Burstein's idea was to lodge the cows in the barn and share any profit with my father. He furnished the cows; my father provided the barn. Almost immediately the cows pushed the loose boards aside like matchsticks and headed for downtown. No one kept cows in town. No one. Only Mr. Burstein would come by a herd somehow and plan to house and milk them in a barn gone to seed, in a railroad town of 28,000, where milk came bottled. When my father saw the cows break free, he got on the phone and soon Mr. Burstein came racing, pushing his glasses up his nose and shrieking. God knows how much money he had tied up in the cows. It was the Great Depression and this looked like another flop. First an apartment house, then a haberdashery; now a herd of cows. "*Mien Gott,* stop!"

Before our very eyes he jumped on the back of the lead cow like a cowboy and wrestled her back toward the barn, the herd following. My father and my older brother, along with Mr. Burstein, flew into nailing up enough boards to hold in the cows. I pleaded for a hammer but Harold my older brother told me it had to be done in a hurry and to forget about it. I wanted to hold a hammer, do a job, and be a man so much.

The cows went. I never got a chance to name a single one or try to milk one. A particular one reminded me of Ernie Banks from school. When it turned its large brown soulful eyes on me I thought of good old Ernie and how he looked when a math problem stumped him and everyone else had the answer. One day the cows were there, then gone. Afterwards came the buggies. It was another inspiration from Mr. Burstein. Only Mr. Burstein could envision buying buggies in the day of the automobile and hope to unload them for a profit. Only my father would be so amused and impressed by the size of his vision that he would go along with it. The buggies were not falling apart like the barn, but they had seen their day. It wasn't time for them to go into a museum, but you never saw a horse pulling a buggy on the town's paved streets. Automobiles ruled.

The buggies stretched from inside the barn to up near our house. One day it was just that old decrepit apple tree in front of the barn; now those buggies were lined up, going inside the barn. Where the buggies came from I never knew. I liked to think that Mr. Greenway down on Market Street might have had a hand in it. Mr. Greenway sold horse collars and bridles in a dim, leather-reeking shop that saw few customers. Mr. Greenway couldn't believe that the day of the horse was over. He still walked down Boone Street every morning, bright and early, a tall, erect, unsmiling man in a tie and suspenders, and stayed in that shop where dust motes fell like snow until evening, and no one came in, or if so, to buy a small leather strip for luggage. The only nag in town pulled an ice wagon, and perhaps the sight of the ice wagon, in the age of the refrigerator, gave him hope. Mr. Burstein had hope for the return of the buggy, too, even as planes flew overhead, taking off and landing in an airfield out in the country that had been a cow pasture.

* * *

I was soon swinging in and out of the buggies, playing games, pretending I was fighting in the French Revolution or in the Wild West. These buggies outdid cars in everything but in having a motor. They had doors. They had shades. The seats were leather. Inside there were glass vases attached near the doors for flowers. I was thrilled to dart around in the buggies, but outside I felt ashamed. No one else had buggies in their backyards. They had cars in a garage. We had no car.

Before long I had company in the buggies, which pleased and alarmed me. Margaret Henry from around the corner started playing in them with some girlfriends. Margaret was ages older, maybe sixteen. She was wild, the story went. Once Mr. Henry, her father, stayed longer than he should at the American Legion Hut, far out on Main Street, and lingered there until the band struck up and the dancing began. Margaret was sent by her mother to retrieve him. The Hut was where men and a few women, sometimes their wives, whooped it up on Saturday night. Mr. Henry was one of the men in town I liked to watch as if I could learn something. He was slight and dapper and used to leave his house in a slow shuffle that picked up steam the minute he got a few yards away, lighting up, squaring his shoulders, nodding, and calling out greetings. Mrs. Henry was formidable, like Maggie of *Jiggs and Maggie* in the comics. You could hear her powerful voice booming through an open window at night. Mrs. Henry had pale orange hair streaked with gray. Her daughter Margaret had a carrot top and was a bundle of energy. She went to the American Legion Hut to retrieve her father and, so the story went, stayed to dance. When they returned in the wee hours, her mother's screams could be heard for blocks.

Out our back kitchen window I watched in fascination as Margaret and some girls her age stepped in the buggies. They had unearthed long dresses and bonnets from trunks somewhere. They were tall enough, filled out enough, to wear their mothers', or more likely, their grandmothers' long-ago castoffs. They were far from being little girls, and they playacted being back in the horse-and-buggy days. I liked the way they lifted their long skirts, put a foot on a step, and hoisted themselves inside. I could only imagine what they were doing inside with the curtains closed. Pretending to drink tea?

After awhile I was recruited to join them. After all, it was my backyard. I in turn coaxed some neighborhood boys my own age to join the game. Jamey Powell was the first. He was Margaret Henry's cousin, and he had startled me once when he matter-of-factly reported what had happened between Margaret and him in her henhouse. He was not inventive, never embellished anything, so his plain words had caused my knees to go weak. Ernie Banks, who had a bevy of good-looking older sisters, was another story. He embellished facts so that his yarns about peeking through a knothole while a big sister took a bath took on Biblical proportions. I knew he made most of it up, maybe all of it, but he needed friends and this was one way to get them. I was mesmerized by his narratives and made him go back to fill in details if he went too fast.

"Stop, Ernie. What'd she get out of? How'd she get in? What'd it look like?"

We all had ideas of what "it" might look like because of outlandish drawings found here and there, but confirmation could only come from those who had been at the front. Wild stories came back, in songs and ditties, and the wilder they got, the better. One ditty had to do with Miss Hart, a sexy spinster down the block. A couplet told how she sat on a rock and every week a barber came by to shave her twat. I imagined old man Lurie from the Congress Barber Shop, a man with a caved-in chest and trembling hands, lathering up and running his straight razor up and down the leather strop, and then, just as he set to work, looking down through the bottom of his glasses at her twat the way he did when snipping my hair.

We all knew the positions in lovemaking thanks to a trio of colored teenagers who had once dropped by the barn to put on a show. It featured one girl and two boys. All stayed fully clothed in overalls. "We going to show you how it's done. That is, if you give us a nickel."

We came up with five cents. The girl, who was wiry and had skin like gray slate and was slightly shorter than the boys, immediately fell to the ground with her legs spread. A boy jumped in between while she shot her legs around him. They went into a frenzy for a while, bucking up and down, and then he alighted and she rolled over on her hands and knees. The other boy sank behind her and the frenzy started all over. There were other positions assumed, we couldn't believe it, all taken in a crisp, no-nonsense way. At the end of the performance, which didn't take very long, one boy said, "Anybody here got hairs?"

None of us had them. None of us knew what to say. We were too awestruck by what five cents had already brought. We never considered asking the performers to show us anything more, nor did they volunteer more. They had their dignity. Playacting was all any of us could handle. If we saw the real thing we might never recover. We must also never tell our parents or any adult about any of this.

It was the same with what happened in the buggies. An older girl would take one of us younger boys into a buggy as her escort or swain or suitor or whatever was thought up. We were playing, as the bright-eyed girl who had selected me said, "a drive out in the country—do-si-do, choose your partner, and away we go!" Her name was Erin and I had never seen her around before. She came from another neighborhood that could have been at the end of the earth for all I knew. She was a vision. I came up to just above her waist, but she took my arm as if I might be six-foot and looming.

"Thank you, sir" she said, as I pretended to guide her into the buggy.

She smiled a glorified smile once inside. She swept off a bonnet and pinned back her hair and I saw that she shaved under her arms. She wore a sleeveless blouse. "Where shall we drive to today, sir? Out in the country? Out for some fresh air? *Out in the woods?*"

"In the woods" meant something thrilling beyond human belief. I couldn't speak. I wasn't required to. Erin put her head out the window and called back to Margaret Henry, who was with Jamey Powell in the next buggy. "Hey, Trickshot's brother and I are going in the woods!"

Margaret Henry squealed behind us. My brother's real name was Harold, the name I called him by. To the outside world, though, he was Trickshot. He was the star athlete in town and had come by his nickname because of the impossible shots he made in basketball.

"Is Trick around today?" she said to me. People who knew him well shortened his name to Trick. I could only shake my head. I couldn't speak. I was still thinking about going "in the woods." Way back I could hear Ernie Banks whooping it up with someone. He sounded hysterical.

"Want to do this?" Erin said, and she reached over, sudden as lightning, and put her lips right smack dab against mine. My eyes stayed open and I saw that hers shut. She had the tiniest of blonde fuzz on her upper lip. I inhaled a scent that took me back to my mother's mysterious dressing table with its array of powders and rouge and perfumes. Erin moved her lips swiftly over mine and then it was done. She didn't give what we had done a name. Then she hugged me and I hugged her back.

She spoke more to Margaret Henry than she did to me. She kept poking her head out the buggy window and looking back. "Hey, Trick's brother and I are having a fine time in the woods! What about you?"

More squeals.

I kept tapping her on the shoulder and making the barest of puckers. She never refused or hesitated. She brought her lips down on mine, squirmed them against each other for a second or two, and then went back to throwing her head out the window or talking about my brother. She wanted me to get out of the buggy like a gentleman and pretend I was helping her down. I can't remember ever seeing her again.

The buggies left the barn and backyard the same way the cows had. Few remembered later they had been there. One day there, then gone. Whether Mr. Burstein or my father made a profit or lost money was unclear; the latter I suppose. It was now just the barn, the aged apple tree, and me. I climbed the roof, took a bite or two of a rock-hard green apple and got back my own private kingdom once again. I could think up my own fantasies and playact all sorts of dramas and depended on no one. I had it to myself.

But I'm forgetting June Lunt. She lived in a rundown house around the corner and several houses down. Every so often you came across a rundown house in our neighborhood. Someone had run out of luck or never had any luck. Mrs. Lunt was a widow lady who was raising a large family. They could hardly fit in the house. To top it off, a poor, hard-drinking man took up residency there on occasion and she had a son by him, a baby who rolled around in diapers that reeked to high heavens. From every one of the few rooms there came a scent of pee that couldn't all be blamed on the baby. I was drawn to the house and household by its anarchy and the notion that I was breaking some taboo by going there. It was thrilling to step inside. But after a while I got the idea suggested to me by my mother that I shouldn't be visiting the Lunts so much. We ourselves had what could pass at times for an orderly household, with meals on time and reading a book after dinner a major form of entertainment. Few came to visit us. What for?

June was my age. We started the first grade together. She had dimples in her cheeks and blonde curly hair like Shirley Temple. The first day in school she helped me color in some drawings. I didn't know what "coloring" was and couldn't understand the teacher's tart words of instruction. June showed me and was patient in doing so. I liked to steal looks at her in first grade and I caught her looking at me. My older brother liked to roll his eyes and whisper "June Lunt" to me at the dinner table. Just that. "June Lunt." No one would be speaking, everyone lost in thought, chewing reflectively, and he'd say "June Lunt," out of the blue. If I held my anger and didn't say anything he would begin singing, "My little June-ey, my little June-ey, my love." I would break. I screamed. My mother would stop us. If she couldn't my father would. The name "June Lunt" was banished from the dinner table. From then on my brother would roll his eyes in the direction of the Lunt house, point quickly with his thumb, and mouth "June Lunt." I would scream and he would say, "What? What have I done? I haven't said anything."

Could he have known? How could he, he never went near the barn, it was way off his beaten track. But I felt he knew. I gave him credit for knowing everything. Somehow, miraculously, he knew about me and June Lunt.

After the cows and buggies had gone, after a period of quiet, June Lunt would wiggle through a small hole in the back of the barn and we would meet. One day it was just understood that this would be so. She would lift her dress and take down her underpants. I would pull myself out, what there was to pull out. We looked. That was it. That was all. That was it. It was our secret.

buck, brownie, and beyond

The idea bubbled up around the time my mother read to me *The Call of the Wild*. I had to have a dog, a dog like Buck, a sled dog that persevered through humiliation and ill treatment and pulled his load and stayed loyal to the one man that cared for him. I dreamed and cried and whined for my very own Buck.

It also happened that around this time my mother said to me, "What would you think about having a little brother or sister?"

My older brother Harold was as removed from me as a star in the galaxy, and the idea of holding a little brother or sister began inflaming my mind. I would protect that newcomer. I would watch it grow and take on an identity, and I would be close to it in a way I could never get with my big brother. I love you, little brother!—or sister, I amended, to be on the safe side. My mother went around in those days with a quiet, reflective air. She kept a faint smile on her face. As for me, I would teach my new brother to play checkers and shoot marbles. We would collect stamps and write to President Roosevelt for his autograph. On the other hand, I would watch my new sister wow everyone with her good looks and smarts, a minia-ture of my mother. I went around with these images dancing in my head until the moment I saw my mother's daily expression change. She stopped being dreamy. She stopped talking about a new companion for me. My father remained stoical as usual, on the sidelines as always.

I went back to whining full-time for a dog—at the dinner table, before sleep at night, on waking in the morning—while being told over and over to hush until one afternoon an apple-cheeked man in overalls and straw hat knocked on our door with a delivery: a dog. It was not a sled dog, but it was a dog. I named him Buck immediately. He was no longer a puppy, but he was small. He was white with black spots, and his coat was made up of short stiff bristles. He was highly excitable as if searching for something familiar, and until finding it, seeking to please the world. You would look at him and he would begin rolling over and over. Someone before may have taught him the trick as a sure-fire way to please a master, and by now a direct command was not required. Give Buck a glance and he would begin spinning.

Commands to me from my folks filled the air. Buck was to live in the basement. He was not allowed to roam and roll over above in the rest of the house. I must keep a water bowl filled for him at all times. I was to take down scraps of food for him to eat. I was to take him out for play and fresh air. I was responsible when he went outside in the vacant lot beside our house for a taste of freedom.

The basement was a world all its own and one I annexed in my own way as I had the decrepit barn out back. Steep narrow steps with a light switch at the head led down to it from inside. There was a coal furnace and a coal bin and a hard-packed dirt floor. A small narrow breeze port, with wooden slats, let in air. You got in through a storm door from the outside.

I flew into the tasks that would make Buck feel at home. I brought him the best leftover meat from meals. His water bowl never came close to empty. I filched one of my own blankets for him to lie on. After school, rain or shine, I took him to the vacant lot to let him be himself. Before bed I switched on the light at the head of the stairs and called down, "Goodnight, Buck!"

Somewhere down there I could hear him rolling over and over.

Buck was too excitable to ever talk to, to tell my troubles to and sympathize with what I assumed his to be. When he saw me coming in through the storm door after school let out, he went into ecstasy, twisting his haunches back and forth like a hula dancer and jerking his head up and down. That was the moment I got the chance to hold him, to get my nose into his bristles, and smell him. He had a rich furry animal scent. The man in overalls who had brought him had the same aroma. They smelled of the country and woodlands. Those from the city didn't smell that way.

Let out on the vacant lot Buck raced around in a large circle, taking time out to leap up and down on me before racing around and around, again and again. Until the moment the arc widened to take him into the street. I called. I screamed. He may have thought I was encouraging him—or he may have loved this taste of free-dom—for he shot his bullet head back to look at me, just before he landed under the wheels of a car. I looked. I put my hands to the sides of my head. *No!* I've just got back from school! I'm just letting him out for air! This is too quick! I saw him rolling over and over as if trying to please the monster above before a wheel came down on him and he lay still for the first time since I had had him.

* * *

"You must stop crying," my mother said later. "Nothing will bring Buck back." My father said little. His own boyhood on a farm had hardened him to any loss of an animal. He was not sentimental.

My own heart was broken, and the sheer grandeur of the epic-sized grief I could throw myself in even dumbfounded me. I was awed by its power. I wallowed in it. It might still be going on to this day except that a new dog arrived to take Buck's place. Another apple-cheeked countryman brought him and handed him over. The bundle was not a puppy but he was not fully grown either, the farmer assured us. He could be "trained." He was mine.

I named him Brownie because he was all brown. Harold said, "Brownie, eh? How original." I was unaware of irony back then and took this as a compliment. I sought my big brother's approval. Brownie took over the blanket in the basement that still held Buck's scent and that Brownie sniffed thoroughly before settling down.

Brownie was not a bundle of energy like Buck, but he was not devoid of signs of affection. I would spend hours with him down in the basement until called above for supper or to do home work. He was not big, he was no Lab, and he cradled neatly in my arms, against my shoulder and cheek, while I talked to him. Occasionally he reached up to lick my cheek in a slow languid motion, which I thought was to demonstrate his understanding of the sentiments I was expressing. I asked him about his day, what he'd found to do in the basement while I'd been gone and at school. Did he miss the farm he had left? He reached up to lick my face the same way he had when I was going on about Mr. Gerwin, a teacher in the sixth grade with Coke-bottle glasses and a pasty face who terrified me with a squinty-eyed glance. I told Brownie about my yearning to play midget football next year in the seventh grade. I told him things I never told anyone else. I kissed him on his wet muzzle and he squirmed a little bit at its unusualness but didn't squirm out of my arms. It was a pretty daring thing to do, I thought, kiss a dog on its muzzle. I wouldn't tell anyone about it.

Brownie did not like to race around on the vacant lot as Buck had, searching for the farm or someone he'd left. Brownie stuck to our tiny front yard that bordered the sidewalk. I never had to worry about his going in the street. He lay in the grass while I banged a ball against the side of the house, pretending I was slinging a forward pass until someone screamed for me to stop. He lay contentedly or frisked around dutifully to stretch his legs and now and then trotted up to me—but his job in the front yard now seemed to be to keep a lookout for intrusion, for someone or something that might endanger the home he was now part of. Or maybe he was just keeping an eye out for someone who might take him back to the farm. He never went after a ball that got away from me and went into the street. He always leaped and greeted anyone in the family, even my brother who had no time for him. Brownie, though, bared his teeth to everyone else—Mr. Winters the milkman, the postman, all neighbors who passed on the sidewalk, and he barked and barked. He never bit anyone, though.

I felt he didn't like being cooped up in the basement. Who would? It might be warm and cozy down there, but Brownie needed fresh air and grass under his paws and some semblance of freedom. I let him have the run of the front yard even while I was at school. When I returned there he always was delighted to see me, tail wagging. Then I took him to the basement, fed him and filled his water bowl, and talked confidentially to him. But something wasn't quite right. I had a dog and I was proving I could take care of him, but I didn't deserve to be so giddy about it. There must be a price to pay. And I was right. I came home from school one bright fall day, when leaves covered the front yard, and Brownie was not there. I ran in the house to my mother. Where's Brownie?

She sat with her hands folded in her lap. She explained quietly that Brownie had been upsetting the neighbors. They feared walking in front of the house because of the barking and the baring of teeth. Brownie had been taken back to the country. "That's really the place for him," she said. "He's not really meant for the city. We had to do it."

I cried. I cried and cried and it went on for days and nights. It stopped when my mother faced me and began crying herself in a heartrending way. I had never seen her cry before. I never cried again over the loss of anything.

* * *

But the yearning to hold and cherish a creature did not die. Ducks followed. I got a drake and a female down on Market Street not long after they had cracked open their eggs and entered the world, when they were fuzzy little peeping yellow things. I figured they would grow up and produce more ducks. I paid a nickel apiece for them. I brought them home in the side pockets of my thin jacket and they wiggled and felt warm in there. At first I kept them in the windowed pantry off the kitchen. As we ate dinner at the round oak table in the kitchen, Harold would look up, act startled, and say, "Hey, who's that going peep, peep, peep? I think I hear peeping."

"You know perfectly well," my mother would say, as I got set to explode the next time he pulled it. I had permission.

Soon the peeps turned to quacks and the pantry couldn't contain them full-time. Whenever their quacks got out of hand I cracked open the pantry door and they paraded through the kitchen, through the hall and living room, to the front bedroom, and then circled back to the pantry. "Those things are looking for a place to swim," Harold said, and hooted. "Where you going to do it? In the bathtub?"

"They do need to swim," my mother said as they squawked and waddled past her.

I saw what might come next: that farmer with apple cheeks in bib overalls knocking on the door. On Saturday before the sun got hot I took a spade and dug a hole in our side yard where the vacant lot began. "What the dickens are you doing?" my brother said, pausing a moment on his way in the house. "That won't hold water for two seconds." He paused a second more. "Let's just eat them for supper and be done with it."

I walked two miles to Patty Lumber Yard on the outskirts of town and ordered up a fifty-pound bag of cement and a hundred-pound bag of sand. My head came just a little above the counter. The man behind the counter, a man with a stiff neck and a distracted air as if looking for something in the distance, didn't blink. He took the change I handed him from the money I'd saved from my allowance, and plopped the two bags before me. Maybe it was too complicated to think of a little boy carrying away two heavy bags. The two bags outweighed me about two to one. He went on to the next customer and didn't give me a second glance.

I hugged the cement bag against my chest, supported in part by my belt, and carried it to the corner, where I propped it against a lamppost. Then I staggered back and struggled with the bag of sand to the same spot. It was not the easiest thing to do. I rested against the lamppost myself, and my heart pounded. But I was going to get home with these two bags, I knew I would. It took me half a day. I weaved down half a block with one, then came back for the other. No one asked what I was doing. No car stopped, no head popped out of a window to ask if I needed a lift. I didn't want help anyhow. I didn't want a lift. I didn't want it affirmed that we didn't have a car at home. I didn't want anyone to guess how much I was beginning to love my two ducks and was going to build a pool for them.

After I dropped the bags next to the hole I'd dug I felt I was walking on air. My arms tingled as if a great weight had been removed—as it had. I didn't wait to recover my full strength. I was too excited about the adventure of making a mix that would turn into hardened cement. I shoveled the sand and concrete dust together in a tin wagon from a Christmas past, ran water from a hose over it, and turned it into gunk. Then I spread it like jam around the sides and bottom of the hole with a large gravy spoon I had lifted from the kitchen drawer. I was so excited I could hardly slow down my hands. It wasn't at all like work. I was doing this for my ducks.

Harold dropped by. "That'll never work," he said. "You need wooden support or mesh or something. That won't stick to dirt."

It did, though. It did. Only now I must wait until it hardened. Right before bed I went out to check on the hardening process in the moonlight. It was like putty still. The next day was fiercely bright and by late afternoon the texture had stiffened to a lighter gray and you couldn't make an imprint with your finger. I gave it another night and then at high noon the following day I filled it with water from the garden hose. I waited, wonder-struck, and the water didn't go down but a smidgen.

I carried the ducks up from the basement where I'd been forced to take them because they'd truly outgrown the pantry and Harold had complained mightily about their parading through the living room when he had his buddies over. Plus, their droppings didn't always find their way to the newsprint I spread out on the pantry floor. Once there had been a squirting, caused by some rich stuffing I'd fed them, that landed as they rounded the bedroom on the way back.

They were happy to see daylight and squawked in my arms as I put them beside the pool that was now theirs. I had named them Pap and Mammy, my first choice being vetoed. I had wanted to call them Tip and Stella, my parents' first names, but when I tried it out on my mother she looked vaguely puzzled. It probably wasn't right to name ducks after your folks. Harold let us all know that. So, they became Pap and Mammy. They went right into the pool with no coaxing, as if they had just been waiting around for it to appear and knew exactly what to do. They had just waited around for me to get the cement and sand home and do the job. They splashed around, went under a couple of times, showing off, then flapped their wings and got out. They lay beside it and made it home and would never return to the basement or pantry again.

However you can love a duck, I loved my ducks. I spent hours by the kitchen window watching how they scratched their small heads set off by piercing black eyes. I watched how they shook all over and ruffled their feathers when they got out of the pool after a dip. I wanted to hold them the way I had Buck and Brownie. I learned how to come up stealthily and grab one and then hold on while it pecked with its funny-looking Donald Duck pale yellow bill all over my face. It hurt and was pleasurable at the same time. I figured the pecking was its way of showing affection and I held on for dear life while I talked to it in comforting tones. I'm afraid I broke Pap's back that way or something. "That guy's got a broke back," Harold said. For some reason I hugged Pap more and harder than I did Mammy. Pap walked behind Mammy always, kept his head down, and didn't, as I saw it, act superior as the haughty Mammy did, who held her head high. He walked like Groucho Marx. After so much hugging from me Pap began to walk stiff-leggedly a few inches from the ground with a developing sway back. He kept going, though, not complaining.

When I woke in the morning the first thing I did was go to the kitchen window and assure myself that Pap and Mammy were still around, that they lay beside the pool, two soft yellow pillows with their bills tucked under their wings. Every day I hosed water in the pool to make up for the slow leakage. And I gave them a steady diet of leftover cornbread, avoiding the squirt-producing stuffing and such. "Hey, what happened to the cornbread?" Harold said, looking for a snack of crumpled cornbread and buttermilk, his favorite. "Some was here just a minute ago."

When it rained Pap and Mammy lay under the eaves of the house. For exercise outside the pool they waddled single-file up and across the vacant lot and waddled back. No one on the street seemed to take notice and I accepted these forays as a normal routine for them to adventure out and back to the pool. I didn't know how you could discipline a duck or train one. I accepted that they would do what came naturally. They got fat on cornbread and I expected them to last to old age, whatever it was for them. I didn't think about it all that much.

But then one day they went on a parade up the vacant lot and didn't come back. Like a police detective I went over their route and down the street from the vacant lot, looking for clues—a loose feather, some droppings, some evidence of my ducks. I found nothing. I shouted their names. I knocked on neighbors' doors and asked if anyone had seen my ducks but no one admitted they had. A few didn't seem to know what I was talking about or were hard of hearing.

I could not cry because not only had I stopped doing that but crying would mean that they were gone forever. I kept looking and looking for Pap and Mammy to come back, to come back home. A winter passed and some snow and then it was spring with daffodils and birds singing. My concrete pool was crumbling in on itself. I couldn't bear the sight. I filled in the hole with dirt I had shoveled out originally, and soon grass grew over the spot. You had to look closely to see the outline of where it had been, but it was there.

* * *

"Doc Powell probably ate those ducks," Harold said. "I saw him eye them the way you do when you want to eat them."

Doc Powell, a pot-bellied man with a sort of duck walk himself, was a plumber who lived around the corner from the vacant lot. He occasionally had a snout-full at the end of day's work and he sometimes entered foolishly into some game my pals and I had concocted on the vacant lot. His son Jamey was my age and my friend. I didn't want to think my friend's father would cook Pap and Mammy, but Harold said it so many times, and so confidently, that I began to believe him, although there was no proof except for the looks he had given the birds. And then, too, and most importantly, I couldn't work up anger or suspicions because new birds now came in the picture and they came from the Powells: pigeons.

Jamey had come by a slew of purplish red-streaked pigeons and Doc, his father, was growing increasingly irritated by their presence. I heard him say, "Those dadburn birds have got to go. I can't sleep at night with all that cooing going on. I mean it. Get rid of them or I'm going to fry 'em up and eat them. The Frenchies do that. It's high on the hog for them. Cost you a lot in one of their fancy restaurants." That gave me a real start.

It wasn't hard to get two cast-off pigeons from Jamey. I think he was tired of feeding them anyhow and making sure their water bowls were full. He was giving his pigeons away left and right, as fast as he could. He sales-talked me into taking two although it didn't take much. "All you have to do," he said, "is keep them in a cage someplace outside your house for awhile until they take it as their home. A couple of weeks should do her. Then you open the cage up, let them fly out, and they'll always come back."

"But won't they go back to your place?"

"Dad's making me destroy their living quarters, every last nail and wire and bowl. They got no home any more here."

I was fascinated by the First World War—Eddie Rickenbacker, Baron von Richthofen, and Frank Luke up in the air and all those mud-splattered soldiers in the trenches who went over the top at the sound of a whistle. Pigeons that flew messages in the middle of battle, dodging rifle and cannon fire, were part of the lore. Pigeons got through. They always came back. That's what I read.

I begged an orange crate from a grocery store up Boone Street and cut a trap door in the side so that I could open and close it by tying and untying a shoestring. The trap door allowed me to feed and give the pigeons water. I hoped that later it would give the pigeons a chance to fly off and come back. I covered the crate's floor with newsprint and then I nailed the works on the pantry windowsill. The pounding caused Harold to fly out of the house. "Whaddya think you're doing?"

"Momma said I could."

"You're going to tear down the whole house before you're through with this stuff."

I gave my pigeons two weeks in their new orange crate home. I could hardly wait to send them out with a message to the front. I put my finger through a slot and felt their slick feathers before they could skedaddle away. I did not name them. I did not try to grab one and stroke it as I used to watch Jamey do. I did not want to love them too much.

I timed two weeks to the minute and then I went, giggling to myself, and opened the trap door. They didn't want to fly out, which I took as a good sign. I had to put my hand in to help them out. They took off in a wild flutter of wings in a straight path, circled overhead, landed for a while on the barn roof and then disappeared on the horizon. I changed the newsprint floor in the orange crate, put in fresh feed and water, and then tied the trap door open for the pigeons to get back in. All they had to do was come back. That was all I asked of them. I expected them in an hour or two. That's what Jamey said it would take. The crate hung out there, its trap door tied open, waiting. It looked lonesome and bereft, if an orange crate could look that way. I called Jamey to see if the pigeons had gone back to him. "No, ain't seen any. My dad says he's going to shoot any he sees, and I figure they sense that. He puts his shotgun out the window every now and then."

I walked outside, looking and looking up in the sky, and once I saw two dark objects dive-bombing in, but they turned out to be crows.

It didn't take much to give up. It took about a week. They were gone. That was all there was to it. What a fool I'd been. Then one night on one of my ritualistic rounds to the refrigerator for a glass of water from the jug we kept there a strange sight appeared. Ever since I had become mortally afraid of being bit by a mad dog, as an older boy had in town while delivering papers, I had gone to drink water in the middle of the night. Word had gone out that if you got rabies you couldn't drink enough water. You couldn't get your fill. I went to get my fill and make sure I hadn't been afflicted although I hadn't been near a dog since I lost Buck and Brownie. The newsboy's screams had sounded through town as he lay in his hospital bed, and I still heard them in my dreams. They caused hallucinations.

But it wasn't an hallucination I saw that night. Having drunk straight from the jug, not being able to drink one drop more, I turned to see a silhouette on the pantry windowsill. It was a pigeon resting there in the moonlight. I thought about waking my father to tell him, but thought better of it.

When you don't think anything will ever come back, it sometimes does. This pigeon had come back. It made its home on the sill through many a long night thereafter. I don't know where it went in the day. I don't know what happened to its mate. I don't know where it thought its real home was.

trickshot

More than anything I wanted to be in his aura, to be included in his world. I remember him coming in the house swiftly and leaving just as swiftly. He was always on the move. It might be football or tennis or baseball or basketball or hanging out with pals who played, but were never quite so good as Trickshot. Or so I thought. It had to do with a ball of various dimensions flying through the air—hitting it, catching it, putting it over a goal line or fence or through a net. All while people gazed in amazement at the tricks he could do with the ball and the enemy who opposed him. He had black curly hair and a loose-limbered, jerky stride. People said he was handsome or good looking, but I couldn't tell. I didn't know what standard to use.

My very first memory of him concerned a tent in our backyard. He was tossing me up near the top, onto stiff canvas, and I would roll down it until I shot off into space. I was hardly out of diapers, maybe still in them. He was twelve years older. He held out his arms and caught me while a small cluster looked on, laughing at the trick. I didn't know enough to be scared. I completely trusted him. Mostly he caught me straight out. Once he turned his back and caught me from behind. This got a big laugh. I was hardly as big as a bucket, but I was in seventh heaven. I felt as safe as I was ever to feel.

Later I was taken by my father to watch him play in high school. The gymnasium glowed like a distant city of lights. A crowd pushed inside. I felt the excitement and anticipation that I felt when the circus was coming to town. We could hear basketball shoes squeaking on court before we got fully inside, and boards creaking. And there he was down below, my brother, running around in a shiny silken uniform, twisting and then tuning and contorting himself, and then flipping a ball against a white backboard that went down and through a net. The stands erupted. People stood. "Look at Trickshot! Did you see that move?"

I was proud of him without identifying the emotion. I was also struck by someone on the team with hairy sticks for legs who never made a basket. He was in serious thought and doggedly went about his business, and no one cheered for him. I felt a kinship, and felt sorry for him, without quite understanding why. Everyone on the floor seemed an age I could never attain. They were old. They were in high school.

A year or so later my brother went on to start for the college right outside town. Its campus began just where houses ended and farmland and woods began. It was a small school, but to me then it couldn't have seemed mightier, with its rows of red brick buildings and clean white porticoes. Impossibly mature girls walked its campus in ankle socks, books cradled against their chests. You might have heard of other colleges with spires and deep bells tolling, but here was the big time in the flesh. Its team was the Buccaneers, the pride of East Tennessee.

One Saturday afternoon, clouds gathering, I walked the five miles to its stadium all by myself. The ticket-taker wasn't on guard. I just strolled in. Rain was starting to come down and people were scurrying about for cover and the game hadn't begun. I found a seat high enough to see the whole field but close enough to really see the players. Those sharp pellets that first stung now flattened out into sheets of rain.

On the green grass out there, with white stripes running through it, I found him—this jittery, well-coordinated figure who barged in and out of my house, slamming doors and no time for a word to me, always in a hurry, my brother. He was swaddled now in helmet, pads, and cleats. I pinpointed him right away. He caught passes, recovered a fumble, and made a block that cleared the way for a touchdown by a lumbering fullback, sending the enemy player flying. "Did you see that?" someone yelled from under a raincoat thrown over his head. "Did you see Trickshot upend that guy? I never saw anything like it!"

They were soon playing in mud. They were covered in it. It gave them extra padding and slowed the game to a trot and a rolling clot of players. The rain became torrential. After every play another band of spectators climbed up the steps and out. It was deliciously pleasurable for me to have lasted through the final whistle, which was hard to hear, and it was hard to see the white stripe-shirted ref who blew it through the mist. I wanted to experience the joy of taking the full force of the rainstorm and not quitting. I took pleasure in pressing my shoe down and watching water squirt out from the soles. I liked not hiding from the rain. I liked putting my face up to it and taking it full on. Not many were in the stands at the end. The Buccaneers won and my brother's teammates hugged and lifted each other and trotted happily off the field. I noticed how their calf muscles bulged.

I was the last to leave. I walked the five miles back, kicking puddles and spectacularly catching passes and leveling tacklers while the stands went crazy and cheerleaders leapt. I darted into the house by the side door, left as little water as possible on the floor, and flew into a bath. I was caught between wanting credit for my hike and sitting through the game, all in a monsoon, and keeping quiet about adventuring so far afield, so grandly without letting anyone know. I was nine years old.

I decided naturally to boast. But by the time I had dried off and donned fresh clothes the chance had passed. Someone else had taken center stage. My brother had burst in the living room, back from the game with a few of his teammates, hooting and hollering. My father, who had just arrived home from work, sat on the edge of his easy chair, peppering my brother with questions about the game, a few of which my brother deigned to answer in monosyllables. A corkscrew of gray rose from the Chesterfield my father held between his fingers as he patiently tried to unlock the mind of my brother. My brother could hardly be bothered. A cigar was clamped between his teeth.

"Boys, please make yourselves comfortable," my mother, in an apron, was saying to my brother's teammates. "Anyone hungry? And Harold, put that thing out. You shouldn't be smoking, should you?"

He puffed mightily. "We won, Mom. Look at this!"

He blew smoke rings that lazily crossed in front of him and then blended with the gray trail from my father's Chesterfield, combining to rise and spread against the ceiling while all eyes went to my brother, who put his arm around my mother's shoulders and winked.

* * *

My brother had a teasing, flirtatious manner around my mother, a stance I could never imagine taking. An example. Once, a house painter, actually named Mr. Painter, who had an almost impenetrable lisp and a strong weakness for the bottle, had been hired to paint our house that sorely needed it. He came cheap, a recommendation that overrode all objections, and he promised to do the job in three days. It was the summer my father was working out of town and my mother was running the house and making decisions. Days passed, then weeks, finally a month, and the job was not half done. Mr. Painter would show up, climb his ladder, furiously slap his brush a few times against the wood, then descend and absent himself in the shadows. Once he was found sleeping on the grass. He would barge in on my mother, face glowing, fumes overpowering, to point out a painting complexity and how he was solving it. Some people, for whatever the reason, fear a German Shepherd; my mother feared a drunken man. When fall approached and only a patch of the back porch was left to paint, Mr. Painter showed up one Saturday and said he desperately needed to be paid in full. My mother paid him. The ladders went away. Then one evening when it was just me and my mother at home the phone rings and my mother answers. What followed became family lore.

"Miz Blowse," a drunken voice with a strong lisp, says. "I'm goin' come by your house. You home?"

"Mr. Painter, please, it's inconvenient. No, please, don't!"

"Yes, Miz Blowse . . ." And then a giggle starts and breaks out into a full throated guffaw. It goes on for some time. "Got you, didn't I, Mom!"

What my mother thought of all that, I don't know. I don't think she was amused. But she had an irrepressible sense of humor. Another evening the phone again rings. It is Harold, on best behavior. He wants something. He wants to bring his coach home for dinner. His coach is an important figure in his life. "Please, Mom, could you just throw something together? You're good at that. I know you can."

And my mother, in perfect rendition of Mr. Painter, says, "Mah bones is achin' and I cain't hardly lift a skillet—"

Harold slammed the receiver down. The coach did not come to our house for dinner that night.

* * *

I knew Harold's teammates, knew them as well as my own smaller collection of chums. I turned the pages of his college yearbooks in a trance. I knew them from their pictures. There was the football team in three rows on the field. There were shots of individuals—Harold prominent, of course. There was the quarterback, Charley Davenport, whose father was police chief in town. Davenport, "Port," has his arm cocked back, about to deliver a pass. He is lithe, intense, and sure of himself. Here is Lard Landis, a lineman, whose father ran a construction firm. Landis is large all over, even his hair is large, and he presents a goofy, good-natured grin to the camera, resting his chubby, uniformed knee on the ground. On and on.

I knew those who didn't play sports because their pictures were in groups called the Thespians or Current Events or Chemistry Clubs. I studied their faces and stances, searching for clues as to their characters. When they wore glasses and checkered sweaters and looked boldly into the camera or avoided it with a smirk, it told me something, but I wasn't sure what. The cheerleaders were shot giving a rah-rah-rah, all girls and one skinny guy with a megaphone. One girl's father, Mr. Doberman, ran a soda fountain and magazine shop by the train station. He had a withered hand and made sodas slowly and painstakingly with his good one. Here was his daughter leaping up in saddle-oxfords and a skirt that showed off her tanned legs, throwing her arm back in a locomotive. There were many inscriptions in my brother's yearbooks and I knew them by heart: "Trick, I never will forget the Emory game and the party afterwards. Be true to Bobbie Sue if you can!"

And many more on the same order. None were complicated or deep and I easily memorized them. I learned more about him from the yearbooks than I did from him. I longed and waited for the chance to learn in person. I longed for someone to tell me to be true to a Bobbie Sue. I wanted to be where he was and learn what it took to get there. I wanted to know what it was all about.

* * *

The night I'll never forget, my mother said to Harold, "I want you to stay in tonight with your brother. He's too young to be left by himself."

She was going to a Franchot Tone movie with my aunt. My father was working out of town. "Sure, sure," or something. He didn't raise his eyes from the sports section.

"Did you hear me?"

"Yeah, yeah, sure," turning a page. He never raised his eyes from the paper.

We were alone and I tried various avenues of conversation. What was he reading? What was in it? Was it interesting? Eyes never raised, words never came. I thought of lighting a match and putting it to the bottom of the paper. I was never, ever afraid of him. He had never said a bad word to me, never, ever been mean, never even had shook me. Both my mother and father had shook me. I just wanted his attention. I once pulled a dried-up corn stalk from the backyard garden, crept behind him while he was reading, and hit him over the head as hard as I could. With his eye on the paper still, he deftly took the stalk from my hand and continued reading.

This night I wondered if he wanted to play a game of checkers. I had gotten pretty good at it. Nothing doing, as I expected, but I never gave up hope. Then a car horn tooted outside and he raced to the curb and came back. "Listen, it's up to you. Lard and Port are outside and want to take a spin. Do you want to go with us?"

I could scarcely believe it! My voice trembled when I said, "Sure, why not? That's what you want, right?"

"I'm supposed to look after you. I can't leave you here by yourself."

Lard and Port, enveloped in bigness, took up most of the front seat. Harold and I had room to spare in the back. But soon there were others. Port piloted us to the college's girls' dorm. But first he had trouble finding the right cut-off. It was his father's car and he wasn't used to driving. He said, having to backtrack, "Shitfire and save matches!"

My brother said in my ear, "Don't pay attention to the language he uses."

And then three girls piled in the car somehow, materializing suddenly from the back of the dorm. They weren't there; then there was a streak and they were inside the car. "Am I squishing you, honey?" A blonde in bangs, with hair curled up in back, giving off a fresh scent of shampoo, came down on me.

"Let him sit on your lap, Bobbie Sue," Harold said.

I didn't want to be thought of as a child, someone who went around sitting on other people's laps, but what could I do? I did what Harold said. My hip went against her flat stomach and I felt the crevice between her legs. It was nothing to complain about. A golden miniature basketball dangled from a thin chain and lay between the two mounds in her sweater. I felt the mounds with my shoulder. I was in horror of wiggling around too much on her. I knew I shouldn't. I stuck my head out the window, making a grand gesture, as if I needed air, but really to show off. I was busy thinking up ways to show off and be included in the fun as an equal.

"Hey, Port," I said, as if I was in the habit of calling him "Port." He grunted. "Where you taking us? You lost?"

It got a big laugh and I reveled in it. Port was not so happy. He actually may have been lost. He didn't answer. He drove, one hand on the steering wheel, the other around a small, dark-haired girl called Small Stuff. I wondered how she felt going around called "Small Stuff." The road became rutted and bumpy and tree branches scratched against the side of the car. We came to a jerky halt, and Port said, "Everybody out." I noticed that he had freshly shaved, the scent of a strong lotion coming off his cheeks.

I rose slightly, bending my neck, the side of my head against the top, and Bobbie Sue scooted out with Harold. Lard Landis got out with a girl as well proportioned as he was and who had somehow been sitting on his lap, and they ambled off, the size of wrestlers. The car had been jammed and full of shrieks; now it was bare and I was alone.

"Stay here," Harold said through the open window. "Don't go off. We'll be back in a few minutes."

"How long?"

"I told you. Only a few minutes."

They walked off into the darkness. They walked off into the woods, carrying blankets.

* * *

There was a curfew in town called the "nine-thirty curfew" which applied to all those under twelve years of age. You had to be off the streets, home, at that time. If you got caught you went to jail. No one explained to me why. The rayon factory whistle sounded at that time, three long, loud, mournful, heart-chilling blasts. Even at four in the afternoon, sitting in a darkened theater on Main Street I felt the fear of it. The fear of it came unbidden. I felt it more than the fear of being bitten by a mad dog, getting polio, or being kidnapped. It had been especially true when I was hunkered down watching *The Werewolf of London* one Saturday afternoon at the

Sevier Theater, where there were deep shadows and hairy faces popping up out of nowhere. I feared that whistle blowing.

Now I sat by myself in the middle of nowhere where a moment before a crowd had been. Wind moved high branches in the trees. Way off I could see a faint light from a farm house. Further away I heard a train's rumble and its whistle. I thought of my father and wished he were here. I heard crickets. I saw the moon above, large and white and of no comfort. I told myself to count to twenty-five before I did anything. I almost got there before rushing out.

"Harold!" I yelled.

Nothing, except the crickets stopped for a moment.

"Harold, Harold, HAROLD!"

From the same far reaches as the train seemed to be, came his voice. Its tone was what he used when he was locked in the bathroom and you beat on the door, screaming, "Emergency!" and the reply came back, "Just a minute!"

I waited and waited and waited, and all I got was pure misery. I was going to end up here forever. Here's what comes from acting like a big shot when all you are is little.

miss mary louise luster

When I first heard the news I felt a little unclean and saddened. But I also felt that here was an answer. Here was the missing link, an explanation, a clearer understanding of Mr. McCorkle, the father of my sometime friend, Eustis. Mr. McCorkle had been caught peeping in a bedroom window at twelve o'clock at night. Another man, a man who was employed to go around town testing the doors of downtown businesses and throwing the beam of a flashlight inside, had strayed off-course for some reason and had apprehended the dignified Mr. McCorkle, crouching in a flower bed, straw hat pushed back on his head, catching stocky Mort Wheeler and his full-bodied wife at it.

The Door Shaker, as he was known, nabbed him and marched him to the jailhouse. Imagine. The Door Shaker, a man who wore a slouch hat and kept a White Owl cigar crammed in his crooked mouth, thought of himself as a law-enforcement officer, although that was stretching it. He was stern about break-and-enter specialists and others in nighttime mischief. Much later in life he himself would be convicted of helping murder the husband of a much younger woman he was involved with. This night he was on the other side of the fence, and hauled in poor Mr. McCorkle, Eustis's father.

Eustis and I had started first grade together and from early on he was the kind of boy all mothers warned you not to play with.

He thought up ways to shoplift in grammar school; he drank beer and smoked in junior high; he never made it to high school. He had a trick whereby he would stick his finger down his throat and throw up on a whim. He liked to do it as a grand finale on Saturday night when boys on the loose gathered under a street lamp, thinking up things to do before having to go home to bed. Eustis was the one who discovered that a neighbor, a traveling salesman, kept his wares in his backyard garage, his product being cartons of chewing gum. Eustis taught us how to pull aside a loose board, crawl inside the dark and dank interior, and help ourselves. I chewed whole mouthfuls of Juicy Fruit until my jaws gave out and wouldn't move. The excitement and fear that the experience brought on was almost too much to bear.

Mrs. McCorkle, Eustis's mother, was a dead ringer for the wife in W.C. Fields movies—buxom, chin raised, an authority making pronouncements while those around closed their ears or scurried away. She was a member of the DAR and an expert on local genealogy.

Mr. McCorkle fashioned snappy hats, bow ties, and two-toned shoes. He wore a gray wispy military mustache. He was a father who didn't seem to have an occupation, but he carried himself as if he were one of the most important and influential men in town—except around Mrs. McCorkle, when he could be sighted darting swiftly around a corner or with his nose buried in a paper, nodding, as she droned on.

The police blotter was a small half column in the back pages of the paper. It was read more avidly than the front page full of war news and national scandal. And there was the item, third down, after one burglary and one drunk and disorderly: Eustis McCorkle, Sr. had been docked for lewd and lascivious behavior. It didn't go into detail and didn't have to. Everyone knew already.

It made me feel the way I felt after I had crawled into the garage and taken gum that didn't belong to me. I felt sorry for Mr. McCorkle, especially since I didn't have any right to judge him. For one of the first times in my life I found myself feeling sorry for an adult. I felt apprehension that someone's secret, an adult's, could come out so openly and shame someone so, although Mr. Mc-

Corkle carried on much the way he always had, as if it hadn't happened. But I could never look at him the same way again. He had a secret, and, well, so did I. I speak of him only to show that the line between me and adults was growing narrower and narrower. This story is really about Miss Mary Louise Luster. This story is really about me and her.

When I finally got to high school, she became my teacher as well as being my neighbor and someone on our telephone party line. She had always made me tingle, but now, gazing at her up front in a classroom, the stakes were raised. She wore blouses with the top three buttons undone, and she was a woman, not a girl. Looking back, she may not have been all that much older—say, ten or twelve years, around Harold's age. She taught math, a subject that bored me to tears, and it was her first job after college. She began to hover as a vision in my head when something flew out of me now, something that smelled like chewed grass, something that came along mostly from dreams, sometimes with help, and I became faint with the scent of Miss Mary Louise Luster, my tenth grade teacher. The twin Bellamy brothers, who were seniors and who shaved, got the idea of peeping in her window one night. They needed company. Everything told me not to go along with them, everything but what rose on its own and unloaded in spurts.

It was a couple of hours after sunset and the Bellamy brothers began arguing over who would go first. Neither one wanted to. "You big old coward, you said you wanted to!" "No, you go. It was your idea!" A few feet from the window they began hitting each other, then going, "Shsss, shsss!"

"Get out of the way," I whispered. "I'll go."

She sat facing a window, reading a magazine. The shade was pulled down to within an inch or two from the bottom. I put my eye there, aware that the Bellamy brothers were arguing and giggling and punching each other behind me. She crossed her legs, in a long, languid movement. The Bellamy brothers shook my shoulders. "Let me, let me," they breathed. I waved them back.

She raised her skirt, rubbed her knee, then pulled the skirt back down. If there hadn't been a screen between us, and the shade up another inch, I could have reached in and scratched her knee myself. I felt guilty, while at the same time I felt that Miss Luster and I were sharing something, sharing an intimacy. Except she didn't know she was. Or did she?

She did fidget about and look up when we giggled once or twice or stepped on a twig. She would look up, and we would duck down. Then back to her nose in the magazine and us back to the window. She did not look at the window. She stood, she stretched; outside, all three of us now crowded at the window with our heads tilted sideways. I could smell the Bellamy brothers' breath, which was not all that pleasant. She had long caramel-colored hair, which she swept back from her face the way Rita Hayworth did. She unbuttoned one blouse button, then another, until her blouse became completely undone, her white bra exposed. I held my breath; I prayed. She strolled to a floor lamp, rolling her hips, stood still a moment and then reached over and snapped it off. But right before, she looked at the window and looked me right in the eye.

After Mr. McCorkle got caught and his name put in the paper, we never went back to the window again. But Miss Luster stayed in the picture. Every time I picked up the phone and she was there on the party line, I automatically spread my palm over the mouthpiece and listened in, scared but thrilled. She talked to a girlfriend, gossiping, talking grown-up stuff—about jobs, pay, difficult supervisors. Now and then came word about suitors or potential ones, and then I held my breath. Miss Luster went on about how someone was cute or snooty or had broken up with someone—and I squirmed and my palm over the mouthpiece sweated. She said abruptly, "*Someone's* on this line. If that *someone* doesn't mind, would that *someone* get off!" I felt she could see from around the corner and down a block right at me on my side steps where I had dragged the phone, and I blushed and gritted my teeth. She never called me out by name as the culprit. She gave me a "D" in math class, which I deserved but didn't think I'd get, and she never called on me or even looked directly at me. It was more powerful that she didn't. It was acknowledging, in a way, that there was something unspoken between us.

* * *

In high school we had extracurricular clubs—Thespians, Current Events, Hi Y, Photography. Miss Luster sponsored the Aviation Club and it had few members, all boys. No one could quite figure out what an Aviation Club was supposed to do. I joined. We met on the grass of a sloping hill outside school once a week and looked up at the sky and felt the wind blow and talked of flying. Flying was dangerous, something you could only dream about, and I wanted to be included. I didn't want to be a Hi Y'er or a Thespian. I got to sit down the hill from Miss Luster, too, and watch the hem of her skirt flutter in the breeze and occasionally reveal a rolled stocking and a glimpse of her white thigh.

One day she said, "Who among us has actually flown?"

A lanky country boy, a new transfer in school, said he had. The rest of us admitted we had not. "Well," she went on, "for those of you who would like to go up, I've reserved a plane for Saturday morning."

An airfield was a few miles out of the town proper and had been cut out of what had once been farmland. Two narrow runways ran parallel for a couple hundred yards right before a cornfield began. Oil streaks and tire marks lay in the center of them. Even though nothing moved on them then they made you feel something dangerous was going on and it made your heart pump. There had been a time, and there would soon come a time, when an airplane would roar down one. It was like seeing a circus tent and knowing that something tremendously exciting was going to happen. There was a whitewashed concrete building near the runways atop which a windsock whipped around; beside it a corrugated tin hanger where the wings of two planes spread out in the shadows. Miss Luster had arrived earlier and stood in front of the hanger. She wore what looked like riding britches, laced boots that came up near her knees, and a leather helmet, the flaps of which hung loosely over her ears. Goggles were pushed atop her head. It was an impressive getup.

"I've talked them into letting me take up Top Hat, boys. What do you think of that? I was afraid they'd saddle us with that old Piper Club I'm so sick of. This'll be a lot more fun. Who wants to go with me first?"

I nudged the lanky country boy. All the way on the bus he had talked about airplanes, how it felt going through clouds, how the earth turned this way and that when you were up there in the sky. He said he had flown hundreds of times when he went to visit his uncle who had a large ranch out west. He said his uncle was rich.

Two men in grease-stained coveralls pushed a bi-plane out of the hanger. The country boy looked at the ground. The other members of the Aviation Club looked at the plane and didn't move. I touched it. It was lacquered, smooth to the touch. It was pale gray with bright red circles on the wings and a Top Hat painted on the fuselage. The rubber-tired wheels were dusty. It creaked as it rolled. We all fell silent, and I was afraid someone might beat me to it.

"I'll go," I said.

Miss Luster was an adult. This field trip had been approved by the school. Or I thought so. Miss Luster had a pilot's license or something like that. What did a license mean anyhow? Half the people I knew who drove cars didn't have a license. There was no speed limit in Tennessee and no gun registration for sure. In any case, this was Miss Luster. Miss Luster! In the soft morning sun her eyes seemed covered with a slight film as if some of the jism that flew from me night and day had landed in her eyes. Or at least the moisture in her eyes reminded me of that.

She easily hoisted herself into the front cockpit. It reminded me of getting on a horse. I struggled into the other cockpit behind her. I now wore a leather helmet and goggles myself. She told me to buckle up in a harness in the cockpit and I had to try several times before I could do so. Miss Luster turned around, her goggles pulled down over her eyes. "All set?" she screamed.

"Yes, ma'am," I screamed, and pulled my goggles down.

A man in coveralls reached up and put both hands on the propeller. I was expecting to hear "Contact!" or something I'd heard in the movies, but it never came. He looked at Miss Luster with what I took as a lewd grin; then he swung one of his legs out and brought both hands down and the motor coughed, caught, and roared. Grayish black smoke streamed from the motor. We taxied to the runway. I had a stick between my legs that moved exactly as Miss Luster moved hers in front. I thought of that stick between hers. She had told me not to move mine, just watch. She would do all the flying. When the stick moved between my legs I thought of her moving it.

We paused at the head of the runway. She gunned the motor a few times and the plane rocked. Then she gave it full throttle and we started off. I waved to the others by the white concrete-block shack. They waved back. The stick came back between my legs and we rose in the air over the cornfield. We bounced a bit and then we got high enough so that people and cars down below became little specks. She tilted the wings and circled the field. I couldn't believe it! I was flying! My mother would be buying Saturday groceries right then. My father would be smoking and reading the morning paper. I'd told them I was going to a school meeting. They had no idea I was harnessed in a bi-plane, up over cornfields and roads and headed I didn't know where, or care, all in the hands of Miss Mary Louise Luster.

Miss Luster pointed below and I looked over the edge of the cockpit and saw the church spires of the town. She roared us over the Central Baptist Church where revivals about hell and damnation that awaited all sinners had scared the near-living shit out of me. I wasn't scared now. I was flying! The danger, or whatever name it went by, intoxicated me. It was the same feeling I got when I had climbed a near straight-up cliff by a rock quarry. I inched up higher and higher although every reason said not to. One slip and I would have tumbled down into a chasm. The danger and the removal from the ordinary liberated me. It was the feeling, too, that I used to get when holding and playing with the .38 pistol my father kept deep in his private trunk. I unbuckled my harness, and just as the wings dipped I buckled back up at the last second. I didn't know why I did that and kept doing that. I liked the risk and the feeling that I was getting away with something. I let my hand hold my stick loosely, thinking about how Miss Luster was holding hers firmly at the same time.

Little wisps of hair escaped from the sides of Miss Luster's helmet. I watched them dance in the wind. She took us over the high school and wobbled the wings. She flew us low over both our houses, which looked nearly side-by-side from up above. I saw laundry flapping in my backyard. I could step out of the cockpit and walk through my side door, I thought. She took us high up through clouds where we couldn't see in front of us. When we broke out of the clouds I looked down and there was the sky! Something's wrong! The wings rolled and the sky went back up above where it should be. I patted my buckled harness as Miss Luster roared low over barns and pastures and then bounced us down on the runway. I climbed out and already a boy was waiting to take my helmet. "Nothing to it," I told everyone. My knees nearly gave way.

Everyone got a spin now that the ice had been broken. The lanky country boy was the last to go and I watched his hands tremble and his eyes tear. When he came back he climbed out and announced that he was disappointed. He had wanted to do a loop-de-loop like his rich uncle on the ranch out west had done with him. "None of you have done a loop-de-loop," he told us all. "That was nothing up there today."

Maybe so. But I was the first to go up with Miss Mary Louise Luster.

* * *

We were not alone together again until one very warm afternoon in summer when peaches grow ripe and you have to pick them fast or they spoil. Miss Luster had a peach tree in her backyard and she called to see if I was interested in picking some. There were far more than she or her mother could ever eat. She never mentioned her disturbed uncle who lived with them and whom she was probably ashamed of. I was welcome to come over and take what I wanted. Somehow I wasn't surprised to hear her voice, or the warmth in it, although she had never called me before.

That afternoon could have happened yesterday for all its vividness. Yet so much lay in the future. I had finished high school and was headed for the army. I had grown, it seemed overnight, to be six-foot-two with no appreciable gain in weight. I had been in love with a girl in high school who carried her books against her chest, who went on Christian youth retreats, who had a rich father, who was a cheerleader, and whom I had never kissed or even held her hand. When I read a Shakespeare sonnet I thought of her. When I saw June Haver on screen I thought of her. I never thought of Miss Mary Louise Luster as a June Haver. She was about as far from a Shakespearean sonnet as you could get. I thought of Miss Mary Louise Luster when I looked at a fuck book.

She sat on a sort of deck in the back of her house, in a chair she had tilted back with her bare feet on the railing, watching me pick peaches and take my time. She wore shorts and a loose blouse, and I noticed when I first showed up with my pail for the peaches that her cheeks were rouged. We talked as I slowly pulled down peach after peach, flipping away those that had become overly ripe with the juice popping out. You wanted them firm but not hard, where the fuzz stood out and you could feel it with the tips of your fingers.

Our talk was not memorable, although endless. Miss Luster had never talked to me so much before, ever. She did most of the talking, and I noticed how Southern and soft her accent was. It was not like the classroom. We were on a holiday from there since I had just graduated. She wiggled her toes and I saw that they were painted a bright red. She had that same moist sheen over her blue eyes that she always had. "It sure is hot now, isn't it?" she said.

"I reckon so," I said. I would never dare to call her Mary Louise, never, ever. But I didn't think of her then as "Miss Luster."

"Nobody else wanted to pick my peaches," she said. "You're the only one."

There had been so many stories floating around about her. One of the Bellamy brothers swore she had invited him into her house and showed him pictures out of a cheesecake magazine. She had watched him while he turned the pages, watched him get a hard-on. I didn't believe him of course; that would never happen, but I savored the memory of it in my mind as if it had. I stood beside her chair, a pail full of peaches in my hand. "Thanks a whole lot for these peaches," I said.

"Sure you don't want more?"

I was up above her, looking down. The open expanse where her blouse went unbuttoned showed dots of sweats and a rivulet wiggling down into the cleavage. She was sitting fully in the sun. She brushed back her hair and smiled up at me. I saw her teeth.

"No, thanks, we'll never eat all these back home," I said.

"I'm so hot," she said. "I'm so terribly hot."

I left. Later I imagined that she took me into her bedroom, pulled out some dirty pictures and showed them to me. What had one Bellamy said to me? He said that she had said, "This is what boys like to look at, isn't it?" I imagined that she had said that to me. I imagined everything in the bedroom, the way the bed sagged, the coolness after the heat outside, the female scents of powder and perfume. I keep imagining that scene over and over, much more vividly than if it had really happened.

Whatever was in her mind that day I never knew, as I've never known really what has ever been in anyone else's mind. Many years later I came back to town from somewhere quite different, and I was different from what I had once been, too, or so I thought. By chance I dropped by a tavern on the outskirts of town and there she was, sitting at a table, drinking a beer. That rich caramel hair I remembered had turned into a mousy fluff. Her teeth, which previously had a fetchingly crooked one in front, had now become two even rows of startlingly white chompers, scary in a way, as if she might snap your head off with them. But there she was, a replica. There was no mistaking her. We were happy to see each other and passed on tidbits of news. We talked about how many had died or become unlike their earlier versions or more like what they once had been. We talked about how you could fly to Paris in no time, and how cheap it was. I still couldn't call her Mary Louise. She had been married five times and now lived in Orange County, California. She had brought her latest husband back to see the old hometown. That man sat beside her now. He carried an unsavory grin and shook my hand with a sweaty palm. He evoked a swinger past his prime, someone who, under ordinary circumstances, I would have avoided at all costs. He wore a pale jacket and white patent leather loafers.

We had a round or two of beers and were running out of things to say when the man suddenly turned to me and said, "I bet that was something to have such a hot-looking teacher way back then. Did any of you learn something more than how to square the hypotenuse?" He arched his eyebrows and his grin broadened. I didn't want to go down that road. I said, Sure, she was certainly something back then.

Miss Luster and I looked at each other, understood each other, and I noted that her blue eyes were moist, just the way I remembered.

Part II

CAUTIONARY TALES

rolf and fuchon

They were different from all others in town and you couldn't help but notice them. You could say their names to anyone—to a preacher, a banker, to a poolroom shark—and they'd know who you were talking about. They were tolerated because they had always been there. They added spice and shook things up in town.

Rolf and Fuchon Kelly had a sort of marriage going. They were brothers who kept house together in Keystone, a tumbledown section on the outskirts of town. Mostly I remember Rolf, the flighty one, the one who'd strike up a conversation with anyone, who glad-handed people on the street as if he was running for office. He got attention. He was tall and skinny and had a wild walleye so you were never quite sure where he was looking. Fuchon was squat and tight-lipped and would look you straight in the eye and almost dare you to say something he could take offense to. Say something I don't like, buddy, and I'll coldcock you, he implied.

They wore old-timey overalls and farmers' straw hats and picked up odd jobs around town. Fuchon worked out of sight as a handyman and leaf raker but comported himself as if a carpenter, with tools dangling. Rolf's principal job was walking around town draped in a sandwich board that advertised the local semi-pro team, the Cardinals—who they were playing that night and what time. It was a way of giving him an income, but you'd think a grown man might be embarrassed to amble around under a sandwich board. Rolf wasn't. The opposite. He was in high cotton. He strutted and bellowed out starting batting orders, the pitchers, and standings in the league. On and on, while children and loafers followed at his heels. He was like a radio announcer or a tent revivalist, a strange sight in a sandwich board. He was entertainment. "Old Carl's going to sling the apple tonight, folks. That old boy's got the stuff, you better believe me! Yes, siree! Seven to three this season! Come on out, come on out!"

Rolf and Fuchon broke the rules and got away with it. No one took any offense because they weren't drunks, and they weren't thieves. They were our court jesters. They presented the alternative, the alternative of slaving away in a standard job and living under repression that would have satisfied Martin Luther. They let it all hang out. They lived as bachelors until Fuchon one day brought home a pale, young country girl, pretty as a picture in a tarty way. Called her his wife. You would see her shopping alone in Kress's, buying hard candy or things that women bought, like perfume and powder. On Main and Market Streets she could be seen with the two brothers close beside her. She seemed proud of herself, delighted with herself and the situation, whatever it was. Rolf, without his sandwich board, would be yapping away; Fuchon would be glancing around, squint-eyed, daring anyone to say something.

I came across them one summer twilight evening as they paused on a corner, waiting for traffic to pass. I felt something was going to happen, and it did. First, Fuchon gave her a squeeze. Then his brother Rolf, with his walleye looking off elsewhere, reached around from the other side and played with her ass. It wasn't done slyly. I was in awe. You might think she would have struck his hand away as you imagined any woman would have. Instead, she acted victoriously. She giggled and looked pleased. Fuchon looked around to see if anyone objected. Not me. Strangely, this threesome always acted superior, as if they were onto something no one else was. They weren't asking anyone's permission for anything or hiding anything. They were flaunting it. They were an example for those who wanted to be liberated and didn't know how or where;

they were also available to be laughed at by those who wanted to feel superior in their church-going, bill-paying respectability. Rolf and Fuchon and the woman who came to live with them knew that they were superior.

* * *

Once the highly aristocratic Senator Estes Kefauver came through town, setting up shop in a suite in the grand Andrew Jackson Hotel, letting out the word that he was there, ready and able to meet the influential. Rolf took off his straw hat and marched through the lobby, pushing the upstairs button. In the suite, he struck a path through dignitaries and politicians, straight as an arrow, a nod and an occasional word thrown out, through the haze of cigar smoke and chatter, past clinking glasses and bowing black waiters in starched white jackets, through it all, into an inner sanctum where the senator sat with a few aides, going through important-looking documents. The courteous, mannerly senator rose, all six-foot-four of him, shook Rolf's hand, and tried to catch where his walleye was moving.

Important figures wore overalls around here. This man with the walleye and the wide smile might be important, you never knew. Senator Kefauver had Rolf sit down near him. He and Rolf talked about various measures before Congress. They talked about the baseball season. They talked about old Harry thrashing Dewey. They talked and talked. Finally, Senator Kefauver caught Rolf's wandering eye. "By the way, exactly who did you say you were?"

"Don't you know? Why, I'm Rolf, Fuchon's brother."

He put on his straw hat, winked his walleye, and marched out like a potentate. He had made a statement, although no one was exactly sure what.

* * *

Later in life, I discovered Henry Miller, who also made a statement or two. I became delirious over *The Tropic of Cancer* and *The Tropic of Capricorn*. In *The Air Conditioned Nightmare*, a chronicle of his journey through America, I was startled to read that Henry (you would never call Henry James just Henry; Miller you would) had come through our town and had stayed at the Singing Teakettle, a boardinghouse up from me. I knew that boardinghouse well. The son of the widow who ran it single-handedly was a chum of mine. I hung out in the Singing Teakettle, watching guests come and go. I like to think that at one time I actually got to see old Henry. I might have watched him cart his well-worn luggage in, with stamps from Paris and Greece and all over plastered on it. I could have seen his baldpate glistening under the harsh overhead light in the dining room. I am happy to think that Henry Miller stayed once in my old hometown. If I'd only known what I know now, I could have told him how happy I was to see how he had torn the chains off and broken all the rules in such a joyous, unapologetic way and had made us laugh about it all. He was an example for us all.

missing

Suddenly Chauncey Deroche was gone. One morning his picture appeared on the front page of the morning paper and that was it. The picture showed an earlier Chauncey Deroche in a captain's uniform of the U.S. Army with a great big smile on his face. He was a Yale graduate, something proudly noted in the write-up. Who'd we ever known who'd been to *Yale*? It was like heaven. You'd heard of it, but no one ever went. After Yale and being in World War II, he had joined his family's insurance and real estate business. No one could remember him as being distraught. The opposite. In retrospect, the people around the tables at the Andrew Jackson Coffee Shop, a gathering spot for the town's elite every working morning, remembered him as being a little more lively in the days before, almost giddy. It was hard for them to put their fingers on, but he seemed to have found the Lord Jesus Christ—or something like that.

Since he was heir to a prestigious business and was part of the town's establishment, we figured he had no room for complaint, certainly not enough to shag ass. He was rich and didn't have to make car payments. He had gone ashore on Omaha Beach and had come out with only a little shrapnel in him. He had been a finalist in the citywide tennis tournament the year before, which had been a great honor. I remember that match. When I think of Chauncey Deroche, I always think of it.

He was all dressed in white and he had a picture-book serve. I liked to think of it as a Yale serve. If I'd ever got to Yale, I would have had such a smooth, flawless serve. The match was played at night under lights on one of the clay courts by the ballpark. It wasn't Forest Hills, but it was something. Small bleachers had been set up around it; the crowd was large and there was much excitement. I still see Chauncey's curly brown hair glistening in the light. He unscrewed his racket's wooden press and took out what looked like a brand new Jack Kramer racket; it glistened like his hair. He carried a slightly bemused look on his face as he warmed up against an unlikely opponent. The man had "country" written all over him, and he wore high-topped basketball shoes and what looked like bathing trunks. He had a potbelly. How he got to the finals was anyone's guess. If he had been playing anyone but Chauncey we might have been on his side, but he was playing Chauncey, who was a World War II vet and hero and whose hair glistened under the lights and who was all dressed in white. The country guy broke nearly every rule in tennis. He didn't use a backhand or seem to know that one existed. He darted around to use a forehand that sliced the ball, causing it to take an odd, ungodly bounce when it landed. He had a pitty-pat serve and he was pigeon-toed. Strangely, he acted as if he thought he had the match in the bag.

Chauncey began by driving shots powerfully down the line, crisply aiming cross-court, mixing up his serve—first a slice, then a cannonball. The potbellied man had trouble covering the court at first and no one gave him much of a chance. It was expected to be quick work for Chauncey, but his opponent didn't seem to realize that. Chauncey won handily the first set, 6–1. In a sort of gentlemanly let up, to not completely thrash an incompetent, he let up and lost the second. It was seen as a gift. Now, we thought, Chauncey was going to bear down and get it over with. But as the third and deciding set got underway, a sense of alarm spread through the crowd, mixed with a strange exhilaration. Could this idiot who'd shown up out of nowhere, who knew nothing about the game, who broke the rules, beat Chauncey, who had gone to Yale? It was unseemly.

The potbellied man began cross-courting Chauncey with his pitty-pat game and using sneaky sliced shots that just cleared the net. He got better and better. Chauncey got worse and worse. Chauncey tried mightily to run down corner shots that landed as softly as rain drops and just out of his reach. Finally, he seemed completely shaken, completely rattled, and began pitty-patting himself. He began playing like his opponent and put his Yale serve aside. The match went on a long time and the potbellied man won. After match point Chauncey hurried to the net first to reach across it and shake the pot-bellied man's hand warmly. It was almost as if he had won. But the potbellied man knew better. He returned the salute with a cocky grin.

Chauncey was different from most of us. That was a fact. There was his name, to begin with. Chauncey Deroche. No one around here had a handle like that. There was but one other Chauncey in town, a highway patrolman, and he demanded to be called Chuck. He was reputed to have one of the biggest dicks in town, and was looked upon in town as you might a movie star. His real name only came out in the paper after he investigated a wreck or something. Then everyone called him *Chauuuunsey* for a while and everybody got a big laugh. He had been brought down to size, so to speak. Chauncey Deroche himself always stuffed a handkerchief in the breast pocket of his suit jacket. Chauncey Deroche didn't shy away from his name. You'd never think of calling him Chuck. No one cared about the size of his dick. He was as close to an aristocrat as we had.

He had married a woman who was on his own social plane and whose family ran the big lumberyard in town. Her name was Alexandra and she was a long, tall drink of water and a classic beauty. But she had a peculiar allergy. She couldn't abide garlic. The mere whisper of it brought on hives and bed rest. She inspected every kitchen and quizzed every cook before she put a bite of food into her mouth. Every spring, when the ramp was in bloom, she fled to New York or some such far place. The ramp was a form of garlic that grew wild up in the hills. There was a ramp festival. No doubt it was painful and maddening to have such an allergy, but people had trouble feeling sorry for her. She had been given pretty much everything already. This was sort of balancing the score. The Deroches, Chauncey and Alexandra, played golf together at the country club. They went to Pawley's Island off the coast of North Carolina every August. They were Episcopalians. They were bringing up a young Chauncey Jr. who was fat and not very good at sports but he was always very well dressed and mannerly.

Now Chauncey Deroche had made the big time. He was "missing." He had gone to one of the TVA lakes to fish one Saturday afternoon, and he never returned. That was the story given out at first by his wife Alexandra. But his motorboat had been found hitched to the dock, rocking in the lapping water, and the deck attendant said he had not seen Mr. Deroche that day. He had not drowned. A follow-up story the next day carried the news that Alexandra had discovered a letter Deroche had left behind, contents unrevealed. If that was not enough, further down it was noted that one Isabelle Johns was also "missing." Then we knew. Then you put two and two together. Your heart raced.

* * *

Isabelle Johns was a sight to behold, at least to me. She had skin the color of the coffee piled high with milk that my mother used to treat me to as a child, letting me feel grown-up. Isabelle's teeth flashed and her flesh bounced and jiggled under her clothes. Her hair was ink-black and never moved in the breeze, looking as stiff as a paintbrush. You imagined she wore no underwear. She had come from somewhere out in the country, or up in the hills, or from someplace no one knew where. After awhile no one much cared. There were enough mysteries in life already. She had just suddenly appeared in town out of nowhere as others had before her—like the Chong family. They were Chinese and had stepped off the train one afternoon because they liked the view outside the window. They never got back on. They opened a laundry. For a short while the town puzzled over how to treat them, as black or as white. Should they sit in the orchestra of the Tennessee Theater or up in the balcony? What school should their son Gordon go to? Gordon had close-cropped hair, a solemn moon face, and the sweetest of dispositions. People just forgot about it. If you don't have to think about it, don't. Don't ever put thoughts you can't handle on the front burner; just let them simmer there in the background, unexamined. That's how it was with Isabelle Johns. The Chongs joined the Baptist Church, and Gordon went through high school, playing the trombone and dating a girl who played first clarinet. He was voted, in his senior year, Cadet of the Year in ROTC.

Isabelle Johns had suddenly shown up in town, and began taking typing and accounting at the "business college," which was three rooms over the furniture store on Market Street. After that she had been hired as a receptionist for Dr. Mock, the lone urologist in town. Before, he had been known as the fellow who had a job no one in his right mind would ever take up; now he was distinguished as the boss of Isabelle Johns.

It was assumed that she was an Indian, but no one checked it out for fear of finding out more. Most dark-skinned people in town claimed Indian blood, but Isabelle never had to. It was assumed for her. She was beautiful. Her looks could hypnotize you. She said "nigger" a lot. She'd look you right in the face and say something like, "The niggers are taking over in this country." It was a little startling. "Whew, glad you're not a nigger," she once said to a phone repairman who came to Mock's office. The repairman felt at liberty then to relax and to work in a word or two himself about niggers, and she went off in a huff. Strange.

She used rather elevated language and her accent bordered on the fancy. She said "aunt" and "can't" with a broad "a," like the English and those from Richmond, Virginia, do, not like those from up in the hills. "I'm afraid we *kaann't* accommodate you," one man swore he heard her say. "We is all booked up." But you believed what you wanted to believe. She was an Indian.

Men of all ages and in all kinds of urinary extremis came to see Dr. Mock. He was a squat, bald-headed man who held a sneer on his face and a hard glint in his eye. He comported himself like an avenging angel. Men sat embarrassed there in the waiting room, an erotic thought the last thing in the world any of them wanted, something that would remind them of the machinery that had caused it all. They watched Isabelle Johns bend over the file cabinet and present a rounded, sculptured behind for view, while from behind a closed door came guttural grunts from someone jabbed unmercifully with a lubricated finger. Dr. Mock was neither artful nor shy in his probings. Some suspected that he was sadistic, only they didn't use that word for it. They said he was a mean son of a bitch, but the only man who could do the job. "Yes, yes, YES!" he'd mumble as he jabbed. He was highly disapproving, too, later on, as findings came in about what had been found out on the glass slide. "There is gonococcus here," he would say, as if looking at a murder weapon.

"I don't know how I got it," he would hear. "I swear it."

"Don't tell me you got it off a toilet seat."

Dr. Mock had no sympathy, gave the impression he found you unclean and a sinner and he didn't know why he was in this business anyhow. And he would assure you, by his manner, that he himself would never stoop so low, you rat, you dirty fornicator.

And it was gleefully rubbing salt in the wounds to place Isabelle Johns out front. Get all worked up by your evil desires, he was saying, And by God, I'll take it out of you, I'll give you retribution, I'll redeem you!

The wallop of redemption was as good as sex. In some cases, it was part of it. The Reverend Wiley, the radio preacher, never caught in Dr. Mock's office as far as anyone knew, raved like a lunatic about the wages of sin over the airwaves. "And you out there fornicating and sinning and . . ." And his voice became a rasp and near left him, ". . . and you'll burn in hell for eternity. BURN! You'll burn and burn and burn . . ."

And the Reverend Wiley ran off with the organist on his show, leaving his wife behind. He returned to his radio audience six months later, abandoning the organist in Cincinnati. In a weepy whisper where there had not long before been a raspy scream, he begged Jesus and the airwaves for forgiveness. It went on and on and on, for those who cared to listen, a slower-than-slow speech, like a motor running down. And for the last five minutes there were no words, only a moan. It was like the last throes of the act of love.

Chauncey Deroche and Isabelle Johns had run off together, no doubt about it. It was expected that the Reverend Wiley would run off with a nubile teenager or someone's wife. He kept doing it. Anyone who proclaimed himself against something so much, and in such vivid detail, must have a weakness for it somewhere—or that was what most people thought, if they thought about it. It was not news. It was not man biting dog. Isabelle and Chauncey taking off was. Chauncey had survived World War II, was an Episcopalian, a Yale graduate, a golfer, a father, a man of taste, etc. He would not join in the telling of dirty jokes. It was all a conundrum. Like the saga of the tall, kindly eyed man who had come to town out of nowhere and got on the police force. He had stayed for twenty years while his hair turned white and he rose to be chief. Then one day a Texas Ranger showed up in town—the first time anyone had seen one—and arrested him. He was wanted back in the Lone Star State for murder. The governor of Texas was beseeched to pardon and forgive him. He had an unblemished history here, was a beloved figure, known and beloved for his gentle approach to law enforcement. He was returned to Texas and electrocuted. How could he be a murderer? Supposedly he had bludgeoned a man in a bar. How could Chauncey Deroche leave everything behind and sneak off with Isabelle Johns?

As far as anyone could recollect, Isabelle hadn't had a man in her life before. No one had ever seen her with Deroche. She took her lunch in Leggett's, which was a few doors down from Dr. Mock's office. The paper stated that she lived in one of the town's several boarding houses, a respectable one. One fellow boarder remembered she always had a smile and a cheery word for everyone, but kept to herself. No one ever came to call. She liked to watch *The Ed Sullivan Show* on the communal TV, and he had thought it strange that she hadn't been there to watch it at eight o'clock on Sunday night. Chauncey Deroche had spoken at the Rotary Club on Friday.

No one had noticed anything different in his behavior. Now they were gone, and leaving together it was all but assured. A mystery.

Alexandra Deroche held her head up, although her eyes seemed to be searching for something a little past her. She went about her usual business, teaching Sunday School, playing golf, and dressing well. She went for periods not bringing up Chauncey's name, and then suddenly—at tea, at bridge, in a casual conversation, she would go berserk. It was Chauncey this, Chauncey that, and ended in sobbing and her breaking out in hives. No one dared to bring his name up around her. She was an attractive woman and rich—and soon suitors, which included some of the town's leading drunks, showed up. But the story went that they couldn't help thinking that someone had left her for another. Plus there was the fact that she went on rants and broke out into hives. Whether she ever got back in touch with Chauncey, wherever he went, no one ever knew. She gave no hint. Chauncey, Jr., who was called Bud, was shipped off to Staunton Military Academy and came back home infrequently. I remember him once at a Christmas dance all decked out in a uniform with shiny brass buttons. Much later in life he became one of the town's leading attorneys and was the first person in town to come out of the closet and say he was gay and proud of it.

Chauncey and Isabelle never age. We see them as they were. I picture Isabelle with that skin the color of the milked coffee. Her hair is black as a paintbrush still. I see her smile. Chauncey I see sitting at the counter of the Andrew Jackson Coffee Shop, sitting there in his bow tie while everyone else wears the straight kind, everyone chattering away around him. He keeps an indifferent smile on his face while he impatiently taps his saucer with his spoon for some reason.

Alexandra ceased going to Pawley's Island in August; after awhile she ceased going much of anywhere. One night she took a .38 and shot herself in the head. *All that money and she did that! Why'd she do that?* But she didn't blow her brains out. She ended up with half her face paralyzed and only able to get out a few unintelligible words at a time. It was the talk of the town, but soon faded in the mist the way World War II had.

We had other things to think of. For one thing, there was the Chicken Little case. His real name was Little and his nickname was Chicken. He was a short happy-go-lucky fellow around town, a bachelor who gave a Christmas party every Yuletide for those without family or close friends, drifters and strangers who needed good cheer. Once he dressed up as Santa Claus. After his death the bones of over twenty unidentified bodies were turned up from his backyard garden. It was all a mystery. Who can say what makes anyone tick?

clark gable

He lived down the block and was a lot older than me, but I never thought of him as an adult even though he was well past twenty-one. He was more like a kid, and he was as fat as a hog. Bill Gahaggen was the fattest guy in town, back when the Depression had left most of us skinny. He was a grown man and still lived with his mother. He tried to fool others, and maybe himself, by wearing pants a good six inches too tight at the waist; it only made it worse. He fashioned gaudy short-sleeved shirts that hypnotized you with their colors so you weren't aware that they held enough material for a tent. The thing was, the thing that hovered in the back of your mind, in his too probably, was that he was normal otherwise. In fact, better than normal. He had a soothing baritone, like a radio announcer's; he had a handsome, clear-featured face, with glossy black hair that he combed straight back like Clark Gable did. In fact, from the neck up he was Clark Gable; below he was Hardy of Laurel and Hardy. On the dance floor he was Fred Astaire. I still see him on the lacquered floor of the Andrew Jackson Ballroom, twirling his partner out, waving his free hand in circles, and shaking his big behind to the beat. I see him flinging open the door of his squad car and springing his heft out. For a while Bill was a deputy sheriff, one of several perks he picked up simply from coming from a respectable family and needing an income.

I understood as a kid that he was not ordinary. He was never "Mister" to me. He was "Bill." One of his girlfriends, if that's the way to put it, was Mrs. Carter. A joke went around that everybody got to lay pipe to Mrs. Carter but Mr. Carter. You had to feel sorry for Mr. Carter. Even though you weren't a master in the art of doing it— in fact, hadn't done it yet—you knew that strong emotional eddies swirled around the act, and that it involved a lot of craziness.

Mr. Carter was an auto mechanic, always in work clothes and grime on him somewhere. He was meek in that he never had much to say, but he was strong-looking, and I guess you could say handsome, when the grime came off. The trouble was that grime didn't come off that often and maybe that was what Mrs. Carter held against him. Or his being a mechanic, something. Mrs. Carter wore high heels and large hats and wafted eau de cologne. Mr. Carter smiled a lot, as if he knew what you were thinking. What you were thinking was, Hey, somebody is banging your wife. How could he take it? Somehow he had come to terms with it. He fixed cars, strolled home to the paper or the radio or mowing the grass, and didn't fool around. Bill Gahaggen fooled around. He fooled around a lot. He acted like a teen-ager. He acted like me if I'd been able to do it.

One summer I was hired as a curb hop at the Sweet Shoppe. I wore a stiffly starched white cap and jacket and ambled out to cars parked on the side street when the driver hit the horn and wanted service. I was amazed to be taken seriously and went about my duties in a startled nervous way. People I'd known all my life now treated me differently. Bill Gahaggen didn't joke around. We conveniently forgot he lived down the street from me. I was now a curb-hop, there to take his order. There he sat, taking up most of the room in the front seat, beside Mrs. Carter. I smelled that eau de cologne that came past the sweat from Bill. I thought I saw the whiteness of her hand resting on Bill's spreading thigh. "Bring us two Falstaffs," Bill said. As if we'd never met.

"Anything else?"

"I need some Camels, honey," Mrs. Carter said in the softest voice. "Could you get me some, honey?" The "honeys" were not meant for me.

"Yeah, a pack of Camels, too."

"And matches, too," Mrs. Carter said.

"And matches, too," Bill said. As if I wasn't meant to hear Mrs. Carter.

I brought them two frosted Falstaff beers, something most people didn't drink at high noon, Camels, and matches to the side. I hooked the tray on Bill's door and didn't receive a tip. Probably he figured he could get away with it since we were neighbors. Maybe he was cheap, too, the way lots of people were in town. The higher up they were, the cheaper they got, I found out. But I got to squint down to where Mrs. Carter's dress was hiked up above her knees, revealing the edge, my God, of pink underwear. It was sort of like a tip. Her hand was definitely on Bill's thigh. That day I remember I went back to my station in front of the Sweet Shoppe and began gabbing with Jimmy, a funny, hyperactive black boy a little older than me. He hung around the front of the Sweet Shoppe, not working, never seeming to be going anywhere in particular. I'd have never gotten to know him or trade stories with him except for this job. Doing menial work, taking orders from everyone, giving them no one, allowed me this association. He just appeared one day, ready to gab. He came up ready to be pals. We were both innocents, as I look back on it. I brought him sodas on the house and loose cigarettes when I could. He told stories in a mock serious way that I couldn't get enough of. We laughed together. We made fun of everybody. We laughed at my boss at the Sweet Shoppe, we laughed at the sorry baseball team in town, we laughed at drunks and crazy drivers and holy rollers. It was liberating to be on the other side of a divide that I didn't quite understand but knew was there. We got away with every subject, fearless and intoxicated, until I made a mistake that afternoon when Bill and Mrs. Carter came to call. "Lookey there, Jimmy, that's Mrs. Carter sitting in that car with Bill Gahaggen. You think he's getting any?"

Jimmy's face turned serious. I'd never seen him frightened before. "I don't know nothing about that. I don't want to know nothing about that. I got to go."

* * *

Bill was the law. He was curiously directed, as part of his deputy sheriff job, to raid a lover's lane on the highway, one in front of a statue lauding frontier days in Tennessee. The composite statue was of a frontiersman in suspenders and coonskin holding a musket, his wife in bonnet and long dress, leading a couple of children into the glorious future. It was mythical Tennessee. The area around the statue was today. It was strewn with rubbers. It was a place where you might get away with doing it. In his gray uniform of big man size, Bill would stealthily pull his squad car into the dark expanse in front of the frontier statue at night, tip-toe his bulk up to a car, and flash his light inside. Chances were he'd catch someone at something. He scared people half to death, but no one got hauled into court. Invariably, the culprits, if such they could be called, got off with a warning. Once in awhile he shared a cigarette with them. Some nights Bill reversed the order and was a culprit himself. His black Chevrolet coupe had been spotted more than once, rocking at midnight. He was doing it or doing something. His stint as a deputy sheriff ended, though, the night he turned his torch on what turned out to be the bare ass of the editor of the local paper, going up and down on his secretary. It happened that the editor's paper was currently having a great deal of fun with the sheriff, mocking his ham-handed attempts to equally enforce some antiquated bizarre drinking laws. (The sheriff didn't drink and was a Pentecostal who had collared a Methodist minister at a bootlegger's.) However, the sheriff mistakenly thought the paper's mockery was praise. All he saw was his name in print. He was the paper's number one fan. The paper's editor called the sheriff immediately after his bare ass had been revealed going up and down on his secretary, and Deputy Bill was fired the next day.

He immediately needed an income. His mother might cook his meals, make his bed, but a forty-year-old-or-so boy needed folding money. You couldn't picture him pumping gas or hauling trash. He might sign on as a census taker or a poll watcher, but those plums didn't come around every day. And no one was going to pin a badge on him again and hand him a revolver. In his heart Bill was an entrepreneur who was chasing the end of the rainbow for that elusive pot of gold.

*   *   *

He was not alone. There were those who put up miniature golf courses on vacant lots or opened chili parlors where once there had been a dress shop or ran a newspaper that had yet to find a reader. I had been bitten by the free-enterprise bug myself. In the sixth grade I had read a library book called *T-Model Tommy*, about a young man who one day ran across an abandoned T-Model Ford, fixed it up and got it running, all by himself. Then he started a business delivering furniture and groceries, you name it, and soon expanded to high heavens. He hired others, he fixed up other decrepit T-Models. He became a millionaire. But, underneath, he remained the same good old good-hearted fellow he had always been. I loved that book. I kept reading and rereading it. I started my own "business" in grammar school.

From my nickel-and-dime "allowance" and from siphoning off some pennies from lunch money, I marched into a wholesale warehouse in town that dealt in confectionary, a closed dark expanse wherein an overwhelming spicy aroma sent you into a swoon, and there I ordered up a few cartons of Three Musketeers, Milky Ways, and Power Houses, going as far as my change would allow. I could tell from the grim looks that met me that no boy had ever popped in before for such an order. No one knew quite know what to do. But candy was legal. I had the money. They were in business. They sold it to me. I carried the bars to school in my satchel and began peddling them on the sly. I cleared a few cents—after all, I had gotten them wholesale—but I didn't clean up. It was work and I ate into my profits, literally. But I got the satisfaction of feeling like an entrepreneur and it was a heady feeling. I was a Henry Ford or an Andrew Carnegie.

I went on to open a soft-drink stand on the vacant lot beside our house in the summer, but it required a lot of heavy lifting and using a lot of space in our cramped refrigerator, plus the fact that my father turned out to be my main customer for the bottles I had not drunk myself—and my entrepreneurial fire began dimming, although was not put out. I had a paper route that required me to rise before dawn, but it unraveled because of my incomprehension of bookkeeping and the fact that a substantial number of customers paid only when they wanted.

My final foray into business was to install a "haunted house" in my upstairs bedroom. With money leftover from my paper route, I'd ordered a kit from a mail-order novelty store. I put up a dangling cardboard skeleton, a big monster head that sprang from a small box and wiggled, and a device that made sounds you might persuade yourself was the roll of thunder and the crackle of lightning. On my own, inspired, I rigged a pitcher of water over the door so I could tilt it by a silk thread, causing water to spill over the head of the unfortunate who might pass below. Admission: twenty-five cents.

I combed the neighborhood and found only one taker, a solemn-faced, tow-headed boy who was amenable to nearly everything. He never had much to say, seldom laughed, never got mad or into trouble. He was always available to pass a baseball no matter what time I came by the cramped apartment he lived in with his mother and father and three sisters. No matter what the weather, even if he was in the middle of a meal, he was ready to go when I came by socking my fist into my glove. I liked slinging the baseball with him, back and forth, easing into a rhythm, nothing too hard or too soft, and not being required to say anything. Other boys liked to chatter and sneak in a hardball when you weren't looking and watch you yelp. His name was Alfred. He came to the house on Saturday morning when I first opened for business, and paid me two dimes and a nickel, solemn as a judge. I told him to wait; then

I raced up the stairs and hid under the bed. As I heard him coming up the steps and coming near, I got the giggles. He opened the door and I yanked the string. I yanked too hard. The heavy glass pitcher left its perch and hit him squarely in the head.

In the emergency room two blocks up on Boone Street, while the gash on his forehead was being sewn up, I tried to give Alfred back his twenty-five cents. He wouldn't take it. He didn't cry or even wince as stitch after stitch went in under a glaring light. I left the business world after that. In high school I became a socialist.

* * *

Bill held onto his dream of an entrepreneurial coup. He had to. He had to dream up a money scheme if he wanted to get around town, and he did. He turned the old barn behind his house, one that hadn't been a real barn in forty years—one like ours—into a henhouse. Sometime later I heard a saying and I thought of Bill. It went, "There are three illusions every man must pass through. One: that love conquers all. Two: that the nation's leaders have your best interest at heart. And three: that you can make money raising chickens." With seed money from a half-focused banker or from his mother, he had the barn fixed up, complete with meshed wire cages, water tanks, and barrels of feed. Soon peeps came from the place and not long afterwards the crow of roosters and the cluck-ing of hens. A scent came downwind and I caught the drift in our house. I thought I could smell it downtown. No one thought to complain. Who were you going to complain to and to what end? No one knew any law against it. There weren't that many laws around anyhow. And no one wanted to run Bill out of business. You just smelled that barnyard smell and made the best of it.

Bill had pulled it off. The hen house had gone up and chick-ens filled it. Bill had done everything to bring it about except one thing: work it. Somebody else had to do that, and, as always, when real work was necessary someone came along. In fact, it was two people: Dicey and Dewey. Dicey was a girl, Dewey a boy. They passed themselves off as brother and sister and maybe they were.

They came from "the country." If you came from town, then people would know your relatives and a lot about you. They came from "the country." They had apple cheeks and rough chapped hands. I don't know where they slept; maybe in Bill's house, maybe in the henhouse. Bill had an "office" in the henhouse where he took a seat in a heavily cushioned, large, wicker-bottomed chair, where from behind a cluttered desk that held a phone, he took orders for eggs and fryers and fowls. Customers walked in, shouting their needs over the din and through drifting feathers.

Dicey and Dewey gathered eggs early in the morning and later through the day did what was necessary to do in the poultry business. They divvied up tasks. One would grab a chicken and wring its neck as if cranking a car. It happened in a blur. I watched them at work once, and one time was enough. The headless chicken zigzagged down a path that had been cleared out and then collapsed. The other one grabbed it, threw it in a tank of scalding water, and then plucked it. The innards were yanked out and put in a little sack. If a customer wanted it cut up, either one did it with a big knife, usually Dicey—deftly, unhesitatingly, with a vengeance. Dewey served as a delivery boy on a battered bike.

Dicey stayed behind in the shop, and there was no doubt that she was a girl. Her nipples pooched out against a sweatshirt and her legs were long and coltish. At times you felt that there might be a better place on earth for her than in a henhouse. She seemed to know that men sized her up when they came near, but she didn't flirt. A man might greet her and say something fresh and she'd stare back and look as if she wasn't above wringing his neck like the chicken. Town girls never acted that way. She acted like a woodland creature or some animal that kept a wary eye out for trouble and the main chance. It was a look that said, if I give you something, if I do something, what do I get in return? It was the look of an animal that would snatch up the meat if you ever turned your back. She gave the impression that life was not altogether worth that much. Chickens and animals and everyone else died. No big deal. There was not a shred of sentiment in her. But, yes, she was a girl.

Bill made money in the chicken business. It may have surprised him as much as anyone else. He started going around in a giddy daze, not quite sure what to do with the good luck that had been preceded by so much bad. It was as if he needed some real bad luck to bring him back to earth. And he got it. In late spring Dicey's nipples began pooching out more and a belly that had been as flat as a board began swelling. There was no denying what that meant. When you were in the hen house your eyes went from the belly over to Bill plopped down like a Buddha in his stuffed chair. He acknowledged the glances, didn't shrug and say, Who me? He acted as if it wasn't bad luck at all. Here was a life-long bachelor throwing in the towel. Here was a man who had been laying pipe in other men's wives for years and now was calling it quits.

Could it be because Mrs. Carter's hair had turned white and her features hawk-like? Mrs. Carter still drove in to the Dixie Drive-In for a milkshake in the evening, looking around as if waiting for someone to show up, but it certainly wasn't going to be Bill. He had ceased cruising, but he remained a gentleman. He supplied Mrs. Carter and her husband with free eggs and a fryer every now and then.

* * *

The wedding took place in Bill's mother's house. The crowd overflowed and from my front yard I could see people milling around the front porch, holding drinks or cookies or something. Dicey wore a dress and looked as stern as ever, as if this was just another event in life's arsenal, one she would get the most out of. She would just take it on stoically. Bill became ecstatic. You might have thought he was going to have the baby. He took Dicey to Gatlinburg on a honeymoon and left Dewey in charge of the business. Dewey was competent, though sullen, and didn't have the easy banter Bill had that drew the home crowd in.

People were glad when the honeymooners returned. The two set up housekeeping in the house like a normal couple, and Dewey was allowed to remain around. We waited.

The baby came. There was hardly a break in the daily routine at the hen house. It was as if Dicey just decided on the spur of the moment to go up to the emergency room and relieve herself of something. She came back with a large object swaddled in a blue blanket. It was a boy and named Bill, Jr. From then on Bill mostly took care of Bill, Jr. in the hen house office. There was a little playpen. There was Bill's big lap. Everyone came to pay respects. I was never big on babies, but whenever I came to get eggs or a fryer, I got up real close to little Bill, Jr. in big Bill's lap and studied him. I couldn't help it. I looked at him and then rolled my eyes over to Dewey, not moving my head. Dewey had a wen above his left eye and the baby had none. I noted how Dewey's mouth turned down at the corners. I noticed a lot of things. Then I looked squarely at Bill, Jr.—and you know who he looked like? He looked like Clark Gable. There was no mistake. You looked down at that baby and you thought he might rise up and say, "Frankly, my dear, I don't give a damn." It was Bill's baby and he was in seventh heaven.

And while he was most happy, at the pinnacle of his life, he suddenly fell over while handing over a fryer to someone and died of a massive coronary. Bill, Jr. had begun walking that week, walking all over the place. The preacher at the funeral quoted scripture and issued the usual homilies and the impression you were left with was that Bill had ended life as a normal human being. He had been to the mountaintop or some such place, he had been in the valley, he had suffered, but he had done his duty. He had died with cherished loved ones.

The henhouse business went under a short time later. Dicey and Dewey took to screaming at each other and no one liked to be around them. Bill's mother couldn't live with them and Bill, Jr. was too much for her, fond as she was of him. The whole kit and caboodle had to pack up and leave. They didn't seem to have planned much for the future, but you took one look at them and knew that if anyone would survive on this earth, it would be them. I had once watched Dicey diaper Bill, Jr., and she had done it efficiently and petulantly in a blur. And with a vengeance. As if she were dressing a plucked bird. As they left for the country, Dicey hefting Bill, Jr.

up, he was about the biggest baby I had ever seen. He was more like a grown boy. He was practically ready to shave. And he was telling Dicey and Dewey in baby talk what to do. There was no doubt who was in charge. They left for the country. Once or twice Dicey brought Bill, Jr. back to visit his grandmother while she was alive but he would break something or he would run out the door and have to be retrieved and they would cut the visit short.

The henhouse that was once a barn was torn down and plowed under like Carthage. Grass soon grew on the spot invigorated by chickenshit. Later, much later, Bill, Jr. came in from the country as a very big man and ran for sheriff. He got elected.

victor mature

Funny about old snapshots and pictures, and even memories, and how they never anticipate what is about to come. Take Harry Tipton. Harry was an outstanding figure—you could say a spectacular figure—in the early part of his life. If fat Bill Gahaggen had been Clark Gable from the neck up, Harry Tipton was Victor Mature all over, right down to his limpid dark eyes and wet, sensuous lips, plus a body right off a Greek statue. He was something. He was an Adonis. In photos, his half-cocked smile looked out from behind glass in the trophy case in the high school gym when I came along. He was around ten years older than me, something like that, and his photos were beginning to yellow. It was fitting that his photos should have aged along with him. It put his story more in perspective. He sits with his legs crossed beneath him in an old-timey football uniform, his hair curly, his shoulders broad. He stands tall and muscular in a silk basketball uniform, in high-top gym shoes the color of his hair. He wears a gray baseball uniform with black stockings, jokingly holding a bat as if about to swing at the photographer. He looks as if he's having a terrific time and ready to take on the world. Those photos and a pile of ancient clippings are about the only historical documents of that earlier life.

Harry's girlfriend during his early heroic period was Cathy Doak. She was a cheerleader. Guys who were cheerleaders were guys who couldn't play sports and were usually glad-handers and politicians in the making. Dismiss them. Their smiles were too white and they seemed to have a sunbeam up their ass. The girls were something else. They could drive you insane with desire. Whoever thought them up? They stood out on the cinder track before the stands at football games, their backs to the green grass playing field; they raced to the side of the basketball court at half-time. They threw up their arms and did the locomotive. And what was the *creme de la creme,* the *coup de grace*, the *coup de main*, was when they twirled and their satin panties flashed. Not a hint, the works. The funny thing was that in ordinary life they went to great length to cover up. They wore skirts that came past their knees, and they were forever adjusting those skirts when they sat. They were so modest and unassertive otherwise. Cathy Doak, Harry's girl, was that way, the prototype: the nicest girl in town. And now here was the only chance you'd ever have in life to look up her dress. Another girl, say, who had the least bit of sluttish reputation, where more than one had lifted her dress and gone under, never got to be a cheerleader.

Cathy and Harry decided to get married right after high school. They must really be in love, the story went. She's not even knocked up. To top it off, Harry had received a scholarship, all expenses paid, to play football for the UT Vols. It wasn't exactly practical to be a married fullback, busting through the line, but Harry and Cathy couldn't wait and they wanted to do it legally. It went without saying, everyone knew, that the only way Harry was going to get past those satin cheerleader panties was to marry her. One look at her enormous doe-like eyes and church-going ways and you understood that fact. She was a determined woman, and she was going to marry Harry Tipton. She saw to a rental of a one-bedroom apartment over a grocery store near Shields-Watkins Stadium in Knoxville. Harry would have a home-cooked meal waiting after classes and football practices. Harry was going to be the next All-American for the mighty Vols in orange and white, everyone was sure, and a moral married man to boot. Could you beat that?

It was late summer, the wedding set, announcements sent out. Then a nagging pain in Harry's right knee, something he blamed on an old football injury kept bothering him. He had trouble walking. Cathy convinced him to go to a regular doctor and not to the old quack Doc Davis who cleared high school players to compete with anything short of compound fractures and concussions that wiped out reason and memory—and sometimes even that. She got him to a specialist and he limped into the office, then he limped into the hospital for a series of x-rays and tests. Cathy saw to it, was with him every step of the way. Cathy was with him when he got the news. He had cancer of the bone. He would have to have his leg removed.

"I should have stayed with old Doc Davis," he said from a hospital bed.

"Oh, Harry . . . *Harry* . . ." Cathy said, beside him.

He had the operation. There then became two Harry Tiptons. The first lived in memory and old photographs. The first Harry Tipton had a cocky, lopsided grin and an easygoing disposition. He was so good at what he did, and accomplished, that he didn't have to brag or act better than anyone else. He was the best.

The second Harry Tipton was angry. It was as if he was searching for the first Harry Tipton and couldn't find him.

"Look, Cathy, listen," he told the love of his life. "We don't have to marry. What do you want with a one-legged guy?"

A nurse heard this conversation and passed it along. What got said and done in town was invariably passed along if there was a pair of ears to hear and a pair of eyes to see. We had nothing better to do.

"Oh, Harry," Cathy had reportedly said, and she had a soft voice, becoming softer still since Harry lost his leg. "I'd love you if you didn't have any legs at all. I'd love you if you didn't have any arms either. I'll always love you, Harry."

Harry tried to be mad at whatever, or whoever, it was that had taken his leg from him. He tried his anger on the medical profession. Had the operation really been necessary? Why hadn't he gone for further diagnosis somewhere else? Why hadn't he gone to Johns Hopkins, where you really got the lowdown? He wanted to redo his decision to let them remove a leg in Tennessee. He wanted to go back. He didn't want to go forward. Cathy kept singing the praises of an artificial leg as Harry was getting by on crutches, his pant leg pinned over his stump. It was how he used to get around with a football injury. He had once had a broken ankle and a ruptured Achilles and used crutches. Cathy was adamant about an artificial leg, and cheerful. Some people you couldn't tell whether they had an artificial leg or not. Some could even tap dance, she wanted Harry to know. Everyone forgot after awhile that the leg was not a real one. It was like glasses. After awhile people forgot you wore them. You must do it, Harry.

Harry did it. It was one of the worst artificial legs anyone had ever seen—not that we had seen that many. There was a Negro man who shined shoes down by the train station who had peg leg that he would twirl on occasionally and do a tap dance with the good leg, but that was more or less the extent of comparison. Harry's creaked when he walked and he had to throw it out in an arc to move forward. The shoe, which stayed shiny and looked small enough for a midget, never bent when he walked. But he was game with it, its creak and the wide arc away from the body it took to move it. But at least he was not on crutches. Cathy saw to it all. She saw to it that he stood up front in formal rented attire, complete with striped pants, as she walked down the aisle all in white at the First Baptist Church. She got them an apartment over a garage in town that was similar to the apartment they had been slated to move into in Knoxville. Cathy went to work as a secretary for a real estate firm.

Harry tried at first to be a clerk in various stores. Everyone tried to help because his aura as a champion still clung to him; on the other hand, you wanted to help someone who'd lost a leg. Harry tried, as a shoe salesman, putting a shoe on someone while his midget shoe stuck out in front of him, his artificial leg unbent. He tried being a stock boy in a grocery store but couldn't really navigate the aisles with a leg that swung in a wide arc. At the Sweet Shoppe where I worked as a curb hop he lasted only a few hours. The Sweet Shoppe was a combined drug store, soda fountain, and beer joint. It sold rubbers under the counter and Kotexes above. It served a lot of needs. It was while Harry was waiting on his third or fourth customer that he came undone, when he tried to wrap up a box of Kotex for a man on an errand for his wife. The customer wanted to make a fast getaway, but Harry kept fumbling trying to wrap it up until the man grabbed it unwrapped, put it under his arm, and hot-footed it out while those nearby sniggered. Harry creaked out not long afterward, not bothering to pick up his pay.

The old Harry, the Harry with two strong powerful legs, had had a different plan for the future. Everyone knew about it. He had spread the story around. He would play football for the mighty Vols, be an All-American, and then be set up in some kind of business by appreciative alumni—say, a car dealership where just his presence and name would sell the cars. Or he would run for office—be a congressman. Or he would be a coach. He and Cathy would have five children. They would have a lakefront home. But first he would have to be a football star in college and charm the crowds. And that was not to be. He couldn't get by with having been a high school star, and now with a terrible artificial leg.

* * *

You just couldn't imagine the first Harry Tipton doing what the second Harry Tipton came to do. After he left the job at the Sweet Shoppe he kept coming back to hang out as a customer and drink the draft beer in a large paraffin cup that the store sold. The Sweet Shoppe was down from the First Baptist Church, separated by the church's grassy slope. He didn't like to stand around in the fluorescent light of the Sweet Shoppe, but would take his paraffin cup, foam sloshing over its side, and go to the dimness of the Baptist church's grassy slope. The slope was like an annex to the Sweet Shoppe where drinkers and gabbers liked to go to get away from prying eyes. Groups staked out their territory there and, as in most areas, the whites had their province, the Negroes had theirs. Of course, the Negroes had to hang out down where the grass was sparse.

It was a Wednesday night that I remember. Prayer Meeting was going on in church, the hymns and sermon and prayers coming through open windows while the beer drinkers congregated on the grassy slope, passing yarns and tilting cups. I don't know what started it. You never know until after it's over, and then the reason seems ridiculous. Maybe it was over territory, maybe some bad-mouthing had got out of hand. All I know is that Harry Tipton stood facing a Negro who wasn't backing down from whatever it was that had come up. A crowd had formed. Most of the Negro men were strangers to me. I couldn't remember seeing them before, but probably they'd lived all their lives in town. The man who faced Harry was as tall as Harry, slim, and had a cautious but determined look in his eye. You could tell he didn't want trouble, but he wasn't going to back down either. Harry was the problem. He was mad as hell—whether three or four Negroes had taken space near him or some looks had passed, something, but he was puffing up his big chest. The Negro didn't budge. Scenes like this happened, but not often. They seemed to come out of nowhere like a summer storm and somehow cleared the air. They were reminders that Negroes and whites lived in separate worlds in town and that it was strange if you thought about it. Negroes had their own barbers, doctors and undertakers. We knew nothing about them. They could have lived in China.

I watched. Naturally, I was not at Prayer Meeting. I could smell the beer that came off Harry. It seemed to come from his very pores. He spoke over the hymn that was now being sung in the church. "I Walk Through the Garden Alone" came softly and sweetly and mostly out of tune. Harry said, his chest puffing out more, "I don't give a Goddamn if you've got a knife or not."

"I don't need a knife," the Negro said.

"Stand there and fight, then."

Harry moved toward him. And I saw that the man saw out of the corner of his eye Harry's artificial leg. It seemed the first time he noticed it. His expression changed. "Ah, shoot, man, go home." And he turned and walked away, leaving behind a dry laugh.

Harry was left with his fists doubled up and nobody to fight. It's strange to think of that encounter after what followed.

* * *

Harry began hanging out in the poolroom where you could drink beer straight out of the bottle and not have to bother with a paraffin cup. Before long he began shooting a game or two to pass the time, and before you knew it, had become the best shot in town. Just like that. Pool was not football or basketball, but it was sort of like a sport with a winner and a loser and you had to have a steady nerve and a good eye and hang tough. It didn't matter that you had an artificial leg that stuck out behind you like a plank every time you bent over the harshly lit green felt table. I ate up the sight of him effortlessly and almost lazily sinking ball after ball, chalking his cue, taking aim and plunging the nine ball straight into the pocket with a sharp snap. He had a neat way of slipping his winnings in his pocket, not bothering to count the bills and verify the amount. You imagined it was the way a real sport did it. He began to make a living at pool. He beat the owner of the poolroom in a match that lasted all night. Then he outgrew the players in town. There was no one left to play. No one could beat him.

If he was going to continue in this career he would have to go where his reputation was not known. But how was he going to get to those far shores? He couldn't drive because he couldn't operate the pedals with his artificial leg and midget shoe. In his former guise, as the first Harry, he had been a daredevil driver. Now he had to find someone who knew the ins and outs of pool shooting and who had time on his hands. Who could drive and had a car. Who knew the art of gambling and hustling. Cathy was out. She could take up the slack in many ways, but not with that. She pretended that the money Harry brought home came from some mysterious but honorable source. It could be from divine intervention.

Harry found Teddy—or Teddy found him. Maybe Teddy had been among the Negro crowd beside the Baptist church. Maybe he had heard of Harry through a pool shooting grapevine. He became taken with him. He followed Harry around, usually at a discreet distance, but there. At first, as the story went, Harry tried to shake him off. Who wanted to have a roly-poly Negro as black as midnight on your heels, especially when you were trying to walk in a dignified way with a god-awful artificial leg? Teddy dressed like a dandy with a flattop hat with the brim turned up and a feather stuck in the ribbon. He had a gold tooth with diamond-like stone stuck in its middle. He was one Negro who was hard to miss. He did odd jobs at the hospital, but mainly he was a professional gambler at illegal punch boards, sport scores, dice, poker, pool hustling, you name it. He drove a rattletrap Ford.

* * *

The Pot Liquor Club, not far from the railroad tracks, was the town's black pool hall. It was on the second floor of a dilapidated building and when you passed you could hear balls clicking and catch the sight of dark figures, some with shaved heads, moving, and you heard rough guffaws. It was a merriment you never found on the street. I loved stealing looks up there, which was a foreign land that offered the promise of breaking free from whatever held you down below. You could throw off the shackles. Teddy helped Harry up the stairs and into it. No white man had ever gone there before probably. Harry took on the best shot there, a shark from Memphis, never defeated in town before, and won. According to reports, Teddy got a cut. From then on Teddy and Harry were gambling buddies, a team.

Teddy drove Harry to towns around the state and down into Georgia. A question hovered in all minds, one never asked, as to where they stayed on the road. A lot of questions about a lot of things hovered over our heads but this one was the most persistent. We figured Harry creaked his leg into Negro homes and lived the life of a Negro. He did have a dark complexion, like Victor Mature. "Harry must turn into a nigger once he gets out of here," more than one said. Teddy sure wasn't going to pass for white. Harry eased off drinking and his face ceased being bloated. He prospered; he came by a fancy personal cue stick that had to be screwed together and was carried in a little black case like a doctor's. Teddy often carried it for him. Teddy did everything but move in.

He would telephone. If he hadn't heard from Harry in a few hours he would call Harry's apartment. Cathy would answer. "Honey, it's for you," she would say. "Teddy."

She accepted Teddy. She didn't understand Teddy and how Teddy fitted in, but she accepted it. She didn't understand a lot of things, but if that's what Harry wanted, that was what was going to be.

Harry was slowly but surely going off the gold standard. He broke free. In fact, he began breaking the law. They said he paid no taxes and didn't have to because he always dealt in cash. He carried a large wad on him at all time, and bet on anything. He once bet on how many birds would light on a telephone wire, and won a large sum. Rumor had it that Teddy had gone up and put something on the wire that made a whole flock of sparrows descend. Harry was hauled into court now and then, but always got off with a small fine or exonerated completely. He creaked in on his awful leg and the judge and jury gave leniency.

I saw him once without the leg. It was at the Sur-Joy swimming pool. He was suddenly there to swim, and I'm not sure what prompted him. To show he still could? To just show his stump off to everybody and get it over with? Here it is, everybody. Look at it. Cathy was with him, but she hadn't changed into a swimsuit. She looked scared and anxious. Teddy wasn't there, of course. He couldn't have gotten past the front gate. Maybe he was waiting in his car.

Harry hopped out from a changing stall in old-fashioned wool trunks that must have dated from his high school years. You could see moth holes in them. I hated to look at the stump and at the same time couldn't look away. I had seen a stump before. A boy in grammar school had had part of his arm torn off by a bull. He used to hold it up, grin, and say, "A bull done it." The stump was small and pale. It was as if it was some sort of joke. With Harry you could see where the surgeon had folded the skin over the bone. The fold was pink.

Harry paused a moment by the edge of the pool, and, as everybody up and down looked embarrassingly his way, dove perfectly in the deep end. He didn't even cause a splash, and he didn't come up. Cathy was wringing her hands and frowning, and then smiling as if holding back tears. No one wanted to get alarmed. Alarmed, you would show you didn't think Harry should be trying to swim with only one leg. You couldn't see very deeply into the water of the Sur-Joy because the water was not all that clean. It seemed like forever that he was down there. Then while everyone stood staring at the deep end, Harry suddenly came up down at the far end by the baby pool. He'd gone the length of the pool, a good fifty yards, under water. He came up and breast-stroked up and down the pool for an hour. When he pulled himself out I saw how well-muscled his good leg was. His chest was as big as they come.

As far as I know that was the only time he went swimming in the Sur-Joy. He didn't need to. He had proven his point. When he approached middle-age he began having girlfriends on the side. He was proving he could do that too. One look at Cathy and the saint-like glow she gave off might be hard to live with, too. It was probably hard to sleep with a saint. But they stayed together, tight as could be. Harry Tipton was the only man ever in her life. He was as necessary to her as the air. It seemed to prove that a good woman never left you once she was yours.

john garfield

War came, and everyone was wondering who Teresa "Terry" Auburon was going to bring home. Shortly after Pearl Harbor, she had gone off to Washington, D.C. to work for the war effort. A few hometown girls did that. It was a substitute for going into the service like the boys, a chance to escape and have adventures. Now word had it that she was bringing a husband back. Terry was deemed a town beauty—black-eyed and black-haired, with a muscular build and a long-legged stride. In town she had strode straight-backed down Main Street with a purposeful air, neither looking left or right. Some said she was stuck up, or crazy, or something. She was different. When last seen she had been going up the iron steps of Number 42, off for the nation's capital. It was a time when people who, if it hadn't been for the war, wouldn't have traveled more than a hundred miles away now were on Guadalcanal or in a Flying Fortress over Germany—or like Terry Auburon going away and bringing a stranger home.

Some went off, and that was it: no coming back. Joe Collins who lived in the neighborhood and had lied about his age got in the Marines at sixteen. He was dead within six months on Iwo Jima. I had played basketball with him in the vacant lot beside my house where I had dug a hole and planted a backboard and hoop that tilted ten degrees off center. Neighborhood boys flocked. Joe had cornsilk-fine hair and a nervous way of brushing it back from his forehead. He had an unorthodox way of shooting the ball, cocking his hand behind his head as if shotputting. Once in awhile it surprised everyone by going in. He had BO. Joe lived in a neighborhood eyesore, a ramshackle one-story house that badly needed paint. The BO that rose from him did have a sweet-sour touch that made you think of the poor. Joe was the only boy in a family of four girls, an exhausted nervous mother, and a father who was dead. I remember one twilight, when a gang of us had been playing for hours and one of the Bellamy boys called Joe "trash."

The breathed word "trash" had hardly left the Bellamy boy's lips when Joe sprung at his throat. Usually when angered and out of control you just hauled off and socked some boy or wrestled him to the ground. Joe began choking the Bellamy boy as if it was life or death, making him fall over, Joe on top, choking him so that Bellamy's head banged up and down on the clay floor. We had trouble prying Joe's hands loose, but we had to because Bellamy was turning blue. Joe never spoke to Bellamy again, nor Bellamy to him after he got his voice back. Now Joe was dead. A gold star went up on his front door window and his picture in Marine dress blue went on the front page of the paper. That's how it went. If you died, say, from a "lingering illness" it didn't give you heroic stature in the paper. You had died from cancer although no one called it that. Joe was a hero—but we never found out how. Joe had died far away. Iwo Jima had done it, but Iwo Jima was halfway around the world, and only those from our region who got to see it were those washed ashore and shot at. Joe was sixteen, although he had passed as eighteen after doctoring his birth certificate. I used to think, somewhat crazily, that no one would ever be around any more to see the brown fuzz that used to cover his legs nor smell his BO. No coffin came back.

Everything was changing. Everything was war, war, war. It seemed to happen overnight. Before it had been a big adventure to simply go out in the country where they used kerosene lamps and slept in feather beds. Football was the big news. Butter came in from the country in pots, so creamy you could scoop it out with a spoon. Now you had oleomargarine where you had to squirt an orange substance on a greasy white bar and mixed it so the result looked like butter but tasted like metal. I noticed women's legs as they walked, and could easily spot those who'd painted their legs tan with a black stripe up the back. Hose were in short supply. Cars had stickers on them that showed the allotment for gas. There were ration books for meat and sugar and coffee. Movies were about war and the diabolical enemy. Tin cans were collected to fight the Japs and Krauts. War bonds were hawked. Blackouts were tried a couple of times whereby all electricity was cut off to get us ready for enemy bombers. It made sense because, to us, we were the center of the universe. We couldn't picture them wanting to bomb anyplace else since we were it. The only benefit to blackouts turned out to be that couples got to go at it beneath tables in the pitch black dark Sweet Shoppe. It was all different in the blink of an eye. They said morals got looser as regards to sex, but how was I to know?

The thing I missed most, when war came, was ice cream. I had taken it for granted. That's what got to me. I hadn't realized what I had. Before it had been so creamy and the peaches and strawberries inside some flavors seemed picked right off the vine. Vanilla tasted like vanilla. It was a taste you never forgot, like an innocence you once had. When war came, ice cream became dryer and the peaches and strawberries inside had had something unpleasant done to them. It was like butter turning into oleomargarine. World War II changed everything we had known before. Changed it all.

I wanted in without having to think of dying. What it came right down to was that I wanted to wear a uniform and salute and, better yet, be saluted to. Before, Main Street had been crowded with men in overalls and business suits, women in loose dresses. Now uniforms were all over—from the Navy, Army, Air Corps, Marines, and Merchant Marines. Uniforms crowded bus and train stations, the streets, the drug stores, the pool halls. Everyone else slinked around. You were awarded privileges if you wore a uniform. My father and I walked once by a jam-packed troop train that was on a siding. He was on his way to the depot where, now that there was a manpower shortage, he worked seven days a week, 365 days a year, and never took a day or holiday off. In the Depression he was lucky if he could find work for a few months a year. A drunk soldier, face flushed, tie askew, campaign cap on the back of his head, called out, "Hey, 4-F! Hey, 4-F!" My father, tall and ramrod straight, didn't turn his head, kept walking. His hearing was getting worse and worse. Soldiers poked their heads out windows. They whistled at girls. "Hey, where the hell are we? What's this Podunk place called?" They all had weird accents.

I couldn't say anything. You couldn't say anything back to someone who wore a uniform. He had all the authority in the world. I nearly swooned when my brother rolled in in the spotless white uniform of a lieutenant, junior grade, of the U.S. Navy, complete with white buck shoes. He went down Main Street in his fast, jerky, athletic stride and other uniforms saluted it. And now at home, in the living room, his pals, once in sweaters with school letters sewn on and in windbreakers, were all in uniform, and it was more than the uniforms that had changed them. Darrel Crowe, curly haired and in specs, was a buck private. Everyone said he had an IQ of 160 or something and had been studying engineering at Georgia Tech when called up. He didn't actually salute my brother or Lard Landis, now a lieutenant in the army, but he was toned down from the boisterous person he had been before. He wore wrinkled khakis now. I eavesdropped, longing to wear the white naval officer's uniform or, second best, getting away with those pink trousers and the olive drab blouse that Lard had on. Those shiny gold bars on his shoulders almost blinded you.

It used to be games and girls they talked about; now it was camps, strange impossible cities, funny characters you'd never find in town, train rides, drills, and—what was acknowledged with an embarrassed ducking of the head—where they might be headed. Lard ended up in England and D-Day and the Battle of the Bulge, receiving but one promotion to first lieutenant. He came home unscratched, only to die of a brain tumor ten years later. Darrel Crowe went down over New Guinea as a tail gunner. My brother went off to Hawaii as a physical training officer who, as far as could be determined, principally helped manage a baseball team that consisted of big league players who found themselves in the military. He left behind sea bags full of black socks and white navy drawers you closed with a drawstring in back and buttons in front. My father and I wore them for years and years. They never wore out.

* * *

When war started I hadn't had the blessings of "hairs." When Terry rolled back in they had come, accompanied by an avalanche of juice. It was another thing that had arrived with the war. Images of Miss Mary Louise Luster might inflame my mind; those of Terry Auburon never did. Terry was not a model for desire—too cerebral, too neurotic, too all over the place and doing what she wanted. She brought to mind Katherine Hepburn. I was fascinated, but not aroused. She took no gruff. I was fascinated by the privileges she had been born into and how cavalierly she threw them away. I loved that she had just pulled up stakes and headed for Washington alone. I would always remember that.

In her absence, I had gone in her father's store downtown and thought about her. I went from one end of the store to the other, trying foolishly to make the salespeople think I might be able to buy something. I had taken a bath beforehand and put on my Sunday best before going in a store where I wasn't going to buy anything. I felt like a thief. Terry's father ran Auburon's, the premier men's store in town. If you were a doctor, lawyer, a professional somebody or other, a sport, you went to Auburon's. It spelled class. I felt scared but richer being there. I drank in the tuxes and the two-toned golf shoes. Glass cases gleamed. Rich striped ties lay spread out like a deck of cards. The finest sea-island cotton shirts— button-down, striped, plain, French cuffed—rose in splendid piles. Auburon's sold dress shoes, not brogans. Elaborate tailoring went on. The war, though, had slowed Auburon's business down to a trickle. While the street in front bustled with uniforms, Auburon's mannequins in the windows were outfitted as if they hadn't gotten the news. Here were mannequins in cardigans and tweed while those who passed wore bell-bottoms and GI issue.

Mr. Franklin T. Auburon, Terry's father, was a moon-faced fellow with large eyeglasses that made him look owlish, and his clothes were rumpled and ill fitting, as if he might have bought them elsewhere on sale. He was tight, everyone said. He was a staunch Presbyterian. He seemed forever distracted by all he had to carry around in his large round head, which was a lot. There was Mr. Harrison Delaney, floorwalker and arbiter of taste, a more dapper man God never made. They said he dressed in black tie for dinner and wore an ascot and lounging jacket before bed—and this was frontier Tennessee! I know that I never saw him without a handkerchief fluffing out of his breast pocket and you could comb your hair by the shine on his shoes. That may have added a Beau Brummel quality to the store; the problem was that he flew off the handle at times, screaming at someone who had shown bad taste in something—"No, no, you cannot wear cordovans with pin stripes! Take them off! Burn them!", he had berated a meek dentist who had braved his way there and then never returned. He grew near to violence if he heard an opinion counter to that of main Republican tenets, too. Further down the line was Russell Owens in men's suits, a bald, eternally cheerful bachelor around whom rumors flew. About twice a year he would show up with a black eye and a bandage if not with a limb in a cast and his neck in a brace. He took beatings and I always felt sorry for him although, since he was a source of ridicule to everyone else, I never got to voice it. Men somehow worried, or said they worried, that he might flip their balls when getting trousers measured for alteration, but no one could ever verify that he had flipped any balls.

Mr. Auburon kept his staff performing not through strictness but through befuddlement. He left them to their own devices. Some people are mean and are born mean. They rule through meanness. Others try to do good, but are so confused and conflicted by what faces them that they only muddy the waters when they try to take a stand so they have learned to back off and let problems solve themselves.

Mr. Auburon learned early to back off from his only daughter. Terry confused and mystified him. He never seemed to know what was coming next. Most beautiful girls in town became demure, accepting their ravishing looks like the gift of sainthood. Their models were June Allyson and Deanna Durbin in the movies. And where most girls took up the piano or violin, Terry chose the xylophone. She banged away at it and yodeled like Jimmy Rogers. She wore slacks like Marlene Dietrich. She rode horses and once I saw her change a tire on the side of the road. None of this turned off a horde of suitors. They came after her, in droves. They had crushes—a radio announcer, a basketball star, a ne'er-do-well son of a prominent family, one after another. Nothing stuck. She seemed bored with the lot of them—drumming her fingers on soda fountain tabletops, looking around in movie theaters, yawning and impatient. Even my big brother Harold had a go at her and got turned down, something that rarely happened to him. That really impressed me. Her eyes, dark and brilliant, were looking elsewhere, past Tennessee, past this little town we found ourselves in. She was older than me, a mature woman in my eyes, but I thought I understood her look. She was unhappy. She was trying to find a way out. I was beginning to feel the same way.

* * *

I was at the depot, keeping my father company while his hand flew at the telegraph key, bringing trains in and out, when Terry came in with her new husband. I first saw Mr. and Mrs. Auburon crowding by the train's iron steps, and I rushed out to join them. While steam blew from beneath the train, sailors, soldiers, representatives of the whole fighting forces swung down, toting duffel bags, sea bags, and officer traveling bags. Those in spectacular uniforms got the longest glances—save those in the Merchant Marines. They were dressed like admirals and we were vaguely aware that they occasionally went down with their ships, but they didn't count sadly enough because they didn't fight. Terry took my breath away when she came down. She had changed. She wore high heels and her skirt was tight. She carried a blue piece of Pullman luggage and a great big smile. I put on an idiot smile myself. Behind her came John

Garfield, a half-cocked smile on his face, glancing around as if unsure where he was, as if he had just popped out of water before an exotic island. He wore the crushed hat of an Air Corps officer and there were twin bars on his collar. A captain! He wasn't actually John Garfield, but you could have fooled me. He looked more like John Garfield than John Garfield. His name, we soon learned, was Dan Goodsaid. He was Captain Dan Goodsaid of the U.S. Air Corps. Terry called him Danny.

Mr. Auburon was in the lead to greet them, Mrs. Auburon hovering behind. There were hugs, handshakes, Mr. Auburon grabbing for luggage and Dan Goodsaid holding on for dear life to his officer flight bag. "No, I can handle it, sir. Please."

"We must—Terry, you should—Train an hour late!—Good weather you came down to— I—Huh?" Mr. Auburon was shaking every hand he could find. He even shook mine.

In the best of times Mr. Auburon didn't seem quite right. Now that war had come he seemed to be losing more of his grip. Everything he was used to had changed. People were dying, not to mention the town's loss of interest in two-tone golf shoes. His black-eyed daughter had gone off in slacks and had come back in high heels, carrying a little blue Pullman bag. A week before he had stopped me on the street to ask me my shirt size, me of all people, who was far from wearing dress shirts and certainly none from the high-toned Auburon's Men Store. "You look like a 14/30," he had said, out of the blue, startling me. "I'm going to get you some shirts. I'm not going along with this government rationing!"

I never got any shirts, but I was touched that he had thought of me. He got Terry and Captain Dan Goodsaid packed in his Chevy—a model from a few years back, gone the privilege of a new Chevy every year now because of the war—and drove through red lights and past stop signs without stopping, up to the imposing home with white columns and a gabled porch a block up from our house. The Auburons' home was a show place in many ways, but still they were Presbyterians and frugal. The bride and groom got a front second-story bedroom that faced the street, overlooking the porch. How do I know? Soon enough I was passing on the street, looking up, my heart pumping in my ears. There was John Garfield! Terry! They were putting their clothes away, talking, laughing—the captain in his undershirt and Terry *in a slip*! They had forgotten to pull the shades or they didn't care. I took a few steps on the street, pretended I had forgotten something, went back the other way, kept doing that. I'd have an excuse if caught, but then I heard someone yelling at me from a lower window. Caught! It was Mr. Auburon with his round head and large glasses speaking.

"Hey, *you!*"

"Yes, sir?"

"Come on in. I've got—Hey!—We—we have a new son-in-law. He's in the service and he's upstairs now. Come in and meet him!" He'd forgotten that I'd been down at the depot. Maybe he'd forgotten that he'd caught me looking up at Terry's bedroom window.

Before I knew it I was in the Auburon living room, which was larger than ours and had a musky scent that ours didn't. I shuffled my feet and watched Terry and the beaming captain, now fully dressed, descend the stairs as the aroma of food began wafting in, the harbinger of an early supper. I said hello to the captain in a daze, smiled goofily at Terry, and was left there shuffling my feet. Mr. Auburon was left with no other choice than to invite me to eat with them. Otherwise I'd just be left in the living room shuffling my feet while they ate.

* * *

We all sat in what I could tell was a seldom-used dinning room, under the pale glow of a large overhead lamp. Usually, I took it, they ate in the kitchen like most of us did in town. You could tell that the best china and silverware had come out, items used only once or twice a year, if that. All women had their specialties in town, a special way of cooking, but the essentials were fried chicken, gravies, biscuits, cornbread, green beans in fatback, mashed potatoes, and iced tea. A silent and bemused colored woman, as elusive as a shadow, hovered in the kitchen. She did the heavy lifting and occasionally glided in with dishes. Mrs. Auburon—blue-eyed and with iron-gray hair—commanded the assault with the raising of a hand or soft words to the kitchen. Mrs. Auburon was as scatterbrained as her husband and as delicate as Terry was tough and needed help in the simplest tasks. She chattered away at subjects that hardly had anything to do with whatever was being discussed at the moment. I said not one word through the meal, but I caught the Captain glancing my way occasionally, and bemusedly, as if we both might be in league as outsiders.

"Mm, mm, this is certainly fine food," he said, chewing away.

"Dan," said Mr. Auburon, "I have this great partiality to fried oysters. Bet you can get your fill any time up north."

"I know a terrific seafood restaurant on the Grand Concourse. When you and Mrs. Auburon come—"

"Dan, you must spend some time in our backyard," Mrs. Auburon said. "It's so lovely and peaceful there. The roses are in full bloom."

"I want him to go to church with me this Sunday," Mr. Auburon announced. "We have this new preacher who's a humdinger, Dan. He's so smart I can't understand him until I get home and think about it."

"Dan and I don't want to go to church this Sunday, Daddy. We have other things to do and time is short. Dan only has a week's leave."

"Oh, I wouldn't mind going, sir," Dan said.

"But we're not," Terry said firmly.

"Terry," Mrs. Auburon said, "I'm so glad you're wearing dresses now. I never did like those slacks although I couldn't bring myself to tell you. Don't you think she looks nice in dresses, Dan?"

Terry gritted her teeth.

"She looks good in anything," Dan said, and reached over and took Terry's hand. She squeezed back.

"I didn't like that xylophone she hauled in at first," Mr. Auburon said. "But you can't tell her anything, as I guess you'll find out, Dan. But, you know, I got used to that xylophone and now I miss the sound of it about as much as I miss anything."

The meal passed. There was a long passage where Mr. Auburon went on automatic pilot and told the old story of his youth on the farm and how he had come to town and learned the dry goods business and how the town had streetcars then and there was an opera house for vaudeville. You couldn't believe the changes he had seen. Dan told about planes and camps, which were as strange to the Auburons' ears as his references to the Polo Grounds, Coney Island, and the Automat. As the talk droned on, the newlyweds' hands went beneath the table. Mr. Auburon was asking a question. He was looking at Dan, then Terry.

"Sir?" said Dan.

"I said, what denomination are you?"

"Daddy, I've told you," Terry said. "You just don't listen any more. He's of the Hebraic persuasion."

"You do what?

"I'm Jewish, sir."

"Huh? You what?"

Peach cobbler and banana pudding came, more iced tea. Mr. Auburon told tales about characters in town, things about Terry that went on and on as if she were included as a town character, which she was. She and Dan fidgeted to get upstairs. As they went towards the stairs, Mr. Auburon put his hand on Dan's shoulder. "Mr. Burstein lives up around the corner. Funniest man I ever met." No more was said about faith. Mr. Auburon's synapses closed on the subject, and whatever subterranean matter swirled beneath the surface of consciousness, it became sealed in the face of the inevitable. Terry had brought home a xylophone and the Auburons would have to learn to love the music. I went home to pick at a second dinner, pictures of Terry and the Captain engraved in my mind.

* * *

During that week the captain certainly made himself at home, certainly in the bedroom. I could swear I heard the bedsprings creaking down at my house in the still air. An intoxicating scent wafted from the open bedroom window—perfume and rumpled sheets and bodies locked in swift pursuit of each other. A Bellamy brother and I were ambling down the street when he stopped me before the

Auburon home. "Smell that?" he said. He claimed to have done it on a family trip to Asheville and knew things a lot of us didn't.

"Yeah, smells funny."

"Well, that's fucking you're smelling."

"What?"

"That's fucking coming out of there."

I can see Captain Dan as if only a moment ago, in the fresh early morning light of summer, coming down the sidewalk to get milk or some muffin or something from the small grocery store on Boone Street run by an elderly couple whose business came from those who needed items in a hurry, in off-hours when regular stores were closed. He wears those long military underpants, like my brother brought home from the Navy, and a loose T-shirt. Maybe it wasn't underpants but some military short pants issued for tropical wear. No matter. In those early-hour forays, when the streets were empty, he made a point, I remember, of cheerfulness. He once sashayed out, as a joke, Terry observing from a window and calling out endearments, in one of her kimonos with his Air Corps cap on backwards. She herself flew to the store in one of his Air Corps blouses that came down to her bare knees, sexy fluffy slippers on her feet. The sight of them made you feel the war might present scary pictures of diabolical Germans and Japs coming after you, but here, as dew lay on the grass on soft summer mornings, they made you feel almost glad that war had come.

Captain Dan immediately made himself at home in the neighborhood. He drifted down to the vacant lot in the afternoon to watch while a few of us boys threw the old apple around, doing pop ups and occasionally playing a lackadaisical game of hard ball. Older men—in truth, boys in their late teens, early twenties, most in service, a few 4-Fs—came by to instruct and comment and watch for nothing better to do. In the past my brother, big and muscular, was notorious for barging up, halting a game, and hitting fly balls. "Throw it to me and I'll show you how it's done." I was proud to be associated with someone who could raise a bat, swing through, and never, ever miss. The problem was—and why my buddies groaned when he lumbered up—was that he knocked the ball, our only one usually, over the high maple trees, past streets, over cars, a house sometimes, then landing out of sight for us to find.

"Over here, over here!"

We'd find the ball in far shrubbery or under a parked car or on a neighbor's front yard. We heard it bounce off house and roof and we went, "Ouuuueeee!" Miraculously it never shattered glass but it once sailed through an open window where it came back out almost immediately, followed by a screaming out-of-control red face. The saving grace of my brother's time at bat was that it was over quickly. He just seemed to want to see how far he could hit, and that was it. We went back to playing our game where the ball was never hit hard enough to go in the street.

Captain Dan stood watching us for awhile in mid-afternoon, a sort of sleepy grin on his face, and we tried to show off for him, show him that some people down here in East Tennessee knew their stuff. Terry wasn't around and he wore crisply ironed officer's khakis, obviously freshly showered, probably half tranquilized by all-night fucking. We soon called him Dan or Danny (as Terry called him) as well as Captain Dan. We were bowled over by the thought of this stranger from way up north, a man, taking an interest in us. He waited a while on the sidelines, and then jumped in to show us some things about baseball. It was obvious right away that he was crazed on baseball. Our real game was tackle football where, on the vacant lot, when the weather turned cool, we banged at each other and saw blood flow. You proved your courage by tackling low and showed weakness by piling on after a play was over and someone was down. Baseball was just something to pass the time in summer—a ball to hit and a ball to catch and a ball to search for in the weeds. Nothing to get excited by.

But it meant a lot to Dan, you could tell. He interrupted our play, but differently than my brother had. He wanted to show us how to field grounders in what we took as a Yankee way to do it. "Keep your back straight, bend at the knee. Slide that glove down and look at the ball. Get set!" We stood in a line and he peppered the ball to us one at a time, back and forth. We wanted to please him, not to flub the grounders, and we squirmed in embarrassment and in secretly deep pleasure that a grown up captain in the U.S. Army Air Corps was whacking us grounders and talking to us. When he talked, he had a fast delivery and a chuckle when it ended. He may have let out a few words about New York but no one could follow him. We didn't have to. He was John Garfield suddenly dropped down in our midst. He *was* New York. I thought of subways, Times Square at night, a sandwich coming out of a slot, checkered tablecloths, a hot dog, a beach, and girls kicking their legs up on stage. Those images flashed through my brain. I was back in that New York that I had once magically seen and lusted to return to somehow, someday. I couldn't get over the way he talked. "How do you like it down here, Dan?"

"As soon as I find a *minyan* I'll let you know."

"Huh?" Why was he laughing? What was he talking about?

"Nothing. It's perfect except for one thing. You can't go out for a paper at night."

"Huh?" We went into something else. "You fly a plane, don't you, Dan?"

"No, I'm a back seat driver. I'm a navigator."

That was how he talked, everything a sort of joke, what I later learned was called one-liners. Before I knew it, I was trying to talk like him, complete with fast delivery. "Hey, jeez, pass the biscuits, Pappy," I said at the dinner table.

"Son, what's the matter with you?" my father said. "Why are you talking that way?" I couldn't get away with it.

And then Captain Dan and Terry were gone, back on the train, up the iron steps, up and away. Once again I was at the depot. Mr. and Mrs. Auburon were there, too, of course, waving and shouting at the train, which was like a troop train, there were so many servicemen with their heads stuck out of windows. Terry and Captain Dan had their heads stuck out, cheeks touching, as close as two people could be without becoming one. The train chugged off slowly, around a bend, past the lumberyard, out of sight. What happened to Captain Dan and Terry after that depended then on reports—as we had to depend on reports to learn of D-Day and the death of Joe Collins. The lone reporters in this case were Mr. and Mrs.

Auburon. We learned that Captain Dan had flown over Germany; we learned that he had not been killed or wounded and that he had come back safe and sound. That was it. There was silence on the marriage, which was not good news, as even I, a teenager, knew.

That was how it was back then. They came in, these people in uniforms, in full glory and regalia, looking as stunned as we were by their appearance. While here they took up a lot of space; when gone, it was a blank. When they came back for good, they told us what it had been like, those who got back. There became a name for it: war stories. We only knew what had happened to them by what they told us. My brother came back and told about playing against Joe DiMaggio in an exhibition game in Hawaii. He claimed he hit a three bagger that DiMaggio couldn't field. What a war story! He had slept on the deck of an aircraft carrier coming home without going into how the stars looked or the air smelled. That was it.

* * *

I did get a uniform, although not of the military. A soda jerk at the Sweet Shoppe joined the army and I signed on for service behind the marble counter after I got out of junior high at three o'clock. It was a step up from being a curb-hop; I was promoted to grown-up. I wore a white starched cap, a white starched jacket, and a big apron that came down over my shoes. I had yet to shave. I drew draft beer into paraffin cups; I sold rubbers from under the counter, cigarettes and cigars and Kotex from on top. I was kept busy. I was half crazy. I never rang up the right amount on the cash register. I became a thief. I slipped bills in my pocket on the sly, an act that had a name—"knocking down." I was frightened of the term, lived in shame that I was doing it, but drawn irresistibly to the thrill and outlaw-ness of it. I didn't need the money at all. I had nothing to spend it on. I didn't care about picking up my paycheck because I'd compensated myself already, but it would have looked odd if I hadn't. I gave money away. I began to feel sorry for the bald-headed owner who was 4-F or too old for the draft. He came by every few days to go over the cash register receipts and cash on hand. At first

I was scared and went in the far smelly toilet to hide, but then I realized that he, like me, didn't know what he was doing. He was a nice man, studious looking, and always a kindly nod to the help. He made a show of carefully adding figures, counting bills, and then—after nodding all around—taking a pile of money away in a tin box. He seemed distracted, though, and the rumor later went around that he was having an affair on the side with a dental hygienist, stepping out on his wife. Maybe that's why he wasn't paying attention. I stopped knocking down. I learned how to smoke cigars I took from the countertop. A cigar jutted out of the side of my mouth every night as I strolled home. I was helping the war effort. I was sixteen.

*   *   *

Two grown-up girls hung around the Sweet Shoppe, too grown-up for me, one blonde, one brunette, and I loved the drama that went along with them. They never drank beer. They nursed Cokes. They played the jukebox where "American Patrol" and "When the Red Red Robin Comes Bob Bob Bobbing Along" were the favorites. Most nights the prettier one, the brunette, would leave with a grown-up, a serviceman or somebody about to go in. On Saturday night when it was very busy and a freewheeling atmosphere crept in, the blonde got taken. They stepped into taxis with their escorts. They went to motels out on the highway. I couldn't get over it. It seemed like a lot of fun. No one looked down on the girls. I loved looking at them when I dished out the Cokes and I couldn't keep my eyes off them while they sat in a booth and waited. What they did in the motels was something I got to imagine vaguely, just as I imagined vaguely what those called to service did in the skies, trenches, and jungles.

*   *   *

And then it all ended. I was in high school, and when V-J Day was declared I was on a Southern Railway train coming home from

Washington, D.C. where I'd spent a summer's week with a chum visiting his elderly grandparents. His mother was with us on the train. Nearly every one else was in service, uniforms everywhere. The train rocked and clicked and was filled with dense tobacco smoke. Sunlight streaked through the windows and every face looked tired and tense. After dark and the yellowish overhead lights went on, word came from the front of the train back through the cars that the war had ended. Faces relaxed. At first calmness, then bottles came out.

Over! All around us men began saying what they were going to do—going to sleep for a week, never going to salute anyone ever again, going to go in the backyard and burn this uniform. "I'm going to put my picture on the bedroom ceiling cause that's all my wife's going to look at after I get back!" Whiskey sloshed. I remember that I left my scratchy, ancient coach seat—nothing seemed to have been repaired or replaced since the war started—and made my way through the aisles, from one car to the next. The aisles, though, were becoming jammed. I ducked in the smoker and sat beside a quiet, lonely soldier. We exchanged a few words about the state of the world now, all in quiet tones, while the hubbub went on around us. We went over our histories. Mine was brief; he had fought in Europe, and there were campaign ribbons on his chest. "It's over! Man, oh man! I wasn't a drinking man before." He raised a bottle and took a long gulp and he changed before my eyes. His eyes rolled back and he shook his head. It was like Spencer Tracy changing from Dr. Jekyll into Mr. Hyde. Soon he was singing "Don't Sit under the Apple Tree with Anyone Else but Me." Lost.

They were singing all over, the favorite being, "Roll Me Over in the Clover." A space was made in the aisle of one car for a couple to dance. The girl, a perky redhead, had a sailor's hat from someone jammed on her head. She was jitterbugging and throwing her hips around, and everyone was clapping. The conductor, a short, stocky fellow, trying at first to do his job, tried to make his way through to take tickets, and his hat was removed and then worn by another girl. He loosened his tie and gave up. He took one or two swigs at a bottle thrust his way and soon was singing, "Don't Sit Under the Apple Tree"—even the engineer, way up front, the man at the throttle, may have been loaded. The whistle began to toot in long and short blasts. I went back to my seat and found a sailor trying to get atop my chum's mother while she pushed from below and my highly embarrassed chum pulled at the sailor from above. His mother was a rather stiff-faced woman who was a pillar of the First Baptist Church. I helped pull the sailor off whereby he offered us a pint that was running low but we all politely declined. He was a service man, entitled to respect, but there was no way my chum's mother was going to tilt back and drain the bottle—although I wouldn't have been surprised that night if she had.

So it was on that the train, whistle tooting, no tickets taken, rocking and leaning around the sharp curves, going deeper into the mountains, that we got the news. It was over.

* * *

Everything in town changed back in short order. Uniforms went away or had a Ruptured Duck on them for a short while and then went away. New Fords and Chevys appeared. Frozen food came in and the GI Bill, vets opened sandwich shops and put up places where you could do your laundry. They joined the Rotary Club and the American Legion. There were marriages and there were babies and it was right back to where they had left off—although of course not quite. There was still the glamour of being, or having been, in service. I made sure I got in, no matter if there was no war. I wanted a uniform. At last I got the real thing. It was not at all hard to do. The recruiters were happy to accommodate. I was disappointed, though, that I couldn't occupy Germany where at least I knew where it was. My orders read Korea. I thought that meant the Caribbean. It was a shock to find the desolation we had come to occupy below the 38th Parallel in that far off land, the Russians in baggy uniforms and looking sour occupying the terrain above. I was lucky to miss the fireworks that came a few years later, but I nearly froze to death the way it was. It beat being shot at, I suppose.

It was then college on the GI Bill, then back to town as if being away from it had been a dream. It was a dream, for the town had never left me. It never would. When I was standing guard on the outskirts of Seoul, at ten below, so frozen I had to be lifted into a two-and-a-half-ton relief truck, I thought that right about now Mr. Winters was swinging up on our front porch, delivering his bottles of milk. When it got cold enough the cream on top would freeze and push the caps up. I would put sugar on the frozen cream and pretend it was ice cream. In college on the GI Bill I didn't think so much about knowledge but how I could return to town and drop the name of Matthew Arnold or some such. There was no other place or people I wanted to impress, no place else that meant so much to me as the town I grew up in. Yet the dream was to leave it, to be somewhere else, to be a grander someone else. It was a state of mind for which I had no solution but which I was powerless before.

Dan Goodsaid never came back. Terry Auburon did. Maybe they had never been married; that was one explanation. You never know about couples. You learn that they can have troubles that you—or even they—never suspect or acknowledge. Terry came back as a mature woman after her parents, Mr. and Mrs. Auburon, had died together when Mr. Auburon drove head-on into the car of another senior citizen coming the wrong way. Terry lived alone in the house with the gabled sweeping porch that soon began showing neglect and needing repairs. You couldn't help thinking that it had once been a show place. Terry had kept her looks, but she seldom went out. There was never any music coming from the house, and one of the few visitors who went there swore she was eating cat food. She's strange, everyone said about her, always had been. The only time she was happy, everyone agreed, was during the war when she came home with Captain Dan.

shards of love, through a glass darkly

Right after the war started but before it got a grip, right when everything was poised for change, I received a clearer picture of my parents one night, one I wasn't seeking. I had just turned fourteen, before curb-hopping and soda-jerking at the Sweet Shoppe began, just before a lot of rules went out the window and independence began. I was in junior high, and it was a Friday night, and I had been out past my usual bedtime. There was no school the next day, no books to study, no need to rise early, so I couldn't see any harm in coming in a little late. I was returning from my first double date.

I had learned about double dating from my big brother, from others older, from seeing it done by Mickey Rooney to a hysterical pitch as Andy Hardy. A pal from two blocks down, George Rupikakus, "Rupe," son of the cheerful widower Greek who ran a beer-reeking restaurant, joined me in taking two girls, both named Betsy, to a movie. They were girlfriends as Rupe and I were pals. I always thought they were tied together because they were called Betsy and no one else was. They were our age, a little snooty, seemingly knowledgeable about courtship procedures that Rupe and I could only guess at.

Rupe and I met on the corner of Main and Roan to go over tactics and have a dress-down before hooking up with them. The Betsys were distinguished by painted nails, fluffy hair, white blouses, and the tendency to giggle. "They know what's what," Rupe said. "You don't giggle like that unless you've had some and want more."

He was more advanced than me, or at least in bragging rights. He claimed to have screwed his second cousin in an attic on a trip to Roanoke. One aspect of his awakened sex drive that he did not brag about, you found out about to your regret if you went to a cowboy movie with him, and certainly not on a double date. A Saturday afternoon Roy Rogers or Gene Autry picture might do it. The scene was inevitable. A young woman, in calico, in a long flowing frontier dress, would rush out the farmhouse, frowning, looking for Roy or Gene to save her or something, and Rupe would secure his windbreaker over his lap and begin beating his meat. "Um, um, um," he would say. "Look at her! Come get some right here, baby!"

Whatever happened under the windbreaker I was just as glad not to know, but he calmed during barroom fistfights or when Gene or Roy flew off a horse and took a rustler tumbling down an embankment. He became as serene as a Buddha then.

Outside, he would say in the sunshine, "Don't tell anyone. I just can't take it when she comes out of that farmhouse that way. God damn it to hell."

Rupe had lost his mother early. It was just him and his father now. His father worked long hours, spoke broken English, and his eternal cheerfulness seemed a cover for some essential, never-ending sadness. Even a kid could sense it. So he could keep an eye on Rupe and because he thought he could trust him with the cash register, Mr. Rupikakus put Rupe to work in the restaurant on occasion. Rupe knocked down anyhow. Rupe was heavy-set with a good-natured, meaty face. He feared, among a host of things, fatness and giving off a smell. "How do I look in this shirt?" he said that night at the corner of Roan and Main. "Should I have worn something looser?"

"No, for crying out loud, you look fine. Let's go. They're out there waiting for us."

"Wait a minute, wait a minute. Smell me."

"I can't smell a thing."

"Get closer. We may dance with them later. Tell me if you smell anything."

"You smell all right, for crying out loud!"

I could get impatient with him, but I was forgetting how long I had spent in front of the old bathroom mirror myself, perfecting a wave to the side of the part in my hair. I thought of it as a killer wave. No one else had one like it. I had mixed together some lard and some of my father's aftershave lotion, my own invention, and it held the wave in place, stiff as a board.

At last, Rupe and I walked up to the Majestic, me a little in front, where the two Betsys already were, waiting. Their faces shone; they were in prettier dresses than they wore at school. Hardly any acknowledgement was made that the four of us were together other than a nod or two and a smile and the fact that Rupe and I paid for the tickets.

It became clear that neither Betsy wanted to end up with Rupe. Neither seemed thrilled to be with me either, but I would do, whereas Rupe was treated as a stranger. I knew in the back of my mind it would happen. I felt sorry for him but was glad it hadn't happened to me, and just steeled myself to get through the evening so Rupe and I could talk about it later. Rupe made cat noises at a prissy actor on screen that got a laugh far back in the audience but not from us. Afterwards, on the walk to one of the Betsys' homes, Rupe suddenly leapt to a tree limb that rose above the sidewalk and chinned himself a few times. It came out of nowhere and no one commented on it.

No adult was at Betsy's ground floor apartment. Her parents were divorced, one of the few divorces in town, and she lived with her mother. The other Betsy lived with relatives because her parents, for some cloudy reason, were not in the picture. The two Betsy's had similar home situations and other unspecified things in common besides their names. I felt, without any clear indication, that they were on to things that were beyond the likes of Rupe and me. They knew, somehow, more about what went on between the sexes. They weren't about to waste too much time on those who were far behind and not ready for the future they were heading toward.

We did dance that night. Frank Sinatra sang at first on the phonograph, but we were too embarrassed to dance cheek to cheek. Later came "American Patrol," and jitterbugging was called for. To my surprise Rupe jumped in, took one Betsy by the hand, and twirled her out and back as if he knew what he was doing. I was partly pleased that he was now included in the frolic, showing he knew his stuff and was my pal, but somewhat saddened that I wasn't the one who could jitterbug like a pro. Once I tried out a few turns with the free Betsy while Rupe was occupied with the other, but it was clear that I wasn't a match for Rupe, or either Betsy for that matter, in the ways of jitterbugging. I didn't think it fair that Rupe could be self-conscious about everything on earth and then effortlessly cut the rug like that. He beat time in a sort of tap dance, shook his hips, looked dreamy, and flicked a Betsy in and out. He even did the dip at the end.

The Betsys served Cokes. They gossiped about classmates. They swooned over Sinatra. One of them turned down the floor lamp a wattage or two. A soft yellow light covered everything. I noted a faint oily impression on the sofa where the back of a head had often rested. Tinted photographs of a man in a uniform rested on the mantel. The time I saw on the clock was later than I thought.

On the street, leaving the Betsys with a handshake, Rupe pretended anger that I had called it quits. "I could have gotten me some, I bet," he said. "Why'd you have to pull out that way? It's early."

"We did all we could," I said. "Don't be silly."

"I just want you to answer one question. And I want the truth now."

"OK."

"Do you think they smelled me?"

"No, no, no. You don't smell. I wouldn't lie to you."

"And I danced lousy, didn't I? Come on, tell me, God damn it, tell me."

I saw what he was after now, and I accommodated him. "You danced great. They were both crazy to dance with you."

"No, they weren't."

"Yes, they were."

He kept it going until we came in front of my house where all lights blazed in the living room. Rupe had no regular home to go back to. He would go to his father's restaurant that stayed open until well after midnight, there to help his father clean up if made to, and to have, I suspected, a second hearty meal and a smoke on the sly.

I went in the front door and there were my parents, facing each other across the living room. My father sat perched forward on the edge of a sofa cushion. My mother sat some distance away in a chair. It took me a moment or two to realize that my father, who seldom showed anger, was highly upset. I took on a burden of guilt because I must be the culprit; I had stayed out too late. My father was smoking. He was nearly always smoking except at the dining table, while walking on the street, or in a car, or in the bathroom, or in his bedroom. He smoked at the depot where he worked. He smoked in the living room which was lined top to bottom with books and where a bluish/gray haze floated from one after another Chesterfield. "How come you're coming in so late?" he said. His pant legs were raised, the better to ease his posture, revealing socks that came up well over his calves, held up by garters. "You're well past your bedtime."

He'd never spoken to me that way before. Usually he joked around, calling me by nicknames, retelling anecdotes about my childhood that I could repeat in my sleep. It was as if a stranger was administering discipline. "I was out with some people from school. You know. Just some people. Rupe."

"You're coming in at all hours. Coming and going at all hours as you please." This was not like him. If anything, he had disappointed me before by not noticing what I was doing or what my concerns were.

My mother spoke then. I saw tears in her eyes. She was not speaking to me or looking at me. She spoke to my father. "It doesn't matter. He's done nothing wrong."

What was going on? I had the sinking feeling that here was an argument that had been going on for some time, and maybe about something else, and had now broken into the open for me to hear. I would die if I was the cause, but I felt powerless.

My father flicked his cigarette over an ashtray on the coffee table, reaching over. He talked to my mother then, not to me. "He has to have some discipline. I have to have some say in this house."

"I'm leaving you," she said all at once, and tears were running down her cheeks. "I'm going to pack up and go live with my brother John in the country."

Everything became still. *No, no, no! Take it back, take it back!* My father flicked cigarette ash over the ashtray again, but said nothing. I felt he was scared, as I was scared. I had never seen him embarrassed or scared before. He took on the air of defeat, whatever their struggle had been about. He never again said a word about my staying out late, then or ever. My mother never brought up moving out again. It was strange that it was my mother who had stuck up for me but it was my father I gave my sympathy to. I connected with him. He was a man, my own gender, and I could understand him, as I never could my mother. He had failed. Maybe I should have been glad that I had more freedom now, but I wasn't. None of us spoke about that evening ever again. It did not go into family lore. But I remember it as well as I remember anything in my life.

* * *

You learn as much about your parents as you need to know in order to love them. I learned that I was loved. I never learned all about them and was maybe just as well off. I observed a myriad of little things: how they treated me, how I came to treat them. Then there was that blank period before I came along. Who were they then, what had made them who they were, what had life been like way back when? I listened to tales that came over the dinner table, in talks with my mother as she rocked in a rocking chair on a summer's evening, from my father as we walked to town to get haircuts together, or on our way to the bleachers to watch a ball game. I drank in their stories.

* * *

There are actual snapshots from the past, yellowing and curling at the edges from age. My mother and father pose by a wooden farm fence, well before I was born, a couple. My mother holds the brim of a large picture hat down over one eye and is faintly smiling. My tall father stands beside her—black-haired then, in a stiff-collared shirt and tie with a fancy stickpin. His hair had started to gray in my early memories of him, but his dress style of shirt and tie continued to the grave. I never saw him in a sports shirt. He shaved with a straight razor, sharpening it with broad sensuous strokes on a leather strap, well into the age of the safety razor. Behind a closed bathroom door he took baths in which not one sound was heard. It was the Great Depression when I first knew him and he worked odd hours or he worked at out-of-town depots on a temporary basis. He took breakfast in his BVD undershirt—before his silent bath, before the straight razor went to work, before the shirt and tie went on. He poured scalding coffee into a saucer and sipped it while it cooled, foregoing use of a cup as people from the country did. He ate the same breakfast every morning all his life: two fried sunny-side-up eggs, strips of crisp bacon, and one hot buttered biscuit after another.

My mother had grown up on a farm, as had my father, but with different particulars. Her father farmed a bit on a small hardscrabble piece of land and brought in extra money the best way he could. He had taught school for a while in the country, for he was a bookish man who knew some Latin. His children called him Pate, short for *pater*. His wife died young, leaving him a widower in his prime. It was, after that, a tough time: a household of father, his three small sons, my mother, and her older sister, living way out in the country with little money.

There was an overabundance of pride, though, and a frontier sense of shouldering through. He had been born at the start of the Civil War, and during his life had done many things besides farming and teaching; he had run a country store with his father (that failed), delivered RFD mail (that lasted), and late in life was elected to the Tennessee state assembly. Principled beyond belief in many matters, he occasionally got drunk and so discombobulated my mother, so young at the time, that alcohol was never allowed and rarely mentioned in our own home. (My father had to hide pints of Four Roses deep in the basement coal bin, like money under the mattress, from which he made discreet withdrawals from time to time.) What was consistent with her father was a love of books, a curiosity about language, and a high sense of rectitude about money and any obligation: pay all debts and lend little money. Do your duty. He never married again, but his eye never stopped roving. He died at seventy-seven as a result of an automobile accident while in the company of a young woman and a rather disreputable man who was placed behind the wheel of the car my grandfather owned but couldn't drive. My grandfather was the only one to die, lingering for a while in the hospital, succumbing to pneumonia. The "chauffeur" and the young woman sued and collected some insurance money.

When my mother and her four siblings were growing up without a mother—I'd hear the story countless times—they would try to stump each other with big words and their derivations. An unabridged Webster's was close at hand and rows of classics on the order of George Eliot and Charles Darwin on the shelves. But then it was hard to reconcile other details of their home life. The walls were papered with old newspapers (from which new words were plucked) because that was cheaper than using regular wallpaper. And out back, to the lasting shame and discomfort of my mother's slightly older sister, my oh-so-proper Aunt Carolyn, an outhouse. Of all things she prized later in life, nothing beat an indoor toilet, with a door that locked, and a warm seat to lower oneself to. Later, even the sight or mention of an outhouse caused her fright and chagrin. The drawing of an outhouse in *Li'l Abner* with the telltale half-moon out front was no joke to her. And she liked to keep the indoor heat up to a near-tropical degree. This was my Aunt Carolyn who came to live with us during the Depression.

Along with wallpaper fashioned from newsprint, an outdoor privy, and stacks of literature all over, was the mode of transport for the children, my mother and her siblings, to school. I might have questioned this oft-told tale as fantasy, save for a yellowing primitive photograph as proof. There astride a horse were four little children, my mother last in line, big dark eyes gazing solemnly at the camera. The eldest, my Uncle Lawrence, stood on the ground, holding the bridle, ready to lead the horse down to where they would learn what there was to learn; then afterward lead horse with brothers and sisters atop back home. I never found out who cooked their meals in a Tennessee home with no running water—water came from a cistern—no electricity, and no mother. Did my mother and my aunt, who were not in their teens yet? Did they have help? Too late to ask my mother. They did grow up. My aunt and mother became schoolteachers. My uncles went into occupations where rectitude was expected and early retirement given, nothing special. The baby of the family, Uncle Jim, went to Chicago and acquired a Yankee accent and a Yankee wife. Uncle John, the closest one to my mother, was gassed in the First World War and later died of lung cancer. Uncle Lawrence, the closest perhaps to my grandfather, delivered RFD mail; one of his grandsons went to Harvard and got a PhD from Yale. Everything respectable, upward, but nothing spectacular.

My mother told me that as a schoolteacher, on her first job, when she was nineteen and not much older than her students, she was shortchanged at the boardinghouse she lived in. "There was only a biscuit for lunch," she said. Sometimes, as a treat, there might be a hard slice of country ham inside the biscuit.

In the wide space in the road that passed for a village, she met my father who worked for the mighty Southern Railway that stopped there on milk runs. She remembered him then with the whitest teeth she had ever seen. He was someone who could make her laugh. That was it. They honeymooned in Oklahoma City. Why there?, I thought to ask late in life. "Because a train pass could get you there, I guess," my mother told me. My brother was born less than a year later.

It was that quintessential time, just before the First World War, when the nineteenth century, for all intents and purposes, was still holding on. They had courted in a rented buggy. There were kerosene lamps in the country, no electricity. Water came from cisterns via hand pumps. Outhouses dotted the landscape. My father got the results of heavyweight prizefights, the Jack Dempsey bouts, and big league ball featuring Christy Matheson and John McGraw from the depot telegraph and spread the word, round by round and inning by inning, to someone who relayed it through the village. He was popular, a looked-up-to man.

His father, my grandfather, died around the turn of the twentieth century. He had fought in the Civil War—fought at Chickamauga in Tennessee under Nathan Bedford Forrest. He would only fight in Tennessee, not elsewhere, and when U.S. Grant and William Tecumseh Sherman ran the rebels out of Tennessee from Missionary Ridge, my grandfather deserted rather than fight for Georgia. He returned to rural Jefferson County to finish out the nineteenth century. He graduated from Carson-Newman College and received a diploma, all in Latin. According to my father, in addition to farming, he practiced a little medicine, from rudimentary skills he came by in the Confederate Army. No medical license was required in those days, back when no malpractice laws were on the books. All you needed was an air of assurance and enough sense not to go too far and kill someone. He came by a large farm and sired twelve children, six girls and six boys, my father the baby, born in 1886.

This grandfather lived until 1905, long enough to become a minor philanthropist, donating money to build a Baptist church near his property. He owned a large two-storied home with many low-ceilinged rooms, most with fireplaces. George Washington would have felt at home. My father grew up there. His mother, possibly worn out by childbearing and farm life, died when he was thirteen. He grew up after that, as had the woman he married, my mother, in a home without a mother. His sisters cooked, kept house, and, as they say, raised him. Throughout his life, even when age assaulted him with disabilities, he carried the remains of once being the baby who didn't mind others taking care of him. But unlike a baby he stoically endured any adversity without bawling and never had a bad word to say about anything other than the

Republican Party, farming, and working for a railroad that had shortchanged him many times. In addition, he liked to practice medicine, and certainly had no license to do so. My mother continually warned me not to take anything he prescribed, which was generally Ex-Lax.

My grandfather lived to see a car pass by the farmhouse, but not much later. He did not live to see the start of the First World War. When he died, the farm was divided among his children. My father wanted no more to do with farming. He might hate the Republican Party with a visceral hot-blooded response. He hated farm life with a slow eternal burn. He flew off the handle if anyone brought up Herbert Hoover. He became silent and brooding if anyone extolled the virtues of good honest toil of the land. Anyone offering praise for a return to nature got short shrift from him. He wanted the bright lights and no early morning chores. To show his contempt for what the earth produced, but also his cranky knowledge, he would not eat a cucumber. I asked him why. "It's the only thing a hog won't eat," he answered, mystifyingly.

He sold his share of the farm to broaden himself and get away. He traveled. He went to the Midwest where he was immediately robbed. He claimed that he was asleep and someone chloroformed him. Glimmers of his past bachelor life came through as mostly of a rowdy nature. Some roustabout cronies put him up to trying on a pair of women's silk stockings before a dimly lit hotel window, so passers by would think it was a woman dressing. He had legs that could get away with it. He and his cronies then went to a nearby saloon to hear fantastic talk about the woman showing it off before an open window. Before his inheritance money ran out he used what was left to learn telegraphy. He was sure it was the ticket to a safe and secure future. It was the means to the open road; it was the calling card to the outside. It would always be around, the instrument of a prized profession.

In Tennessee he met and married my mother. They fashioned a life together that lasted through thick and thin. My brother got typhoid from bad cistern water a year or two after birth and almost died. There is a picture of him in a baby's nightdress, as bald as a cue ball, looking solemn and world-weary. A shock of curly black hair would later rise from his head. My father prospered along with the country in the 1920s. The family moved to a real town on the Tennessee River into a big house with running water and electricity. There I was born, twelve years after my brother. My father sold life insurance as well as being a telegrapher. Money was no problem. Anecdotes and reminiscences had him holding forth in the drug store, on street corners, at ball games, getting off a good one, always ready for a nip when well away from my mother. No need to think it would not continue this way forever.

Then the Great Depression came, right after I did. The Southern, going by a seniority system, put my father temporarily at out-of-town depots when he outranked some poor soul for the moment. Reminiscences paint a most dark picture of this period. There was the WPA that was supposed to get America back on its feet, but all you heard were jokes about how no one worked. There was shame attached, an admission of being poor and broke and all hope lost. There was the CCC that stigmatized any young man who joined up. There was the black NRA eagle with a shaft of lightning going through it that flashed on before a movie began. There were Fireside Chats on the radio from the president. Everyone was hard up. Those who lived through it, like my father, had their spirits dampened forever. They were like war veterans who couldn't forget the battles and only spoke of them occasionally because the memories were so painful. Money and the loss of it and how hard it was to get stayed with them into better times. The pictures of the Great Depression of bread lines and apple sellers were only pictures to those who hadn't gone through it, just as pictures of D-Day and Guadalcanal are only pictures to those who weren't there.

*　*　*

To conserve money my family combined households with my mother's sister, my Aunt Carolyn, when I was three. We had left the small riverside town downstate and moved to a city of 28,000 where my aunt taught school and my father found temporary work at the depot. This would become my hometown. The city had four movie theaters, two colleges, a towering brick hotel, a railway depot where my father sat with earphones on and busily clicked away at a telegraph key.

Moving gave us a new set of neighbors. My mother was instrumental in getting us, kit and caboodle, into the reputed first home of the first mayor of the city some time before. My father, in his crushed financial state and misery, never knowing if he'd be jerked from one depot to the next in the rocky seniority system, would have been just as happy with a ramshackle house by the railroad tracks. It would have been closer to going to work. As long as you had any sort of money, though, it seemed you could move into any vacant house. The ex-mayor's house with the barn out back, far from its former glory—paint peeling, floorboards buckling—rose on a tilt next to a vacant lot. My Aunt Carolyn left her small apartment to move in with us and allowed it all to happen. Her meager teacher's salary made the difference. My father never had a bad word to say about her. "Your aunt is as solid as a rock," he would say, at the least opportunity. "She saved our lives."

Thus, we moved into the Andy Hardy series. My father was no Judge Hardy but he was an older dad who passed on wisdom I seldom followed but couldn't forget. Here in our house, Andy Hardy, me, had an older brother, not a sister. There was a schoolteacher aunt. We all sat around a dining table at meals. My aunt and mother, two sisters, had grown up on nineteenth century literature and learning the derivations of words, in a house wallpapered with newsprint and having a Webster's unabridged on a stand. They sat near one another after supper, making references to *Mill on the Floss*, obscure words, and aphorisms of Dr. Johnson. From meager savings they ordered books from New York. My mother got *Blackwood's* magazine that came by boat and then rail from England. She subscribed to *The Nutmeg* that Heywood Broun put out. She quoted Christopher Morley.

The Sunday edition of the *New York Times* was wedged in the wire attachment beneath the mailbox every week. I became more knowledgeable about Broadway openings than about the schedules of local baseball teams. I had a starched Eton collar put on me for special occasions, something that I yanked off as soon as possible and complained about so much that it only sprang to life if I sat to have my picture taken. I was taken on cool summer evenings to the junior high auditorium, large and magisterial to me then, to watch productions of Broadway plays that the roving Barter Theater Players of Abington, Virginia, brought through. I writhed in ecstatic pleasure hearing actresses in finery say, "God damn," draw on cigarettes through long filters, and talk about "affairs." Roy Rogers never did that. Perfume filled the air. I counted the days before the Barter Players rolled into town. Shortly before the Second World War my mother took me to hear Paderewski play at the UT auditorium in Knoxville. She took me to hear Carl Sandburg play the guitar and offer homilies there. I heard Harry Elmer Barnes, a well-known columnist at the time, talk about Japan. "One thing I can assure you," he said. "We'll never go to war with her. What do we want with a little burnt-out island?"

My mother bought me an Underwood Noiseless Portable and saw to it that I learned to type. She gave me a guitar when I became fixated on the glut of singing cowboys onscreen. I never learned one chord and only pretended to play. Benny Goodman onscreen led, though, to a clarinet, which I did learn to play, and play well. I held first chair in the junior high band, but gave it up to be on the basketball team. My mother gave me a fine red Parker fountain pen that had a replica of my signature etched on the gold band around its cap. I wrote stories with it.

My father had hardly any of his friends visit our house. Once in a while he opened the door to a few railroaders, very few, or a jovial long lost relative from the country who straggled in for an hour or two in the afternoon. No one stayed for dinner. We never gave parties. We were self-contained in whatever private closed drama was going on inside, the adult side I only got glimmers of. All I know is that I was tremendously happy within it. I never felt so relieved or safe as when I could come back to it from wherever I had gone. In the evenings there would be my mother and aunt springing words on each other. My father would be stretched out on the sofa after supper reading Dickens. He continually read the works of Charles Dickens, from beginning to end. He went through Dickens' entire work, from *Sketches by Boz* through *Edwin Drood*. He was not interested in any Dickens memorabilia, no biography, any literary critique. I suspect he was caught by the stories of boys who had lost a mother and were forced into cruel early labor by sadistic, manipulative adults. He liked to quote Sam Weller who said, in *The Pickwick Papers*, that he gave his son the best education in the world by throwing him in the streets and letting him shift for himself.

Away from prying eyes he slipped detective magazines into the house, kept out of sight beneath a living room side table, where on top lay *Blackwood's*, the *American Mercury*, and the Sunday *Times*. I liked to fish around under the table and pull one out from time to time. There were articles of Dillinger being gunned down, a drab housewife or two who spiked a mate's coffee with arsenic, a citizen who shot up a brothel. The photos were so realistic you felt you could step inside. The crime scene had superimposed black dots that led to an "X", where a bloody hatchet or a dropped revolver lay. Photographs of the unhinged culprits showed plain ordinary people you might pass any day on the street.

Over time, in an out-of-the-way space in my mind, grew a silent, persistent, heartfelt sympathy for my father. My father was tough, no doubt about it—never complained, never took one sick leave day from work in his life, always had a joke handy—but I felt an underlying sadness about him. He hadn't quite caught up with a life that was posed to forever shortchange him. Paradoxically I got the same feeling through many subtle moments from my mother, that she had been shortchanged from what might have been. But my mother was of another gender, in a world of flowery scents and delicate ways, and I really couldn't be a part of it or understand its subtleties. I was drawn to her, though, in ways I never was with my father. When I was a little tot I slept with her, a country custom, until I had to be pried away like a slug. I remember how it felt to hug her in the dark of the night and the security it gave. On a summer evening, as crickets sang outside, I stood behind her chair as she sat reading and combed her long black hair. I loved her.

My real love for my father came after he had reached his fifties and had been tempered by crises and disappointments, and the cataclysm of the Great Depression. I did not know him when he had a strut. I did not know him when he had a profitable insurance business. I remember the day when, long after he had lost that business, a young pathologically cheerful insurance agent somehow wormed his way in the living room that saw few visitors. He went through his spiel about annuities and some such and my father listened politely and nodded and drew on a Chesterfield and never let on that he had once produced the same bullshit that the ebullient man was now throwing. In parting the salesman could not find his snappy straw hat. "I know I had it," he said. His words were not part of his chipper memorized pitch and were a little alarming. My father rose. He had been sitting on it. It was crushed to the size of a Buster Keaton pancake hat.

* * *

And so memories of dislocated actions and events careen around in my head, some cloudy and with no reason for being there, but all as stark as if they'd happened five minutes ago. Among the unexplained in there: I am shrieking and wailing going up the stairs—I could have been eight or nine—when my mother who is ahead of me turns and gives me a smart, well-aimed smack. I was never so surprised. In every other memory when I am with her I am being coddled. Maybe my wailing had finally worn her out, but why this time and not others? Maybe she was upset over something else. What I learned then was that love comes with surprises. That was a pretty hard smack.

* * *

The night I came in late I sensed, without putting it in words, that my father had lost a power struggle with my mother. He had tried to show he could discipline me and he had failed. I was embarrassed for him, and I sympathized with him even though I was the one he was trying to hold in line. Maybe it was a male thing. I bled for his ineptness. I thought I could understand his emotions, and I sympathized with what he was going through. I loved my mother, but not enough to take away my sympathy for my father. Women you loved but could never completely understand. Men you never loved in the same deep way, but you understood them. It was part of being a male.

My father never tried to discipline me after that night. Not that he'd done much of it before.

* * *

No matter what happened out of sight between my parents, their marriage kept going. Late in his life my father's inviolate nightly ritual was to bend down, nearly always falling over, to kiss my mother, who sat engrossed in a book. Then he laboriously climbed the stairs to bed. "Goodnight, honey," he'd call. She'd follow soon. In her mid-seventies my mother was struck by a farmer's pick-up while she was walking to town in the bright sunshine of an April's spring day. She lay in Intensive Care where machines hummed and tubes rose and where my brother and I sat beside her and begged her to wake. My father was infirm by then, too wobbly to navigate the stairs and elevators and intricacies of Intensive Care to see her. He sat silently in his easy chair at home, waiting for news. Once I caught him reading the Bible. She never woke. She was buried in a country cemetery by the graves of her father and her brother John. As her coffin was being lowered, my father, who had to be helped into a chair, rose on his own and shouted into the quiet sweet air, "Goodbye, darling!"

* * *

The girls named Betsy came and went quickly. In high school I fell in love with a girl. It was all in my head, of course, but it was total. I had never been affected this way before. I was swept away before I knew what was happening. She had straw-colored hair and widely spaced eyes that looked searchingly at you. She cradled her books in her arms and she wore clean, slightly scuffed saddle-oxfords. I blushed around her. I stammered and froze. I melted when I saw her, but I was not on her agenda. She was a cheerleader. She went on Presbyterian youth retreats in the mountains. She drove one of her family's Chevrolets to school now and then. Her family had money and position in town. We had one date, to a movie after school, in which all I could think about was, should I make a move to hold her hand. My own hand sweated. We never touched. We never kissed. I fought against having any erotic thoughts about her. I prayed to Jesus to keep those thoughts away. I never really knew anything about her beyond the clean, slightly scuffed saddle-oxfords and her well-to-do parents, but I loved her in a way I had never loved anyone else.

* * *

And then the inevitable. It certainly wasn't going to happen with any girl in high school. Right before my senior year I lost my virginity. It was how it was done in town. I went with Rupe to the Dixie Hotel near the train station where we knew prostitutes were available for five dollars. We went through the nerve-wracking pretense of registration, some dialogue with a colored bellhop about what we wanted and could expect, and then before I could sort out my emotions, I was in a room with a stark naked, blonde-haired woman reclining on a bed. Somehow I got my own clothes off.

She was mostly bored but vaguely amused. I couldn't get over the fact that at last I was looking down on a real live naked woman. There was no doubt about it. There was that lightly colored triangle with the pink pouched out lips within, the breasts and nipples, and a large deep belly button. *My God!* I kept looking and looking. I could have looked all night. It was my first naked woman up this close. I was mesmerized and paralyzed. I didn't know what to do. She said, "Don't tell me you don't know how to fuck."

I didn't. I got on top and did what I'd pictured many times was the way. My main inspiration came from Tillie-and-Mac eight-pagers. It ended quickly and I was greatly relieved that I'd come though. So that was it? I was more relieved than satisfied. We had done what you were supposed to do.

Rupe then barged in without knocking, with a proprietary air, making a big show of zipping up his pants. He had been down the hall with a woman I'd considered not half as attractive as the blonde who now was spread out on the bed before us. He must have come through himself, had proven his worth, because with high confidence he marched over and jiggled one of the blonde's big tits. He hadn't been invited. He just must have felt he had earned the right. "How'd he do, baby?" he said, jerking his thumb toward me. "Was his whang big enough for you?"

"He had a big enough whang," she said. "And he did everything just fine."

I never learned her name. Never learned where she came from or where she was going, but I loved her at that moment.

Part III

THE TENNESSEE WALTZ

It is the Great Depression. I am on the floor, crawling along. Women's legs are all around me, legs sheathed in silk, belonging to those mystifying, alluring creatures who sit on sofas and easy chairs high above and shower down attention. I know how to act so as to get it, and I'm punch-drunk with power. The light is lemony, the world filled with perfume and powder. I never had so much pleasure in my life. I am three years old.

One early afternoon in summer, a year or so later, my mother says, "Let's have a picnic, why don't we? Just you and me." Dark-haired and green-eyed, she is a dead ringer for the pretty maid on the box for Sun Maid raisins. I think of her every time I see the box. She makes deviled eggs, potato salad with little chunks of onion, and lemonade. She arranges it all on plates. We go outside and she spreads a cloth over a large flat rock in the side yard. It is our table. Clouds billow and float under a delicate blue sky. A car slowly drives by. The air is so still, the grass so green and soft. Down the hill looms a sturdy two-story building, the jailhouse, with bars on the windows, through which men yell at night. I can hear them from my bed when the night is soft and at a standstill. At that dark hour train whistles come from the distance. My father works for the railroad, and I pray he gets home safe.

Beside the flat rock, I look and look at this woman who has set out this picnic for the two of us, and I think, without anyone preparing me for this moment—I love you. I know what love is. I will always know. I will die if she ever goes away.

When I am first permitted to walk two blocks by myself to a small store around the block, it is a huge treat and adventure. She gives me some change and says, "Here, go buy something just for yourself." I think and think on the way, and when I enter, I order a bottle of milk. For her. "No, no," she says, when I bring it back to her to show my love, "You should have bought something else. Something for yourself."

sunny

"I love you," I said, but didn't mean it. I just said it.

"You're a great lover. I can tell," she said.

What was she talking about? How could she tell? I didn't even know where the clitoris was. I didn't know there was one. None of my buddies did. The girls obviously did but may not have known what they'd found. In East Tennessee back then, we knew a quarterback's position better than where the "little man in the boat" sat, or what he was doing down there all by his lonesome. And that's just the start. Folk were probably better informed in the Middle Ages. My prior experience came from grindings against girdled loins and Wagnerian humps that lasted all of one minute and never called for repeats. And, of course, there were those you paid and never got to kiss. What a mess. All we had to go on was instinct. And youth.

Her name was Sunny. It was on her birth certificate that way and wasn't short for anything. Her last name was Dale. Sunny Dale. It all happened in the early 1950s, in a few short months in our small town in East Tennessee, in a time when, as everyone well knows, we were all supposed to be buttoned up and locked in mind-deadening conformity. Oh yeah? You think so?

It was back then that Sunny and I boarded a rocket ship. She had been programmed, I came to realize, that when the time came to scoot beside me in an automobile the time came to fulfill some eternal un-

spoken need. Hey, I thought it was all fun and games with an escape hatch as usual.

How was I to know? She may not have known everything—who does?—but, as I learned along the way, she knew more. How were we both to know we'd be changed forever?

* * *

The first step came with the car. It stood in the sunlight: a brand-new, glistening green 1951 Plymouth Cambridge. I went in the showroom to ask a few questions. That simple. Years before I had bought a shiny phonograph on a similar impulse with savings from my paper route, longing to hear *Gaîté Parisienne,* that I'd only heard on the radio, and the Andrews Sisters do "Bongo, bongo, bongo, I don't want to leave the Congo . . . Oh, no, no, no, no. . . !" But my father had made me take it back, saying, "They'll try to foist anything off on a kid."

No one could stop me now. I was twenty-three, the possessor of a fresh degree from the state university, thanks to the GI Bill of Rights. At the university I had made acquaintance with Thomas Mann and Marcel Proust, could order a ham sandwich in French, had made friends with a Turk from Turkey, had ridden a horse at daybreak onto campus after an all-night toot, could talk about Montaigne and Sophocles and tell you the difference between ATO and SAE and ZBT. My qualifications did not set the world on fire, and I had to settle for what I could get when it came to making a living. I came back home. I joined the workforce of our town's Tourist Welcoming Center in the Andrew Jackson Hotel at fifty dollars a week. The Center occupied roughly the space of a bedroom and faced the street. There was Curt, my boss, and secretary Flo. I had to move back in with my parents.

Now, a brief hour or two after stepping into the salesroom, I held the keys to this Plymouth with a green sheen and a new car smell. All I had had to do was walk over to the bank, talk to a man I'd seen around at the Baptist church, back from when I was going there, and sign some forms I didn't read. Everyone was affable—in the sales room, at the bank, me most of all. I smiled like an idiot. I received a book of blue coupons, from which I was to tear off one every month and hand it to the bank along with half my salary. I got a supply of self-confidence along with the car, too.

I saved money the best I could. I chose not the Plymouth-recommended radio but a cheapo silverish product with outsized black knobs. I hoped no one noticed it wasn't standard. The Plymouth itself was not perfect. When it rained a slight leak came down over the edge of the dashboard. No one anywhere, although many tried, could find the cause. But it was a car, it was a first, it was mine. I awoke at three in the morning and looked out the window at it in the moonlight and it was mine. The job that paid for those coupons to come off once a month was worth it—but barely.

At the Tourist Welcoming Center I was at the beck and call of anyone who could walk or be wheeled in from the street. We boosted free enterprise, dealt out highway maps and brochures by the ton, and lauded "freedom." The businessmen of the town, our sponsors, took for granted that we hated the federal government as much as they did. We smiled at each other and joshed about the waste of government, the laziness of those on its rolls. Government cut into our "freedom." No one suspected that this baby-faced boy, a native son, me, had savored the dialectics of materialism, the struggles of the proletariat, the adventures of the Soviets, right down there at the state university, inside its fake Gothic buildings. Made sense to him. From each according to his abilities, to each according to his needs. How about them apples? On paper, communism seemed okeydoke to me. I didn't belong to anything, but I had to hide my feelings. As far as government was concerned I could only say a good word about the FBI. Forget unions. Find communists. And show someone how to get to Gatlinburg.

A beaming man burst in and asked if I had let Jesus come into my heart. I assured him I had. Then he wanted to know how you got to Chattanooga. I went over which roads to take, their conditions, and heard from him about his gallbladder operation. Citizens who weren't going anywhere, who had nothing to do (as I did), came by to hammer away at various topics: being stationed at Pensacola during the Second World War, last Sunday's sermon at the Methodist Church, and today's story about Mr. Pearce the jeweler who had keeled over at the ninth hole from a heart attack and had to be taken away by a golf cart. Here was an open door. Here was the culture of the times. Invariably the culture of the times is insane. It was so during the French Revolution, the U.S. Civil War, and the Raj in India. Here was an open door. Those who entered were all nice enough, deserving perhaps of an ear and correct road information, but, sitting there, stuck, I got a whiff of eternity in hell. Worse, strangely enough, was when no one came in. I had to sit there and pretend to be thinking up ways to improve the town and welcome people to it. I didn't know what I was doing.

My boss Curt was an addled but nice enough man who took great pleasure in the rituals of smoking: lighting up and waving the burning match a second before it burned flesh and then inhaling deeply and directing a plume to the ceiling. I was comforted by its regularity, so that when he once blew smoke rings I was taken back. I also noted how he would sink a hand deep in a front pocket and shift his balls to the other side in a little dipping motion—and think he was getting away with it. He pored over diagrams of vast warehouses in town that had been vacant since before the Second World War and plotted how he could lure outside industry in. He received no interest anywhere. It gave him something to do. I read the paper. I listened to the radio in the hotel lobby. I watched the thin ass of Flo, the eternally cheerful big-lipped secretary, as she swished past and past again. To while away the time I thought of how she might suddenly throw those long legs over my shoulders and we'd waltz around the room. I sat in the can in the hotel's marbled men's room, my chin in my hands, and moaned and prayed for a way to escape. To where, I had no idea. New York was best, but anyplace than here.

At the stroke of five I was set free. I put a dollar's worth of gas in the car and drove. In the summer the air was sweet and I drove around on country roads, the tires clicking. I smoked and listened to Guy Lombardo and his Royal Canadians on my silverish bolted-in radio. I watched the coupon book go down slowly but surely.

In the fall, with the weather turning crisp, it all changed. Sunny came along. The moment arrived. It happened that Curt my boss was drawing on his ever-present Camel, shooting plumes above, and tossing around ideas about how to get people interested in the upcoming Thanksgiving Parade down Main Street. It would be modeled after the Macy's Day Parade in New York. The prospect of the high school band leading our bald-headed mayor sitting in the back of a convertible and waving wasn't going to do it, though. We needed something fresh. We needed publicity. We needed a gimmick. Why not some . . . some *cheesecake*! He looked at me. "Well? You're single. You should know someone."

Someone popped to mind, someone I'd recently met. Her name was Sunny Dale, and her father was J.C. Penney's new manager in town. She had already turned me down for a date, quietly informing me that she was going with someone. But if I now called and asked if she'd like to pose for a publicity shot, that wouldn't be the same as asking for a date, would it? I wouldn't run the risk of being turned down twice. And I had the hunch she might be interested in me, as astounding as it might be. I had caught the sparkle in her green eyes when we met by the magazine rack in Liggett's drugstore where she was flipping through a movie magazine, and I was thinking up ways to get my foot in the door. She was beautiful. She strutted. She must be hard to get. I had no chance. *But I had a car now!* I wasn't some poor dumb fool without one. I could drive her to a photographer's studio where she could pose. She answered the phone in a quiet, practiced way, as if playing a part, and I later learned that she indeed had dreams of being an actress. She thought a moment about the prospect of posing for some cheesecake, giggled some, and then said, "What'll I wear?"

My boss Curt hadn't told me. I babbled something about something skimpy, acting wise, but not really knowing what I was talking about. She took it from there. She said, "Will shorts and a sweater do?" I said fine.

When I knocked at her front door she appeared almost immediately in a raincoat and high heels. She smiled and nodded and her mother in the background appeared mystified but faintly smiling too. We drove to the photographer's and she sat against her door with the raincoat tightly buttoned. I noted again how pretty she was. Her legs were bare and crossed at the ankles. We smoked and talked about nothing, but as the smoke rose and then raced out the open window I sensed that something irrevocable had happened, that I was passing not down Market Street but into a vast gauzy landscape up in the sky. The spaceship was taking off. She had dark hair and those green eyes and she looked at me out of the corner of those eyes with a look I'd never seen on a woman's face before. Was it suspicion or—dare I hope?—some interest? I was driving a new car. I was wearing a suit and tie. I had set up the cheesecake shoot. I was somebody.

The photographer was a country boy, as indeed I was, except he was a photographer and had a studio and had Sunny Dale shed her raincoat as if he were Yves Saint Laurent or Hugh Hefner. She revealed herself in high heels, in shorts as snug and brief as a bathing suit and in a sweater that looked two sizes too small. It was an image I would keep in my mind forever. Soon two live turkeys came scratching and squawking on the scene to lend the atmosphere of Thanksgiving, but they raised so much hell that a boy in overalls was called to arm-lock and carry them away. Sunny sat on a high stool, cradling some corn stalks in her arms and told to smile. The photographer then raced behind a Matthew Brady–type box camera on a tripod. She was not embarrassed or confused at all—by the turkeys, by the photographer, by anything. The photographer wanted this and that pose, the chin raised, the head a little more tilted up, the smile increased, and she complied. He threw a black drape over his head and clicked away, saying, "Perfect. Hold it! That's it!"

I stayed in the darkened background, a goofy smile on my face. I felt I had pulled something off, something above and beyond the shoot. My boss would be happy with the pictures, but that was a small benefit. I was thinking maybe, just maybe, I had a chance after all.

She put the raincoat back on and we had Cokes afterwards in a drugstore on Main. She didn't want a sandwich. She sucked daintily on her straw and looked up at me from time to time. I hemmed and hawed around and then struck: was she still going with the other fellow?

She took a pull on her straw and said, No, she had stopped seeing him. No more than that. I conjured up images of him, someone I knew slightly. He was a tanned, white-toothed fellow who cut a swath through the beauties in our region. His range extended into nearby towns and valleys, and I had a picture in my mind of him in a white dinner jacket dancing with a blonde beauty queen in Knoxville. I tried a few scenarios in my head of what might have come between him and Sunny. I settled on boredom. Even a shadowy sex scene was replete with boredom. I was a master on boredom and felt I had a Geiger counter to reveal its presence.

I drove Sunny home in my new Plymouth. We smoked a cigarette together. As she snapped open her door the raincoat came open enough for me to see her bare thigh. And I had a date for the weekend. I drove back to the hole-in-the-wall office to report to my boss on the successful picture taking. But first I stopped off in a diner and had a cup of coffee and smoked another cigarette. That was what I liked to do in town, stop off some place, have a cup of coffee, be alone, smoke a cigarette, and think. It was how I used to sit atop the barn in the old days and think. I thought in wonderment of this Sunny—with and without the raincoat. I liked the way she talked and kept a cigarette between her teeth at the same time. I liked how she could shed that raincoat and pose. I liked her self-confidence and daring. I liked that her home was no grander than mine. She didn't come from a fancy part of town. I liked that the tanned fellow in the white dinner jacket had been drawn to her as he had to other beauties. It was like having the Good Housekeeping Seal of Approval. I liked that I had a new car to take her out in. I had set it up for the weekend. I had a date. And I had a little strut to my walk now, because I had pulled off a caper. I was an impresario who could lay some claim to getting a desirable woman's picture in the paper.

Thus, it began. There were rules. She was a "nice" girl. She went to church. She didn't mind working. She made a pretense of working in one of the dress shops in town. She knew clothes. She knew the rules. She knew how to sell. I liked that "nice" girl aspect. In my new car and in my new respectable persona, on our first date to a movie, with a Coke and sandwich later, we talked knowledgably about who our favorite composers were. "Oh, yes, Beethoven. And Brahms," I said. "Do you like them, too?" As if I was in the habit of throwing a master or two on the turntable. We discussed our fathers' occupations and our parents' dispositions, and got that out of the way. Neither one could lord it over the other. She had a dog. I let her know about the two dogs I'd had as a boy. I played around with letting her know about the two ducks, but didn't know how without making it sound peculiar. At parting, at her doorstep, a nod and a handshake and the promise of another date. By then I had her aroma stored away. I knew her perfume. I had kept the wraps on and hadn't done anything silly. Dignity all the way. I wore a suit and tie. Sunny wore hose and pumps and a silk blouse.

We progressed. We ate out together in an actual restaurant and I put a napkin on my lap and knife and fork side by side on the plate when finished. It was as if the town's elders had prepared a script for us. There were rituals you followed—if you wanted to be respectable and admitted to this society. Indian chiefs around the campfire, or Kurdish warlords, couldn't have set the tone for the young and upcoming any better. I was talked into umpiring a Little League game in my sacred off-hours. It was part of being a member of the community. It was part of fitting in. My boss Curt took me to a remote mountain village that had commercial ties with our town—to keep him company and to offer support while he made a disjointed speech to some community leaders. There was a Negro in a tuxedo on the dais with Curt, there for some reason, a businessman of sorts, a sight you didn't see every day, a harbinger of things to come. Every so often he turned in a white-toothed glow, and a giddy exhilaration passed through the audience. A minister prayed. A stout man in a tight suit gravely introduced Curt, looking down at some notes for guidance, and doing well until he called him Cal. Curt rose, cleared his throat, and started to plunge a hand in his pocket for a little pocket pool but instead had the presence of mind to wipe the side of his pants. He said, "I can't tell you what a pleasure it is to be here tonight with you fine people. Driving up here through these great mountains made me think of many things. The potential for industry we have here. The cattle. I saw herds of cattle in the valleys. I saw the possibility of tremendous growth. I saw sturdy men in work clothes. I saw proud women of good old Celtic stock, from those that once drove wagons into this promised land and made it their own. I saw where we have nearly every good thing on God's green earth already right here. Why go elsewhere? Why would anyone ever want to leave?"

I was thinking of ways to leave. I was thinking, too, of Sunny, of proud Celtic stock and what a fine ass she had. I was thinking about how miraculous it was that I was connected with her. On the trip back, burnt out from blather, I looked for something to talk about. It wasn't going to be about free enterprise. I talked about Henry Miller. It just popped up. A professor at the university had lent me the *Tropics* that he had smuggled in from Paris. Curt surprised me by being interested in Henry Miller. And with no formal declaration Sunny and I became a couple. It became as natural as slipping into a suit and tie before going off to work. As natural as diving into clear deep water. We began, as they say, going steady.

Curt and his wife invited us for dinner in their small apartment. It was another ritual. It seemed to say that here, in such a small apartment, Sunny and I could be in short order if we went along with things. We could join them. Some day we, too, could have our own small apartment. I could spend my nights there with Sunny, my days thinking of ways to bring industry into eternally empty warehouses. Sunny made a to-do over their small daughter while I minded my manners.

We ate the food and said how good it was. We talked about free enterprise, the horrors of socialized medicine, and what car got the best mileage. Once when Curt went to replenish our iced tea, I caught him out of the corner of my eye grimacing and shaking his head, as if to drive away a thought. Maybe he wanted us out of there so he could have a beer or something and unbutton his belt. My neck began to ache. My cheeks were sore from forced smiling.

But I must admit that I was glad to be included in a family scene with Sunny, to be thought worthy. To be respectable. Then we were outside, waving to them in the lighted doorway, as they stood there with their small daughter between them.

We were alone in the car at last. There was a mercifully quiet moment while I shifted gears. Sunny scooted beside me and placed her hand way way up on my upper leg. I turned on the radio; she turned it off. She said, in such a soft voice, "You know, I know how to make you hot."

"Huh? Yeah?"

"Only not just yet. Not tonight. Let's wait a little while. It'll be better that way."

Better that way!

That night came. We parked high on a hill, up from her house, away from traffic, away from everybody. We could look down on the lights of the city below where everyone was going about their business fully unaware, eating apple pie a la mode or catching the news or something. Sunny reached over and took charge. Her hand went here, her mouth went there, and I nearly went crazy. Only a few nights before we had been talking about free enterprise, talking about schools and children, and drinking iced tea. I came out of shock and began going to places I'd never been before. She removed my hand from here, from there, and everything dropped back to normal, like a steam gauge dropping to zero. It had lasted all of ten momentous minutes. "No, not just yet," she said.

Sunny read the syndicated columns of one Dr. George W. Crain in the local paper and liked to enthuse over them to me. Dr. Crain—the "doctor" came from a PhD—was a booster, an answering machine for all that ailed us. He burned me up with his digs at "social engineering," his waving of the flag, and his simplistic take on most things. He was no Macaulay. Every time Sunny brought up his name I began to sigh. But secretly, despite myself, I wolfed down his column myself when he offered advice to a woman on how to treat a guy. Be mysterious. Tease him till he is half out of his mind. Dr. Crain was a sexual fixer-upper. Right there in the paper, under medical authority, he advised women to wear black lace panties and think of ways to entice and then satisfy and to keep him coming back for more. Good old Dr. Crain. He advised women to pay strict attention to the sexual side of marriage in keeping a man in harness. It was not the best thing. It was the only thing. Forget baking bread.

The night after our brief but hot petting, we kissed goodnight at Sunny's doorstep and there was a twinkle in her eye.

* * *

I had met her father, a brooding man with a sly smile. He liked to sit in an easy chair while I sat in a straight-back facing him as we both waited for Sunny's golden appearance from her bedroom, like Loretta Young coming into view on TV. We talked about Hereford cows, about the only thing we could think up. Her mother never sat when I came to call but stood in doorways wiping her hands on her apron and being cheerful. I met Sunny's older sister Emily, who was not married. She had been born with a splattering birthmark over the bridge of her nose and there had been an operation where a piece of skin had been taken from her forearm and sewn over it. It was a shade darker than the rest of her face and tiny hairs grew there. I made as if not to notice. Emily was attractive otherwise. Sunny told me the story of the botched operation, and, just by telling me, going over the whole story, made me feel as if I was included in her family. I felt happy.

I saw Sunny in all her clothes. Her outer clothes. There was not a dress I didn't know. When she wore the red dress I looked for the small hole she had repaired near the hem. The patch was the size of a dime and had been skillfully sewn. I knew the way she closed her black coat, the one with the curly wool collar. She held the coat in place with her left hand and buttoned expertly with her right. I knew her shoes. I particularly liked the black flat ones with the tiny flap over the middle. I had once seen an ancient pornographic photo of a woman on her back wearing the same kind of shoe. I knew how she squatted to pet her dog, how she stuck a piece of gum in her mouth, how she laughed. I knew her jokes, her political opinions, which I didn't share, and where little nicks and scars were on her body that weren't covered. I knew more about her than any person I had ever known and it had only been a couple of months. I knew—or thought I knew—about all her past boyfriends. But once or twice she'd think of one she'd forgotten. She was all-revealing, and yet all-mysterious. She did Dr. George W. Crain proud.

I asked her to marry me. It just came out; I didn't mean it. I was high and dancing with her and I just leaned back, looked her in the eye, and said it. I felt I could say anything to her. I had that much confidence.

She said, "No, I won't marry you. But I'll have an affair with you."

She had a flair for the dramatic. People might do it, but they didn't call it an "affair." Only in novels did people have affairs. As for marriage, only a handful of my friends were married—but it was a handful. I took for granted that she didn't mean what she had said about an affair any more than I did about marriage.

In the car I liked how she took a pint of Jack Daniels I had, up-ended it, and took a swig. It was done with style. I felt there could never be anything awkward about her. Then one day I was slouching down the street by myself, stopping on a corner in a dark mood that came and went with me in the town when, lo and behold, she passed in her father's car. He drove and she sat against her door with her head tilted in woe. She didn't see me. She looked tired and dissatisfied and gloomy; or maybe she looked that way to me because she wasn't looking at me. It was fleeting, just the swift passing of her face against the side of the car window. She looked downright ugly to me. I was as surprised seeing her that way as I was by my reaction. It came suddenly out of the blue. I resented her.

We called each other every day. It was satisfying to do and to have done. I thought up things to do: drives in the country, miniature golf. I was on an unknown path but it beat, by far, anything else I'd ever done. I steeled myself and brought her home to meet my parents. My father surprised me by being lively and my mother served lemonade and cookies. Sunny sat in her formal best, her hands clasped on her lap, ankles crossed, her chin tilted up. I felt a test had been passed as we drove off silently. Not far off the mood changed swiftly. With a little grin, she said, I heard her, "Let's take him out."

She unzipped my pants, moved her hand around inside like a wand, and then brought out what was then firm and held it as no one had ever done before. We drove down Main Street, both looking straight ahead. That was all. It didn't go further that night. I kissed her at her doorstep.

We exchanged Christmas gifts. We went to a roadhouse for New Year's Eve, and there, on the dance floor, in the drama of the occasion, it just suddenly came out. I said, "I love you." It was so easy to say. She just looked at me; she didn't say it back. I noted that. She didn't say it back.

* * *

We went on double dates. Timber Ted, who was more an acquaintance than a pal, had a girlfriend whose father was the superintendent of a German plant in a nearby town. The whole family was German. You couldn't get more German than that. Her name was Heidi and she had breasts that bounced. Timber Ted sat in the front seat with Heidi, Sunny and I in the back. We were on a double date. Which meant you went to a roadhouse, sat across from each other, and told dirty jokes. My then-favorite one was about the Old Log Inn . . . *Fellow gets lost on a dark road and is trying to find it when he spots a parked car off in the woods. He sticks his head in and says, How far is the Old Log Inn? And a guy gets out and beats him up* . . . I laughed more than anyone. Timber Ted wasn't a joke teller. He was loud-mouthed about his enthusiasms and desires, such as the one for shrimp cocktails, but he couldn't get outside himself for a joke. It had nothing to do with morality or distaste. It was as if he had a moral center for his own concerns, and it was unshakeable.

Heidi told one about a farmer knocking on the door of a convent full of nuns and went on from there. She was Catholic. Then came Sunny's turn. I waited, seeing how she'd do. Sunny told one about a black couple, using dialect. She did it in a black woman's voice . . . *My boyfriend invited me up to his place for a little Scotch and sofa. Well, I got up there and there weren't no Scotch . . . there weren't no sofa . . . and boy was I floored! . . . That excited me.*

Once started, we drank continually on double dates. Total respectability on the outside one moment, outlaw drinking un-limited the next. I pulled on bootleg Jack Daniels in the back seat, thinking to pass it to Sunny after every second swig or so. I couldn't get over how she would tilt up the bottle and take it neat. She knew what to do. She could do anything, go anywhere. Fog descended on the curvy, narrow road. We plowed through without loss of speed because we knew the road's every turn, even blindfolded. We only half-remembered the fatalities that had happened to others who knew the road just as well. A few years earlier three contemporaries had left the road and struck a tree, killing two, one the owner of the car. The third, the driver, was inexperienced but behind the wheel because he was less drunk. His head bandaged, he was a pallbearer at both funerals.

In our car, the heavy, not unpleasant scent of a run-over skunk came and went. The moon appeared when the fog lifted, shining through tall trees and lighting homes and country stores closed for business. I could hear Timber Ted talking from behind the wheel. It was as steady as the clickety-click-click of the tires. It was about how the Dixie Drive-In had better shrimp cocktails than the road-house we had just left. He knew his pleasures. He had let a few select friends know that he was—could it be?—slipping the pipe to Heidi with the bouncing breasts. He hadn't stopped with that news flash. He went on to describe the beatific aura she gave off as she brought her knees up and he went in full fathoms deep. It did seem a little base and crude to let us know all that, but apparently Timber Ted couldn't keep it to himself. He was too much an enthusiast to keep his big mouth shut. He wore a beatific smile then himself.

We had known since adolescence, from sightings in the school shower after gym, that he carried more timber than any of us. Thus, "Timber Ted." He was now engaged to Heidi. She seemed so happy as she turned to speak to us in the backseat, her wheat-colored hair swinging. I wondered for a second if I might be cutting myself off from girls like Heidi to now be tied to Sunny Dale. I hated to think it, but was something better down the road? Someone like Heidi with breasts that bounced and hair that swung? Was I stuck with Sunny Dale? What had I done? Had I cut all avenues of escape? I resented her then, and she had done nothing to deserve it.

But I needn't worry. I didn't have to think. It, whatever "it" was, had its own momentum. It said we should double date, and, when it was just Sunny and me, that we should go for a restaurant spaghetti meal or to a movie. Sunny was the guide, the one who knew every step of the way, as if the plan had been embedded in her genes. I needed a guide. This was all new to me. What were the rules? Every now and then, as we drove along of an evening, she did that trick of looking out the window one way and taking my dick out with the other. It was a sleight of hand. It was radical. It took my breath away. This was Sunny Dale, a nice girl. This was not someone you paid so you could get on top. There you jumped on, wiggled around, and then got off. In Korea when I was an eighteen-year-old soldier boy who had learned everything he knew about sex in Tennessee, it didn't seem unusual to present a carton of cigarettes to a singsong girl in order to lay atop her on a frozen hillside.

There had been a girl later in college, Lettie Lou, who ground against me on the dance floor—no mistaking it, by God. She was strong, stronger than I. In a fight she would have pinned me flat, I was sure. She was tall, rawboned, and had biceps that knotted. She majored in physical ed. In the erotic winds of a dimly lit dance floor, while a spangled ball turned above, we found all sorts of tricks and maneuvers to disguise the way our middles did their own dance as I looked over her shoulder and she looked off in the distance. Our middles were socked together. Sooner or later she began breathing heavily, going, "Umm, umm, umm." Once I came in my pants. Refreshed in the bathroom, back at table, there was no signal between us of what had happened. We chatted away with others at the table and didn't look at each other.

Lettie Lou and I were creative with clothes on. She would do anything with clothes on. Then one night, in a parked car behind the fraternity house, for no reason I could discern, she allowed me to raise her skirt and do the real thing. It threw me off stride. Why this night? Why had she automatically pushed my hand away at other times? Clothed she had been a whirling dervish. Now laid back, bare, it was as if she had been shot and put to rest. Before, on the dance floor, she had grinded away like an Egyptian belly dancer. Confused, I did what I was supposed to but it was nowhere near the excitement of make believe. This was real. This was a chore.

Sunny Dale was something else. Even though my hand hadn't stolen beneath a garment, hadn't squeezed a breast, things were getting serious. I would tell her things, like my admiration of socialism—yes, socialism—and how blacks should be given a fairer shot, matters I kept hidden in public. She disagreed with my pronouncements, but then said that her father had noticed a slight change in her political beliefs and wondered where it came from. She confessed things to me. She confessed that she wore sponge-like contraptions inside her bra, falsies. So that was why I hadn't been given a feel. And it also explained why one day she took on the proportions of Jayne Mansfield and the next there was hardly a bulge there. She told me about a summer when she slept most of the time and thought she was dying. She revived in the fall and never learned what had been wrong with her. Her mother said her blood had thinned—a country diagnosis—and that was the end of it. She told me that her mother's parents, her grandparents, lived in a cabin in the mountains and that her beloved grandfather could hardly read or write and chewed tobacco, keeping a smidgen in his mouth when eating. Those things hit home.

* * *

I watched her, amazed that we were now a couple, that people considered us so. One of the Bellamy brothers said with a grin, "You better hang on to that one, buddy. You're never going to do better."

I remember standing on the street and watching her inside the dress shop. She waits on a customer. She doesn't see me, and I relish the fact that in a couple of hours we will be together. She turns, sees me, and her green eyes flash.

I am hit by a thunderbolt.

gilmore

It wasn't so much his looks but an accumulation of subtleties that made you think of someone reclining on a sofa, bangs falling, an intelligent, knowing look on an elfin face. You would think of Truman Capote, for a host of reasons, and then Gilmore Polk would open his mouth. Out came a basso profundo with the rolling thunder of blackfaced Orson Welles in *Othello*. It was confusing. Gilmore was one of my oldest and best friends and unlike any other I ever had in town. He occupied a special place. I had known him forever. I knew him back when we both wore corduroy knickers and sat in the Sunbeam section ("Jesus wants me for a Sunbeam!") in Sunday School at the First Baptist Church. Gilmore seemed to know all the parables before Miss Holly, our spinster interlocker, got a chance to drone on about them. He quoted them. Uninvited, before Miss Holly could stop him, he even enacted them, taking various roles. For the one about the Good Samaritan, he became the one set upon by robbers. He pretended being hit over the head, gazed up to heaven for a long dramatic moment, and then fell straight out flat on the floor. You never thought about the Good Samaritan the same way after that. Miss Holly didn't know what to say.

Gilmore never roughhoused. He never played an improvised game of touch football on the long grassy slope down from the church after we were let out. He never siphoned off a nickel from his "offering" to buy a Coke or play the pinball down at the Sweet Shoppe. He didn't do what most of us did or think the way we did, and I turned out to be his principal friend back in those early days, well before his basso profundo entered. Maybe it was because we had a lot of books at my home and my mother and aunt subscribed to the Sunday *New York Times*. Maybe it was because I never made fun of him the way all the other boys did. I wasn't exactly bowled over by all his chatter, but I knew enough to act as if I knew what he was talking about. I figured he was having a tough time of it and being his friend back then (maybe his only one) was the right thing to do. It was what the parables were trying to teach us to do. Good Lord, I was doing what they were trying to teach me in Sunday School. Also, visiting Gilmore's home had its cachet.

Mrs. Polk, who was called Kiki, picked me up in her big black Buick. Gilmore and I sat in the back, Gilmore bubbling over with enthusiasm at the sight of me, and that pleased me. It's good to be wanted. His mother was a sexpot. There is no other way to put it. You didn't want to get all worked up over someone's mother, but you couldn't help it. When she walked down Main Street an awed silence followed her. It was like watching Mae West stroll by without underwear. Everyone was struck dumb. She was respectable, of course, she was a mother, but there was something of a tart about her. She had a long red mouth that turned crooked when she laughed in a throaty, sort of lascivious way. Her eyes were a stark blue, her body something else, and she was a blonde. There was even a fetching beauty mark by the corner of her mouth that struck a note of naughtiness. Gilmore got his looks from her. But the awed silence that followed him wasn't of the same order as that which followed Mrs. Polk—or Kiki as I learned to call her.

Those trips to the wooded enclave where Gilmore lived spanned many years, much history, many changes in fortune, first as Mrs. Polk drove and then as Gilmore commanded the wheel as his feet barely touched the pedals. He didn't bother with a license. We drove through snow, through rain, through bright cloudless skies, and through falling autumn leaves. My journey with Gilmore started at the tail end of the Depression, sailed through World War II, and lasted through the adjustments to adulthood. In the beginning, in the back seat, Gilmore would tell me about his new train set, where bells clanked at crossings, lights flashed, and real smoke came out of a toy engine. He would inform me of the latest episodes of *Jack Armstrong, the All American Boy!* (We didn't even own a radio in my home then, let alone a car.) His home rose on the outskirts of town like Tara. There was a narrow road that led to a large circular drive sprinkled with crunchy gray pebbles. The house was brick, two-storied, and with brilliantly white windowsills. It smelled throughout of money, privilege, and security. Inside the floors gleamed where not covered by deep rich rugs, not a speck of dust anywhere, and the furniture and pictures on the walls seemed better placed in an English manor house than in Tennessee.

Through all those years I could count on one hand the times Gilmore visited me. I felt shame, then guilt for feeling shame, for the sagging creaky boards on our front porch, the peeling water-marked wallpaper in the living room where books rose galore but hardly left room for a train set even if I'd had one. I must say that Gilmore carried himself off as if right at home there. He comported himself like a forty-year-old. He sat with his chubby legs crossed and talked railroad lore with my father. You would have thought he might have once been a section hand or conductor. He talked to my mother knowingly—or pretending to know—about the mayor who was said to have built our house long ago. He talked about Christopher Morley and the Algonquin Round Table. He mentioned Harold Ross. He gave the impression of knowing everything and being able to do anything. I thought that any moment he might go to the broken down piano in the front bedroom and bang out a Beethoven sonata.

I noticed that my parents looked at Gilmore, even at this early age, in a way they didn't look at my regular chums. You would think they would be pleased that I'd hooked up with such a well behaved kid, and rich! But their faces took on a wary, guarded quality. In one way or another nearly everyone I came across when with Gilmore took on this look. It continued over the years. I just accepted other people's reaction to Gilmore and put it aside, never questioning what it meant. I relished his company too much. He was the only boy who seemed to know there was a larger world out there.

At home Gilmore and his mother never stopped talking while never listening. They flew like two fast trains on parallel tracks. When they baked a cake, which was something to see, something incidentally you'd have to put a pistol to my head to do, they took separate tasks on cue, practiced to perfection, as smooth as Fred Astaire and Ginger Rogers. At times it seemed the same body going to town—a hand mixing, another hand sifting, another hand coming out of the blue to pour the milk. It was a juggling act by two practiced professionals. You forgot whose hand belonged to whom, all while the chatter ratcheted up and down. I had heard Gilmore's stories more than once, but his mother Kiki's ramblings could startle me—that is, when I could stop peeking at her boobies, God forgive me! Somewhere along the line she mentioned that she'd been in a beauty contest in Atlantic City, losing out by a whisker to a girl who later became a movie star. "Did that really happen?" I later asked Gilmore.

"Of course not," he said immediately. "She makes things up."

Well, Gilmore made things up, too. Oh, boy! He said he had written a story and the *New Yorker* was considering it. He said the New York Yankees might make him a batboy. He only had to beat out one boy, like his mother only had to beat out one girl to win the beauty contest in Atlantic City. He told this story in various versions. I never believed him. Everything was theatrical, wild make-believe in the Polk home, including the home itself. But perhaps the most theatrical of all was now the last to arrive—Gilmore's father.

I would be sitting cross-legged with Gilmore on the living room floor while he acted out an Edgar Bergen/Charley McCarthy routine, his mother popping in and out with chatter about *One Man's Family* on the radio, when Dr. Polk would burst forth like an explosion from the front door. He immediately sucked all the oxygen out of the room. He was tall and gangly with a rush of brownish gray curls that rose from his head. He kept a bemused smile on his face, like someone who held a bomb that he could let off any time he pleased. Gilmore and his mother became startlingly quiet, which was scary in itself. Their theatrical routines ceased. Dr. Polk's time on stage had arrived. "Whadda we have here? The Wednesday afternoon sewing circle?" he drawled, then howled. He acknowledged me with a wink.

We lived in a dry county, only beer was sold legally over the counter. For hard liquor adults went to bootleggers in the poor section of town or out in the country. It was high-priced. That was usually how it was done. Dr. Polk would immediately pour himself a tumbler of amber liquid from a beveled decanter, then swish the tumbler faster than a Joe Louis hook under a faucet. I loved to watch it. He had style; he was not sneaky about it. He poured one like Humphrey Bogart. He carried a drink in his hands every time I visited the Polks, and I thought of how my father had to hide his pints of Four Roses in our coal bin in mortal fear of my mother. Gilmore proudly told me that his father drank Scotch. "Single malt, too. He has connections in New York."

A few descriptive words always followed the mention of Dr. Polk in town: "He drinks, you know." But that was invariably amended to: "I'd rather have Doc Polk operate dead drunk than anyone else cold sober."

Dr. Polk was a surgeon. He "went in." He was highly successful, an artist in the OR. Many left-for-dead crash victims walked around town singing his praises. He made, as legend had it, no distinction between complicated brain surgery and an appendectomy on a nine-year-old girl. Everyone who needed repair had to have Dr. Polk, and he never turned anyone down. He couldn't resist the theater of the OR. I noticed, as his hand held a tumbler, that his nails had been nearly completely scrubbed off. He squinted a great deal, either from hours under the hot lights or to bring someone or something into fine focus. "He has 20/40 vision," Gilmore told me. "You can't see any better than that, except if you're an eagle."

Sawing away at an etherized body, Dr. Polk could do no wrong. The body lay still, its mouth closed, under the harsh light, and a phalanx of attendants handed him tools, which, they say, he called for like a drill sergeant. He had music piped in while he worked—

Boccherini, according to Gilmore. Even his music showed a special taste. No Roy Acuff or Ernest Tubbs like the rest of us had to put up with, night and day. But Gilmore could have made up that about Boccherini, just to show he knew about him. You never knew about Gilmore. But one thing was certain: Dr. Polk didn't like, or trust, the medical field outside of his specialty with scalpel and thread. Maybe, just maybe, he didn't know anything about that other side of medicine or had forgotten what he had learned at Harvard Medical. When someone slipped past barriers into his inner sanctum with a general medical complaint, Dr. Polk didn't know what to do. He would be faced with general practice, internal medicine. "Doc," it went, "I don't know what's with the matter with me."

"What do *you* think is wrong with you?"

He let the patient diagnose all ailments that didn't call for the blade. He himself kept an eye out for home remedies. Once someone caught him with a paper bag over his head. "Fellow told me this kept his asthma at bay," he said, lifting it off, not embarrassed at all.

Everyone knew that Dr. Polk, whose forebears went a long way back in Tennessee, one reputedly a former president, had met his sexpot wife, Kiki, in some far reaches. One story went that he had caught Mrs. Polk's "dance of the seven veils" when she performed at the Boston Gaiety, been struck dumb, and soon made it legal. He left Harvard Medical for a residency in surgery at Bellevue, administering to a gunshot, knifed, and smashed public. Gilmore had been born in New York City, something he never let you forget. But he couldn't have remembered much because Dr. Polk brought the family back home when Gilmore was two. That didn't stop Gilmore, though, from graphic descriptions of subway rides, the Automat, and plunging up and down on Coney Island's Cyclone. He'd make you think you were there. It almost didn't matter if he'd been there or not—but not quite.

The Polks settled down in Tennessee, Gilmore joined me as a Sunbeam in church, and eventually along came World War II. My father continued as a telegrapher during the war. Gilmore's dad served as a battlefield surgeon in the Third Army under General Patton. After the war, when I was at the Polks' and the doctor was well into his second or third scotch, a cigarette burning in the ashtray, Gilmore would prod him: "G.W., why don't you tell us about Patton?" Gilmore was the only boy I knew who called both his parents by their first names. I could call Mrs. Polk "Kiki" but my lips wouldn't move to call Dr. Polk "G.W."

"What do you want to hear, son?"

"Tell us about how he used to speak."

"Well, old Georgie"—*Georgie!*—"had this high-pitched, high-strung voice. That might throw you. But the son of a bitch was a soldier, I'll say that. And he looked after his men and was very noisy about it. I had to throw him out of the tent more than once for barging in at the wrong time."

"It was hell over there operating, wasn't it, G.W.?" Gilmore's basso profundo rumbled.

"Well," taking a sip, then a long drag. "It was nothing compared to going in the Ardennes in one of those tin-plated Shermans. A fellow could get roasted alive in there. Maybe I shouldn't bring it up now, but we're having a roast tonight. Let's eat!"

I always got well fed at the Polks'. Their food was nothing like mine at home. We more or less lived on fried chicken, beans in fat back and potatoes, biscuits and cornbread and plenty of fresh milk. When steak came it was beaten so thoroughly that never a pink spot showed and you had to chew forever before swallowing. The Polks drank wine and Gilmore always demanded a glass, which was cut in the beginning with water. When the Polks offered me a glass I refused. I feared the wrath of God, and was sure I would turn into a drunkard at the first taste. What would my mother say? Nothing here was like home, not the long polished mahogany dining table, not the arches over doorways, not the candlesticks. I sat mesmerized as Dr. Polk took charge of the carving. He sunk a big fork into a carcass, a rump, or a roast, and then the blade went to town. He made quick, precise cuts, turning out very thin juicy slabs of meat in a flick of the wrist. I pictured him dealing with a stretched out body that way.

Dr. Polk was not squeamish about anything. He was one adult that didn't seem to censure any thought or hold back any vivid language. That may have been the surgeon in him or due to his military service. Once when Kiki was out of the room, just Gilmore and me there sitting with him after dinner, he raised half a cheek and blew a fart. *"Pardonnez-moi, mes enfants,"* he said. "I just had to let that one loose."

I got the giggles. Gilmore, straight-faced, said, *"Pas de tout, mon père."*

I figured right then and there, so help me God, that I was somehow going to learn how to *parlez-vous.* That was the most sophisticated thing I'd ever heard. Where had Gilmore picked it up? Undoubtedly from his father, who had served in France. His mother Kiki's expertise lay in other realms, the actual theater, for one thing, and piano playing. Gilmore was in all the school plays. He even directed some. In one production about the founding of our nation he set off firecrackers onstage to simulate gunfire and scared nearly everyone to death. While they exploded he played the *Warsaw Concerto* off to the side on the piano. You never knew what to expect with Gilmore.

It was a shock when he went off to military school about the time high school was to start. I took for granted that Dr. Polk wanted to make a man out of him. I was wrong of course. It was Gilmore who had talked his father into sending him. "Do you know why a boy would want to do such a thing?" Dr. Polk asked me one day, cornering me on the street. "Why in the world would a boy who has all the comforts of home want to be lonely and harassed and woken up at five in the morning? Just to wear a *uniform*? Why?"

"Maybe he wants to be like you," I said. It just came out.

"Yeah, you think so?" Dr. Polk said. "Well, God help us all. I'll miss him, I know that."

Usually someone got shipped off to military school when something was going wrong—someone caught in thievery or piling up failing grades and disciplinary measures were called for. Shape up or ship out. You didn't just go there because it was a fun place. You also had to have money. You couldn't be poor and a thief and get a ticket.

Dr. Polk certainly had the money. Gilmore went. But Dr. Polk had been against it. "You'll be lonely down there, son," he said, within earshot. "You have a good home right here. You have excellent grades here in town. They'll bust your balls down at Sweetwater."

What they did was put Gilmore in a snappy uniform. He came home on vacations in a brown tunic with gold buttons gleaming, shoes shined, bangs gone and a crew cut in its place. He larded his language with "take five" and "go blow it out your barrack's bag." He also carried home a fellow cadet or two—guys interchangeable with one other—always a handsome, taller figure resembling Tab Hunter. The girls in town went crazy for these Tab Hunters with a passion that lasted for all of five minutes. Gilmore never showed the interest in girls that my other chums did. I went to bed with a boner and woke up in the morning with one—pictures in my head of a teacher's ripe breasts and bottom, girls in their tight gym clothes, spreads of laughing females in *Life* magazine, selected actresses on screen, even sultry voices via radio. Eight-pagers with Blondie lying back, saying to the Fuller Brush Man, "Give it to me, big boy," nearly did me in. They all spoke of one thing, of pussy one day to come. I learned from the earliest never to bring up pussy around Gilmore. Never. I got the message when he turned his head or immediately changed the subject. I figured that the idea hadn't come to him yet, or that his idea of girls and why they were put on God's green earth was different from mine. That is not to say, though, that he did not *act* as if he had passion, but his passion seemed no more real than his putting on a military school uniform made him a real soldier.

Through a mystifying period he became obsessed with a thin blonde girl in town, a judge's daughter. She was no Kiki. There was not a curve on her body and she had the habit of fainting during dramatic moments, as when the Pledge of Allegiance was given during assembly. I liked her, but couldn't imagine anyone enthralled. She did not spell "pussy." Gilmore found a way to bring her name up in any drift of conversation. We might be talking of a cold snap, and he would say, "Gail goes to Ft. Lauderdale with her family every January, you know." His eyes would follow her at dances, but he never broke in on her to dance. He never had a date with her. When she ran away with a strange Brazilian she'd met in her freshman year at college, Gilmore said, "My life is ruined, you know."

"Come off it. You never really had anything going with her."

"I guess you're right," he said, in a sad, broken-hearted way. "We had difficulty communicating. Remember, that's the most important, if not the most difficult, thing in a relationship. Never forget it."

It was as if he was a counselor dissecting a marriage between a middle-aged couple. It was like something he'd read.

Polly was another case, a long, tall drink of water, the daughter of a sad-eyed, stoop-shouldered man who ran the third best theater in town. Rumor had it that rats ran around in the darkened orchestra, but I never spotted one, although I was on guard and couldn't relax when there. Polly's father was sunk in depression and some of it may have rubbed off on Polly. But when she and Gilmore got together they ignited each other to a feverish pitch, and Polly acted as if she'd been released from some deep, dark cavern. When I heard their rapid-fire gab, I turned giddy, too. I kept a knowledgeable grin on my face, but felt unworthy to express an opinion on anything. They jumped from the fashion statement made by Oveta Culp Hobby as a WAC, to the latest on Broadway, to *The Magic Mountain*, to the grand movie theater on the Queen Elizabeth ocean liner. I knew that Gilmore had never sailed the Atlantic, probably had seen a picture of the theater in *Life*, but I let it go. Gilmore never went beyond talk with Polly, you could tell. It was unthinkable that they would even hold hands. "*Date* Polly?" he said, when once I suggested a double date. "Go out on a *date*? With *Polly*? No, I don't think it'd work, *mon ami*."

Polly went on to Wellesley on a scholarship and later in life published a novel about an oddball movie theater run by a picaresque loner in a small Southern town. Gilmore was in and out of town, in and out of uniform, in and out of different kinds of mufti and schools. Much went on with him over the years I knew nothing about. There were periods when I neither saw him nor thought about him. He could be in town; he could be elsewhere. I myself could roll in from somewhere and never think, or want, to call him. Frankly, at such times, I didn't want to talk about *Aida*. I didn't want to fall, over a cup of coffee, into French. I felt more at ease talking about UT football and running a rack of pool with loafers.

After military school Gilmore claimed he had a congressional appointment to West Point, but had failed the physical. "I was a quarter-inch too short," he said. "Do you know what that's called? That's called chickenshit."

He enrolled himself, again over his father's dissent, at the Citadel in South Carolina where he came down immediately with a mystifying illness and was sent home, bed-ridden. When people got sick in town it was generally mystifying. People never used the word "cancer" any more than they did "the clap." If no one said it, no one had it. When people died it was caused by "a lingering illness." Unless they were mowed down in full sight or dropped by a heart attack. But how could Gilmore be dying if the birds were singing in the trees and the sun was beating down fiercely at high noon? But there he lay, staring at the ceiling and breathing through his mouth. He could only smile wanly when I said, "How tough was that Citadel, Gilmore?"

Kiki drove me over, but she never went in the sick room while I was there. I took it she didn't like to go in sick rooms, even her son's. She chattered away outside, as if everything was the same as always. Act the same; then nothing changes. Dr. Polk went in and I'm sure that he, like the rest of us, didn't know what was wrong with Gilmore. I opened the door softly, not making a sound, as you do when entering a sick room, and heard Dr. Polk speaking, bent over a silent, laid-out Gilmore who looked near death's door. His eyes stared vacantly, and, despite myself, I thought of Greta Garbo in *Camille*. Tears ran down Dr. Polk's cheeks. He held Gilmore's hand. "Oh, Lord, let my boy live and I swear to thee that I'll never take another drink of whisky as long as I live."

Gilmore recovered. He rose like Lazarus. His clothes fit loosely on him for a while; then he filled out to his natural plumpness and began strutting around much the same as always. Dr. Polk went guiltily back to a few tumblers of scotch in the evening, gradually filling out his quota the way Gilmore filled out his pants. I ran into Timber Ted, a reliable source of gossip and what's what, on Main Street one day, and he said, "You know what was wrong with Gilmore? He got shell-shocked down there at the Citadel. Any person in his right mind would be. It was psycho–*so*–matic!"

Gilmore himself rattled off a string of fancy maladies as likely candidates, many in Latin, and I could tell he had made them up. They sounded dramatic, but I was sure no one had ever had them. Finally he said, "You know what? I think I got just plumb tuckered out." He put on a hillbilly accent. He liked to do that.

* * *

We were called the Silent Generation, although we weren't so silent or lethargic. We bridged the closing of the Second World War and the start of something new. We were all conditioned and affected by the war and a few of us got in it. We jumped—or were forced to jump—into the giddy postwar period: shiny new cars rolling around town (one of which the bank and I now owned), new businesses popping up (Laundromats, frozen food lockers, etc.), old-timers looking lost, and at times you felt you were in *Gone with the Wind*'s reconstruction scene in downtown Atlanta with hammers flying and a new world a-coming. You didn't know what to expect. You didn't expect the Korean War, I can tell you that. Most of us thought the Second World War had solved everything.

* * *

I was sitting in the Welcoming Center, mulling over what I could get Sunny Dale for Valentine's Day—a Zippo cigarette lighter with "Sunny" engraved?—when a presence loomed before my desk. It took a moment to fit the pieces together and figure it out. There's someone in a blue enlisted man's Air Force uniform. He was smiling.

"*Bon jour, mon ami.*"

"*Mon dieu*, Gilmore! You get drafted?"

"I'm in for a week. Emergency leave. I'm in the 82nd."

"Gilmore, you're in the Air Force. You're in a blue uniform. What are you talking about?"

"Don't let appearances fool you. Pretty soon I'm off for Benning's Jump School. A transfer between services. It's difficult, but it can be done. Don't let them tell you otherwise. But first I've had to come home on this other business. Let's not go into it. Did you know G.W. knew General Gavin at Normandy?"

Months would pass—sometimes a year or so—and then Gilmore would pop up, or the other way around. One of us would be here. The town was our home base. We had been Sunbeams together and there was a lot I knew about him, a whole lot I didn't. One thing I knew for certain was that he was not going in the 82nd. The last time I'd run into him he was in the uniform of the University of the South at Sewanee. On the street he wore white bucks, a tweed jacket with tie. I was in Levi's. At Sewanee I'd heard they all wore cap and gown the way they did at Oxford. I couldn't get over it. In the hills of East Tennessee. "Is it true, Gilmore?" I asked.

"Certainly. It's tradition. Tradition is the glue of civilization. Don't ever forget it."

* * *

Now I finally had a car, my green Cambridge Plymouth. No one had to chauffeur me. I can't tell you the relief. With wheels I was a grown-up at last. I drove down tree-lined streets, cut into the wooded alcove and pulled up on the crunchy gravel before the Polk home. I slammed the car door shut and the sound broke a deep, spooky stillness. Gilmore was at the door. "Come on in," he said jovially but softly. "You haven't been out here in awhile. Everyone is really eager to see you."

Kiki sat in the front room alone. Everything was immaculate as always. No dust motes floated. A grandfather clock ticked in the hall. Kiki had aged somewhat, I noted. Her curves were fuller than before, diminishing desire rather than enhancing it. She chattered away at me as usual without asking a single question. I let her know that I was back in town more or less permanently, second-in-command at the Welcoming Center. "That's nice," she said. I don't think she knew what it was.

When I turned my head, Gilmore slipped off on tiptoes. He returned from a far room wheeling in a shrunken figure with a shawl over its shoulder. It was what was left of Dr. Polk. It took a moment or two to drink him in. His brown grayish curls seemed to have melted, hanging limply and thinly from his yellowish skull. His hands had become bony, almost skeletal, and they clutched the arms of the wheelchair. His jaw jutted out as if some bridgework had gone awry or he was reaching for something with it. All the while Gilmore and Kiki smiled and nodded, keeping up the pretense that all was the same as always. Dr. Polk did not speak, but he turned his still-bright eyes on me for a second. He seemed to be signaling that we were both in on a secret—whatever it was.

Gilmore took charge of all ceremonial duties. He pulled himself up straight, glanced at his watch, and announced, as if the Mercury Theater Players were coming on the air, "Attention, ladies and gentlemen and all ships at sea! The sun has now passed the yardarm. At least somewhere it has. Time for a bracer!"

Gilmore mixed and poured with the aplomb and almost the dexterity that Dr. Polk had once shown. "Ready, G.W.?" he said to his dad. And he ever so gently placed the rim of a tumbler of scotch on Dr. Polk's lower lip that jutted out. He held the back of Dr. Polk's head gently with his free hand while he did so. No one spoke about what was wrong with Dr. Polk, then or later. What you saw was what you got. I thought of wheelchaired Monty Woolly in *The Man Who Came to Dinner*. It was as if time had simply come for him to go into a wheelchair and be struck dumb and that was all there was to it. A full diagnosis would be more than anyone could bear. I thought it polite though to ask him a question, but he simply smiled at a spot over my shoulder.

Our talk resumed. Kiki informed us about the latest Little Theater Production—*Private Lives* by Noël Coward. She went into detail about the struggle to gain production rights. She was going to play the lead. Gilmore let us know that in basic training real live ammunition had been fired over his head as he crawled along with his rifle cradled in his arms. I let it go that he was in the Air Force.

* * *

Gilmore and I hung out a few times during his emergency leave. It was the least I could do. I gathered that it was a way for him to avoid dark forebodings and I was there to help. It also gave me a break from the roller coaster ride I was on with Sunny Dale. With Gilmore I didn't have to bring flowers or remember special occasions. I didn't have to make a date. All I needed was a phone, on the spur of the moment. "Hey, let's see what's happening in town."

"*Mais d'accord.*"

His French got out of hand now and then, especially after a few beers. In a backwoods roadhouse we were checking out, he suddenly reared back and began bellowing out "La Marseillaise," banging on the table. I knew it was a mistake. Men in overalls with shaggy beards came to attention. We were in Tennessee, after all. One came up. "What'a think you're doing? You a communist?"

We left. There were not that many places in town set aside for a discussion of, say, the *New Yorker*, Gilmore's favorite magazine, that came a month late, sometimes not at all, to the newsstand by the depot where my father worked. There were movies to go to. But Gilmore couldn't sit through one without complaining, in his Orson Welles voice, about an idiotic plot or a vapid actor on screen, and all around would go, "Shsssss!"

We had no friends in common. Most real-life subjects were off-limits. We were not intimate. Sunny Dale knew more about me in a half hour than Gilmore had learned since we were Sunbeams. At times I wondered what I really knew about Gilmore. I knew I liked him enormously. I knew I had felt elevated in his company since the time he showed off his elaborate toy train with fake coal smoke coming out of a tiny engine. Too, Gilmore was always glad to see me. That was no small matter. It was as if I were eternally walking in on the polished floor of his hallway, the grandfather clocking ticking away, amber scotch in a crystal decanter in the cupboard, Gilmore coming forward with a smile on his face and his hand outstretched. Here was someone sophisticated enough to call his father "G.W."

* * *

"I've heard of this new place," he said. "It's supposed to be pretty wild. Want to give it a shot?"

"Sure. Why not?"

It irritated me to be nearly always following his lead, but in our relationship that was usually the case. It was understood—at least by him—that he knew more. The new place sat off the road leading out of town. A fading Miller High Life sign flickered over a steel-trap sort of door and the place had no name that proclaimed it. It would be something that Gilmore had heard about. A steady, low-level hum came from within, like the hum from a beehive. All shades were drawn. It had the welcoming air of a tomb although the parking lot was full. Gilmore led the way. Inside we were met by the familiar beer joint blast of stale beer and waves of gray smoke. The jukebox played. Coins rattled. The patrons were all men. For some reason, most were smiling crazily. A man with slicked-back dark hair and in a Hawaiian short-sleeved shirt showing off bulging muscles stood near the bar checking out all who entered. He gave us a thin, knowing smile, a cross between a greeting and a show of contempt. I remembered him as being connected to a string of beer joints along the railroad tracks that dealt in tip boards and betting spreadsheets. Here was a real criminal if I'd ever seen one. I wouldn't want to cross him.

Inside, surprisingly enough, I recognized several happy guzzlers although I'd never run across them in a beer joint before. Here came a Methodist minister up to where Gilmore and I had taken a booth. The last time I'd seen him he had given a speech at assembly in high school. He reminded me of Abraham Lincoln, the same weary look, the same long, drawn face. "Evening, boys. Tell me. Think the rain's going to ruin the rhubard?" He chuckled. How's that again? Then he passed along, giving benedictions left and right to the booths around us. My God, there was the drugstore delivery boy—actually a man in his thirties or forties—who was the fastest bicyclist in town. He passed every car on the street and some on the highway and once I saw him peddling backwards without using his hands. Here he was, hair sparkling from goo, in lively conversation with a dentist who never seemed to have any patients. I spotted one of the chubby Newcomes, from a family that picked up garbage in town, now in a clean shirt and with a washed face. I knew what had brought this collection together, realized it after a moment or two, but I wasn't going to say so. It was up to Gilmore, he had brought me here. I was not comfortable. "Look," he said. "That man over there is staring at me. Look out the corner of your eye. Tell me what you think."

Huh? A man in a business suit was indeed staring, now at me. He was wetting his lips and now and then raising his eyebrows up and down. Christ, now I know what a woman feels like. "Gilmore, let's get the hell out of here."

"Well, I should think so."

Outside, the steel-trap door clanged behind us. I said, "Listen, I have a date tomorrow night."

"Anyone I know?"

"No, she's new in town. Her name is Sunny Dale." I felt a shiver go through me just saying her name.

"Sunny Dale. Oh, I know her."

"How?"

"She went with my roommate down at the military school. He was first captain."

I simply had to hear more about Sunny Dale and the first captain. We drove along, looking for another beer joint, not mentioning for the world the one we had just left, when I said as casually as possible, "What was the first captain like, this roommate of yours?"

"Oh, he got a lot of honors. I don't know how."

I waited awhile, looking out the window, fiddling with the dials on the radio. "Did he look like Tab Hunter?"

"What a weird question. As a matter of fact, the exact opposite. More ordinary. Like you."

I let that pass, though it stung. More glances out the window. "Were they close, this first captain and Sunny? Anything like that?"

"He took her to the spring prom, and that was a big deal down there. That was the next thing to being engaged. They came onto the gym floor through a row of cadets holding sabers overhead."

"What was she like then?"

He drew his breath in and let it out, his lips vibrating. "Will you stop? She was nice. She was very, very nice. That's all I know. Can we talk about something else?"

The next night, with Sunny beside me in the car, I said, in as off-handed a way as possible, "I hear you know Gilmore Polk." I didn't know what I was hoping to discover.

"Oh, Gilmore. Sure. He's a funny fellow."

Did I imagine she seemed embarrassed? She blushed slightly. I pictured her and Gilmore's roommate, the first captain, going down through the row of sabers held overhead, her in a strapless evening gown, him in dress whites. I couldn't help that my next fancy was of the evening gown going down above, going up below, in the backseat of a car. Those things happened at randy military and prep schools, I'd heard. I longed to fill in all blanks about her life. Sunny Dale had sprung out of nowhere and I had fallen in love. I couldn't control myself.

* * *

It was old Timber Ted who sidled up beside me on Main Street. I generally tried to dodge him because he was never the bearer of glad tidings. We could double date, sure, because he had a car, but he was no one to hang out with outside of that. Once he had sidled up and said the craziest thing. He said, "You know something? I hear Gilmore Polk squats to pee." He had laughed his horse laugh, spittle flying. He was not a joy to run into. Now he said, "How's Sunny doing?"

"Fine."

"You better hang on to that one. Someone's going to take her away from you if you're not careful."

"Thanks for the tip.

"You know she went out with Corporal Parsons, don't you? Went out with him before you came along."

Corporal Parsons! Some veterans came back shaken from the war and never wanted to hear another word about it. They repressed the craziness that had gone on and what had been done to them. From then on it was the picket fence for them and *Leave it to Beaver* on TV. They brought up a generation who broke out and became the hippies of the 1960s. Then there were the crazies who came back from the war and didn't repress a thing. Corporal Parsons was in this latter category. He was a Marine Corps veteran of Iwo who had returned to scorch the landscape of any moving female target. Corporal Parsons kept his military rank before his name, like Captain Butler of *Gone with the Wind*. Why he wanted to be called by this rather lowly rank—after all, it wasn't of officer category—was beyond us all, but since he was rather unbalanced we went along with it. He could have meant it as a joke or was serious. We never knew. He carried the flag on Memorial Day and occasionally made speeches at the high school on the value of patriotism and what it was like to be washed ashore at Iwo and was drunk three or four nights a week in the American Legion Hut. Corporal Parsons had once been extremely handsome, having Robert Taylor and Farley Granger looks. He could still get by, although not helped any by the chaws of tobacco that often swelled his cheek or his putting away caseloads of beers. Women were still drawn to him, at least for one evening, and he pinned the panties of his conquests to his bedroom wall, to go along with captured flags of the Rising Sun and samurai swords.

As Timber Ted gave me the news on the street, I died a death. I tried to keep a tremor out of my voice. "She went out with Corporal Parsons, you say?" Smiling, ho-hum, isn't that interesting? "Er, what happened? He say?"

"Well, what do you think?" he said, with that distinctive, deep-voiced chuckle that I hated so much. I could have strangled him.

When I went to pick up Sunny that night for a spaghetti meal, I trembled. I squirmed in exquisite pain, thinking about how Cor-

poral Parsons may have pulled down my Sunny's pants with his cal-
loused mitts. It was like imagining your home burning down. Over
the meal, I looked past Sunny's shoulder and said, "Oh, by the way,
you know Corporal Parsons, don't you?"

I noticed that she flinched a little. "You mean *Sam* Parsons?"

"Yeah, we call him Corporal Parsons."

Her color rose. "I know him."

I said, as if in someone else's voice—and it just came out, not
the circumlocution I had in my mind—"Ted told me about you
and him."

"It's not so," she said. Neither one of us had to spell out what we
were talking about. I was surprised she wasn't madder. She didn't
seem mad at all. The closest she came was to frown. She didn't ask
any questions. Nothing. And that ended it. His name was never
brought up between us again. Later, Corporal Parsons invited me
on a tour of his distinctive room in the home of his long-suffering
and bewildered parents. It was as if he was showing off his Bruegels
and Modiglianis. "Lookey here. Here's a pair I'm really proud of.
These are off that blondie out at Don's drive-in."

"You mean Wanda? The night waitress? *Don's* girlfriend?" Don
was a narrow-eyed, hot-tempered, squat fellow who favored gang-
ster-like silk shirts and had shot his own brother in a disagreement.

"Yeah, reckon so. Wanda."

He unpinned them from the wall and smelled them. They were
pink and looked as delicate as a rose. "Want a whiff?"

"No, that's OK. Thanks, though." Later on I was a little sorry
not to have given it a little try.

I got him to identify other flimsy trophies on the wall, and they
came in all shapes and styles and shades. There were a few brassieres
thrown in for good measure. I waited, my breath coming sharply,
as pair after pair went past. He paused. "And this here's Suzanne
McCorkle's. We were on her front porch swing last July."

"*Suzanne McCorkle's!* The preacher's daughter?"

"Yeah. Man, oh man." He paused again before a pair of white
ones that might be a possibility. He dallied, reached into a striped
Beechnut pouch, and extracted a substantial load between his

thumb and first two fingers. He opened his mouth and lodged it inside. He chewed, spat in a can, and shifted the cud. I was going crazy. "Yeah, this pair. Guess who."

"Corporal, I wouldn't have any idea." Would I grab a samurai sword and ram it into him?

"I got 'em off Miss Josephine Turner." Could you believe him? She was the high school gym teacher, stacked like a brick shithouse. We had reached the end of the line. Any from Sunny Dale never came up. I left confused, but happy I guess.

Gilmore was departing town, leave up, and we were saying our so-longs, I had one last chance to work in a few more questions about Sunny. I wouldn't get the chance again. He might be shot raising his head on the training field, rifle cradled in his arms. Who knew? Now was my chance. I forced myself to make some flattering comments about Gail the wispy judge's daughter to smooth the way, then:

"Gilmore, was Sunny in love with your roommate way back when?"

"No," he said sternly. "It was the other way around. He was crazy about her."

"He was?"

"Yes. I think she ditched him and no girl had ever done that to him before."

"She did?"

"He wasn't too intelligent when you came right down to it."

"What else?"

"That's all, for Christ sakes! That's all I know! *C'est tout! Complet! Mon dieu!*"

"Well, *au revoir!*"

"*À bientôt!*" And he marched off in his wrinkled blue Air Force uniform, catching a bus. I noticed that his ears were dirty. I would sorely miss him. Actually I enjoyed his company as much as Sunny's but in a much different way—a way devoid of the erotic excitement and pleasures unknown and unexpected. Hanging out with Gilmore was like going into retirement.

Sunny Dale tolerated Gilmore. She tolerated my brother, my mother, my father, the university I had gone to, the books and movies I touted. She tolerated them. She even tolerated Hemingway. "I read him but I can't figure out what he's getting at. It seems like some child wrote it."

She came alive when she picked up a baby—any would do anywhere where one might pop up, my brother's, her aunt's, a married friend's, a perfect stranger's in a restaurant. She would coo and tickle and ask to hold it. Granted permission, she would rock it to and fro. She asked if I wanted to hold it. I tolerated the experience. But I couldn't understand the attraction of holding a red-faced, squalling bundle in my arms, something I was in terror of dropping. When Sunny lifted one up to me, a light in her eyes, something deep inside me said, Get out of here! Retreat! Cover your flanks, men, and head for the hills! *Incoming!*

When it was theoretical, beautiful, sexy, and nothing spelled out, I was up for adventure and chance. I loved having Sunny Dale on my arm. I loved being able to recognize her perfume in a room. I loved this jog into the unknown with her. I loved not thinking about consequences when nothing real was in front of me. And the days and weeks piled up. In November she had posed in shorts and a tight sweater. Now we were approaching Valentine's Day. Would I spring for a big box of candy or a steak dinner? How about that Zippo lighter with her name engraved? What would I come up with—or her to me? I had been seeing Valentine's Day come and go forever, and it hadn't meant much since grade school when you were measured by how many cards you got and who from. It was all commerce and vanity. This one would be different. This one would change the landscape forever. I had flirted and professed love before this. Little did I know.

I picked up Sunny Dale on Valentine's night and she wore a black skirt and white silk blouse buttoned at the top. She wore heels and hose. She was all dressed up, as if for a ceremony. I was in an itchy suit. She bent over and kissed her father goodnight as he sat in his easy chair. He seemed surprised. She waved to her mother in the kitchen. She even squatted down and ruffled the ears of her little dog that squirmed and yapped in ecstasy. It was as if she was leaving them in some final, deciding way. She looked at me, smiled, and her color rose. She knew. I knew. We both knew. It didn't need the exchange of candy or card. This was it, and it didn't need a seduction. I didn't have to talk or plead anyone into anything. I walked out the front door after her on a cloud. I walked with a mixture of excitement and fear that almost capsized me.

In my car, she sat against her door, not closely beside me as she usually did and her eyes were on me. I drove so slowly that a man walking on the sidewalk passed me. I cut over the railroad tracks, just letting the car drive itself in a way, like a horse finding its way to pasture. The sun had just set and the air was a little sharp. I had the heater going and it sent little puffs of warm air over our legs. "I love you," I said.

"Do you?" she said. "It's very important now."

"I do. Do you love me?"

"I do."

The road we took—or that took us—rose on the outskirts of town toward a wooded cove. On it we passed the elementary school, a church or two, a grocery store, one-story homes spaced well apart, a park—all I'd seen many times before. I had ridden my bike here once to deliver papers. I had bought sodas at the country store, had been an ineffectual laborer in building one of the churches during summer vacation. I knew the route like the back of my hand. All past associations were now washed away. Here on a chilly February evening in Tennessee I was driving off to make love to Sunny Dale.

the thunderbolt

She slowly took little bites of cherry pie, raised her eyes and blushed, but she wasn't shy. We sat in my Plymouth in the Dixie's BBQ drive-in. I could only manage a few sips on a 7-Up loaded with ice in a paraffin cup myself. I couldn't believe my eyes, could hardly believe what had happened scarcely an hour before. Everything outside was going on normally: cars backing up or moving into place; the red neon sign proclaiming the Dixie BBQ. The moon was up there somewhere. Faint car fumes were in the air. We didn't say much. We just looked at one another. In wonderment, on my part.

I was a different man now, would be forever, than the one who had driven such a short time before into the woods of a farm on the outskirts of town. She was not old enough to vote; I had just reached the age but saw no reason to do so. Republicans ran everything in town and lived in the finest houses and always won, so what was the use? I wanted more; more than anything, I wanted to break free. But the world this night was far, far away. In the woods that night the moon had been big and it had been our only light. We had taken off our clothes in the front seat with hardly a preamble. We did it cheerfully and with alacrity. We understood. She got out of her skirt and blouse and did the unsnapping of a small white bra. I took off her last garment, a symbolic gesture of some sort, I suppose. She was completely bare, totally, everything off, and I looked and couldn't believe it. This was real, but not real; this was how a dream came. Dreams came unexpectedly and were like nothing ever before. Her skirt was familiar; also the blouse. They were gone. For some reason, perhaps symbolically, too, I left my T-shirt on. I didn't take every last stitch off as she did. And then:

It had been a miracle. It was like being a stumblebum, a devoted but unpracticed enthusiast of the dance, and then whisked to a ball and waltzing away. Where had she learned to do all these things that I'd never even had the wit to imagine? Her mind was free. I could still worry. A twig snapped. "What's that?" I said.

"Nothing," she said. "Do you like it like this or do you like it like that?"

"Like that."

"Go ahead. It's not my time of the month."

We went twice that night with but a pause for half a cigarette and to note the rustle of a cow outside the window. At times it was like barrel-rolling in the bi-plane with Miss Mary Louise Luster. I didn't know what was up or down, whether the sky was below and the earth above. I saw parts of the car and flesh I'd never seen before. We put our clothes back on with far less alacrity than we had taken them off. I was given the honor of snapping her bra in place from behind—she just turned and expected it to be done. I acted as if I'd snapped many a bra before. I hadn't. This was my first, but somehow I managed after a few trys. The way she turned her back and lifted her arms, bra dangling, signified something important to me. Trust? Familiarity? We were in this together. I felt like a hero. I felt like a conqueror. I had won her love.

Back in public we sat chuckling in the car, realizing that we had pulled something off and no one that passed our way had any idea. You get married and have a honeymoon and then everyone knows. No one knew. I called her first thing next morning, still awestruck, and there were pauses, things said and unsaid, everything low-key and soft. I didn't know about her, but I had never been happier in all my life. I wished, somewhat crazily, that we could stop right then and there, that we wouldn't go further but would just savor what we'd pulled off. It was like a grand heist, a stickup at Monte Carlo, and we could retire on it and mull it over for the rest of our days. Nothing could top it. But the next night, after we drove around a bit and I thought two nights in a row might be too much, I drove up before her home. She touched my leg. "Not yet," she said. "Let's go back to where we were last night."

I dutifully drove back to the same spot and the same cow thrashed outside the window. I went back to where we had left off, still lost in savoring the previous night's extravaganza. And panicked. What if I couldn't? I forced myself to think of the behind of Miss Tillie Johnson. She was the town librarian. Anything to arouse myself. But it was only for a moment, and it was unnecessary. Sunny wrapped her arms around me, and we were off and running. Our roller coaster ride plunged ahead.

* * *

We kept the wooded cove in reserve, but found other venues. We found the drive-in theater. I paid the couple of bucks and then nosed into an empty slot as far from other cars as possible. I bought no popcorn. Motor running for awhile, heater perking, we got out of our clothes routinely and expertly, as if ready for athletics. We were limber, able to swing over the front seat into the back. The front seat was showing tracks of past frolics that no matter how hard I tried to erase in daylight remained. In seconds we flipped into the roomier backseat that had no steering wheel or pedals. We could hear other motors running, other activity, and then we heard nothing else. A gun could have been put to my head and I wouldn't have stopped. Limbs akimbo, all flesh revealed, rising and falling before the steamy windows, must have been some sight for anyone who cared to crawl up and peer inside, but we didn't care. We rested, we smoked, and then we started back up. Doing it once we considered too tame. Finished, we drove out slowly, clothes on but wrinkled, faces as beatific as if we were leaving church. In the early phase I had no idea what movie we had been given fleeting shots of. While

Indians galloped around a circle of wagons or a couple rode in the backseat of a New York taxi—we flew into multiple positions.

* * *

I had gathered some intelligence earlier. Ernie Banks, who had once cavorted in the backyard buggies with those older, alluring girls, passed on some technical know-how. He had recently been at it for a month or so with an older woman in his father's car, and he let a few select friends of his know about it. Later he had to marry the woman and had a nervous breakdown, but before that happened he was able to give us some mechanical advice. He said, in his happy Southern drawl, as if he was savoring country ham and red-eye gravy, "What she does is get right up there on top of you in the front seat, puts her knees right down there on either side, and then comes down like a pile driver. Man, oh man!"

"What about the steering wheel?"

"You scoot over. Toward the passenger seat. I mean, it's something. She can wiggle around like she likes. Some women just know how."

I wondered about Andy Hardy. What if it had been real life then, and not the movies? Bow-tied Andy would pick up big-eyed Polly Benedict in his old jalopy. "Shucks, Polly," he'd say. "Let's skip the soda and the drugstore tonight. Let's go do some parking."

"Oh, boy," Polly says, lowering those big eyes. "Say you love me, Andy Hardy."

"I love you, Polly Benedict."

They park in the moonlight. Back home Judge Hardy, old Lewis Stone, is passing on homilies and the biscuits. Mom is fretting over Andy and worries that he will stay out too late. Sensible Aunt So-and-So says there is nothing to worry about. This is a fine new generation. Andy's gang is at the soda fountain thinking up ways to get Andy elected student body president. Andy is now trying to peel off Polly's rubberized panty girdle. Andy can hardly crank up his jalopy to get it going let alone roll down a chastity girdle. But after some suspense and broad comic turns that you can always count on from Andy, the job gets done. You can always expect some exasperation from Polly. She's never quite satisfied about anything. "Can't you get it in, Andy Hardy? Here, let me do it."

And Polly, with naked knees astride naked Andy, comes down while putting one tit and then the other into Andy Hardy's big mouth. She goes side to side in a shimmy. "Hot dog!"

* * *

When the weather had warmed a bit we cracked the window to let in the sound of crickets and the croak of bullfrogs from a nearby stream. We watched the start of movies. We watched June Allyson and June Haver and Doris Day being virginal and unattainable, and then, having enough, we let fly. We saw Ma and Pa Kettle, two obsessively endearing hillbillies, grapple with life on the farm. "Ma, you shouldn't be pulling that plow anymore, you know. You ain't as young as you once were," Pa said, and we laughed, and said it to each other, and then went at it.

Another time, up and beyond me on the screen loomed the large moist head of Somerset Maugham, introducing a movie based on a quartet of his stories, called *Quartet*. Here came that silken cozy English voice, full of privilege and worldly advice, with stories to follow. I wouldn't mind seeing some of it. It was my birthday and she had given me a shirt with a little loving note slipped in the pocket. "I have another present for you," Sunny said now. I reached for her. "Not just yet. Waiting is not so bad." I got to watch *Quartet*, about couples and desire and misunderstanding. And then Sunny let my hand roam free, and I breathtakingly found that she wore no underwear. "My present," she said.

We broke free of the confines of the drive-in and the woods and driving around. We tried to break free of sex for a change. We attempted a turn at religious services on Sunday. For adventure, for novelty, we went to Mass at the only Catholic church in town although we were as far from being Catholics as you could get. We threw ourselves into being pious, practiced worshippers. We genuflected and crossed ourselves to a fare-thee-well. Then we sat back angelically. Outside, in the sun, alone and out of sight in the car, services ended, she lowered herself on me, her wide brimmed church hat going up and down. Another day, on a picnic up a mountain trail she slid under a blanket, leaving me above and wonderstruck. Some hikers passed and I cheerily passed a quick pleasantry or two while she was busy down below. Parked in front of her house one night we got caught in the same arrangement. A neighbor just poked his head through the open window and said, "I seen you."

What do you say to that?

Sunny rose with dignity, smiled, and said, "Hi, how are you this evening?"

He walked off muttering.

The secrecy, the furtiveness, always being on the outlook, did get to me. I wanted security. "How about driving in my backyard?" I said one evening. I was thinking of where the old barn had once been. No one could find us there.

"No, not there," she said.

One morning while I smoked and moaned in boredom at my desk at the Welcoming Center she called and said, in her girlish trill, "Come over to my house and we'll have lunch."

"Where's the rest of your family?"

"Gone."

"Sure?"

"Positive. Don't worry."

"I'm on my way."

She met me at the door in a long, blue-quilted bathrobe that parted as she strode to the kitchen, giving me fast glimpses of her bare thighs. I had seldom been in her kitchen, certainly not for a meal. I can still see her, decades later, taking slow suggestive spoonfuls of bright red Jell-O. She would hold it in her mouth, look me in the face, green eyes flashing, smile, and swallow. Right then I knew love, knew it as if the word had just been invented and didn't do whatever I felt justice. I didn't eat and followed her into her bedroom as she carried a bowl of Jell-O. She placed it on a night table and took off the robe. She wore nothing beneath. In my mind I see her as I see the Jell-O. It was the first time I had seen her full body in full light. Her hips flared and her stomach was flat as a board. I could encircle her waist with my two hands. I took off my clothes and she helped me with my T-shirt. On the bed she took the Jell-O in her hands and hovered above me, taking slow bites and transferring some to my open mouth. She put more in her mouth and then went down below the border. I couldn't speak. She uprighted herself and squiggled atop me. She looked me in the eye, amused, and we began. I said, "Stop."

She stopped, still amused, which almost sent me over the top. I looked away and made myself think of baseball. That worked for awhile, until she did a secretive something or other with an inner muscle but not moving her body. "Stop." It was as if I heard a bird call or the sound, God forbid, of her father's Dodge pulling up. I made myself think of my old high school principal and drew myself back from the brink.

Soon enough, though, I said, "Is it O.K. now? You know, the time of the month?"

"I'm due tomorrow. Go ahead, darling."

We made love four times and I didn't have time for lunch. Back in the office I gazed out over my Welcoming Center desk, satiated, as if I had been to Lourdes and had received a miraculous cure for terminal horniness. Whatever or whoever was in front of me made no difference. "Young feller, are you listening to me?" someone was saying. "I want to know how to get to Andrew Johnson's cabin. It's advertised right here in this brochure and I'm lost as daylight . . . young man, what's wrong with you? Look at me. Young man, young man."

I got through the day as best I could. That night we drove off into the woods for more. We wanted to get one more in before it was time-out.

* * *

I was being given firsthand instruction in what went into making a woman. Where had I been? I had been too busy turning into a man. I was again in her kitchen and the rest of her family was scattered elsewhere in the house. She stood before me in a white tennis outfit, the kind she'd seen Elizabeth Taylor wear in a movie and she had to have one. She was bringing milk from the refrigerator to pour us both a glass. "Hut, oh," she said, the bottle in hand. I saw a crimson drop escape from the whiteness of her outfit and run down her leg. Then a circle of the same hue spread on her linen white shorts. I watched as she calmly put the milk down and go off, saying cheerfully, over her shoulder, "What if it had happened on court? Wow-wee!" We were in this, this cycle of nature, together. Only I wasn't doing the bleeding.

When she didn't come around was the time for me to bleed. She told me over the phone in a voice I hadn't heard before, "I'm late. I should have started by now. Maybe we figured wrong when we could and shouldn't have." She did the figuring. What did I know? I supplied the latex during the fertile period and occasionally it broke. And she didn't like latex and I didn't like latex, so there we were. When I got the news, I drove by myself around town, gazing at homes and stopping at red lights. Everything took on a cloud of doom. I couldn't picture an actual baby. I pictured a cramped apartment over a garage. I pictured the big event of the week being a Saturday night party with liquor in brown paper bags and everyone cursing the government. I saw a hammer coming down over my head. I was never going to get out! I was never going to get where I belonged, wherever that was. I was never getting to New York. We went out, we ate meals, we talked about everything but what was on our minds. And I held her hand. I knew deep down that we were a team, I would stick with her, we would stick together, until they drew and quartered me, chopped me up into hamburger and fed me to the dogs. But I'd rather that didn't happen. She knew this, too. But she was not as relieved as I was when she called one late afternoon, right after I got home from work, and said, "I've come through. It's started."

"Wow-wee, baybee! We have to be more careful!"

"I know."

I immediately went in the backyard, lay in the grass, puffed on a cigarette, and looked up at the blue, blue cloudless sky.

A night or two later, we were back at it. The flow be damned! I could really let loose now because I knew I wasn't in danger of knocking her up. Besides, I got to marvel at the sight of her blood on me. It was as if we were bleeding together. We were connected physically and otherwise. I knew so much about her: the times she had been sick in childhood, the boyfriends she had had and how far they'd got, her relatives in the country. I learned just how far Gilmore's roommate, the first captain, had got. Not far. ("I could tell he would never make a good lover. He didn't kiss right.") I heard how she had lost her virginity one night on a couch to a sailor who was going overseas. I knew she was allergic to coffee. I knew she had played basketball in high school. I knew her politics, her scent, the ways her toes went, the tiny beauty spot near her right eye. I wanted to be inside her as far as possible. I wouldn't have minded crawling in completely and hibernating for the winter.

When we weren't at it, I was either thinking of what we had done or when we were going to do it next. Every time I sat in a straight-back chair in her living room, waiting for her to enter, facing her father who was sunk in a easy chair and going on about Hereford cows, I was thinking, Sir, in scarcely over an hour, I'm going to be inside your daughter as far as I can get. I wasn't proud to think this, but I couldn't help it, it was so. While she performed onstage in one of the local Little Theater productions of missed lines and falling scenery, I had a similar urge. I wanted to stand up, wave my arms and call for quiet. She stood up there in perfect beauty. I wanted to shout, "That's my baby! We're doing it!"

She sang, she danced, the footlights made her face paler than it normally was, and her green eyes sparkled. She held a cane out with both hands, a top hat cocked on her head, and kicked first one leg out, then the other, and looked at me down in the audience. And an hour later we were in the woods, clothes off, at it. Did Shakespeare make love this way? Did Mickey Rooney?

It was spring in Tennessee. No need any more for the heater in the car. Wild onions sprouted. The Ramp Festival came. The turned earth was black and loamy. Birds woke you at sunrise. The mountain air was sweet at night and the sun was warm at high noon and the streets downtown were dotted with tiny specks of light. Sunny joined me on a walk and took my arm. She pulled me over before a jeweler's window and wordlessly pointed to the array of gold bands and crystal rings. They glistened, almost wagging a finger for us to enter. She caught the stunned look on my face. "Well?" she said.

I turned my head and shuffled my feet. I turned back and saw a stunned look on *her* face, a stunned and hurt look I had never seen before.

Those rings meant unconditional surrender to me. They said you'll be wearing a suit and tie and coaching Little League in this town for the rest of your days. You'll never get out. But I went weak at the knees at that look on her face. "Come on, honey," I said. "Let's walk some more in the sunshine."

"OK," she said, and was silent. She was holding something back that was threatening to break out. She had a temper. She had an unforgiving sense of right and wrong and I didn't want to cross the line.

Love gave me confidence, an assurance that I could bring down Goliath and do no wrong. That was one of the many reasons I had to love Sunny Dale of Tennessee. She gave me my manhood. We had a date scheduled once, and I was supposed to call a day before about what we would do—a movie or eat out or miniature golf, whatever. It didn't seem that important. When I called just before time to go out, she was steaming. "You should have called earlier," she said. "I don't think I'll go out with you tonight."

"Aw, come on," I said softly, a little taken aback, but confident I could win her over. "Come on, baby. I'll be by in fifteen minutes."

"I have a good mind not to."

I picked her up, she sat silently against her door for a few blocks, and then gradually the storm clouds cleared. But I had had a taste of her righteousness. I had had fair warning. She did not appreciate being wronged. She stood up to her boss at the dress shop who'd promised her a raise and hadn't followed through. She stood up to a bank manager who figured something wrong and claimed he was right. She stood up to her mother over everything. I had trouble with such absolute morality, particularly when I considered the wide parameter of our lovemaking and how liberated I felt in breaking the rules. She explained, "I can do all these things because I love you. You bring it out in me. No one else ever has before."

I believed her. I was tied to her. But I wasn't tied to this town. I had to leave or lose all hope of a larger life. I would die if sentenced here. I looked for ways to show how I felt. When she once complained of bills, a rare occurrence, I gave her my paycheck—minus car payment. She came back and said she had opened a joint account. I said it would be our getaway money. She began acting as much as a wife as a lover. She did surprising things for me. She gave me perfect neckties. No one except my mother had ever given me a necktie before. Every time I put a regimental stripe on, I thought of Sunny. I rubbed the material between thumb and forefinger, tied the knot, and smiled. I watched her pick up her small dog when it yapped. I would have slugged it. She cradled the thing in her arms, brought her cheek next to the dog's ear and caressed it.

We visited my brother Trickshot—ex-athlete, former wower of females, presently married and a new father. Sunny held the baby and bounced it on her knee. The apartment was cramped and small, and my brother got me off in the abbreviated kitchen. "If you can make it through your twenties, you've got it made."

What was he talking about? He had the tendency to jump right into the middle of his thoughts, with no preamble. I noticed that his once-dark, curly hair was thinning and one of his front teeth was discolored. I had never noticed him looking tired before. "What are you talking about?"

"Marriage. You're weak now. You'll succumb if you don't watch out. You'll be home free if you can last past thirty."

I couldn't remember him giving me advice on anything before. He wouldn't even let me drive his car, back before I had one. What was he doing? Making sure he was the only married son with children in the family, a star still? I got mad, but mainly because he had struck home. For awhile in private the song I sang to myself was "When I Was Single, My Pockets Would Jingle," and the old saying "a rolling stone gathers no moss" came easily to my lips.

* * *

I sat behind my desk in the Welcoming Center, day after day, chained to my chair, watching those at leisure pass on the street. A leading citizen, a florid-faced man, a hardware tycoon, entered once, swinging the door nearly off its hinges. "I want to tell you the most marvelous thing I ever witnessed in my life," he said, with no preamble, in the manner of my brother, as if he had been talking to himself on the street and came in to finish the sentiment. "It was down at Knoxville at half-time when everybody stood up and prayed. All those fans, thousands, stood up, bowed their heads, and prayed to the Lord Jesus Christ. They thanked God they were here on earth, right here in Tennessee."

"Yes, sir," I said. Jesus, I thought. Let me out of here! How much longer was I going to have to sit behind a desk in a Welcoming Center and listen to such stuff?

I loved the countryside and the crops laid out on it. I loved watching farmers in overalls bring in fresh vegetables for sale on Market Street, and loved how they spit tobacco juice out the side of their mouths. I loved skillet cornbread, biscuits, and anything fried. I loved walking down Main and seldom passing anyone I hadn't seen before. Such things I assumed would always be there, and I could always come back to them. But right now I'd had enough of angry Republicans who went beet red at the mention of the New Deal and grown men who wanted to pray at half-time, and sinking in a sea of them with no relief in sight. One day I came upon a car with a man I remembered just having seen a short time before going into a movie starring the Range Busters. Now he was slumped back in the front seat, his face twisted and his eyes open and not blinking. Some young country boys were peering at him and shuffling their feet, seeming to start to run, changing their minds, coming back. "Hey, mister," one of them said. I had suddenly become a "mister." "That there man looks like something happened to him. He looks dead."

I knew I had to find an escape hatch before I slumped over myself. I had to get out. A likely conduit, I thought, might be through one of the many promoters who came through town, hawking something or other, messengers from more storied heights. A hearty, rotund man, an executive and spokesman for a large steel company, came through. He wore a tailored gray suit with a boutonniere. He made speeches at our grade schools on the glories of free enterprise and the dangers of the income tax. I could have done without any of that, but he did come from a big city and a big outfit and there was that carnation in his lapel. I called his hotel room after he'd finished a full day of speeches. He seemed a little tipsy. "Sir, I was wondering if there might be something open in your organization," I began.

"We have nothing," he said in a slurred voice. "Could you please tell me where I might purchase a bottle of your fine bourbon?"

"This is a dry county, sir. You have to know a bootlegger."

"Could you please connect me with such an individual?"

I gave him a number. One after another they traipsed through—the out-of-town speaker for Spring Cleanup Week, a droopy-eyed man with his face blotched by scrofula; a vaguely smiling woman who was doing a magazine article on life in the Appalachian Mountains and who also needed a bootlegger bad; and a dapper man with hair slicked back like Adolphe Menjou who had been imprisoned in the Soviet Union and came to us in the hills to describe life behind the Iron Curtain. He was advertised as PR for something called Freedom Now, an organization that solicited funds for the tearing down of the Curtain. I liked the sound of being in PR but was unsure of what it involved. What did people in PR actually do? I called his hotel and believe I took him from the potty. There were bathroom gurgles in the background. He was most pleasant and seemed to get immediately what I was driving at, that I wanted to escape, as he had escaped from Russia. I was unsure if he was American or not. What was he doing getting imprisoned in Russia anyhow? He gave me his number in New York, but when I called a week later I was told the number had been disconnected.

I wouldn't stop trying to break out, though. I would take Sunny along. We could both escape. I imagined it. We could go to LA and she would cock the top hat on her head, kick her legs up, and get in the movies. I would shuffle papers around, work in a factory, pump gas, do something. They said jobs were easy to find out there. The only trouble was that it was three thousand miles away and we didn't have gas money to get past Murfreesboro. But I daydreamed of an apartment by the beach for Sunny and me. We talked of it. It was easy when it was only daydreaming. It was intoxicating. "I could live on beans with you," she said.

"I love you so," I said.

And then . . . then I just did it. I woke up one morning, looked at the ceiling, told myself to remember this moment forever, and decided to get out, to go find something else—to go alone. *A rolling stone gathers no moss!* I came from frontier stock, didn't I? I came from people who just left everything, went out there, and laid claim to somewhere else. The men had simply left, went off alone, and *then* sent for loved ones. I could do it. Sunny would wait for me. I would be a man. Why not Washington, DC? It was a day's drive away. It was bustling. There must be work galore. There were the arts. There was sophistication, one notch below New York, on the way to getting there. I could get a room somewhere. Sunny could join me later. Why not?

Sunny didn't argue, although she wasn't as enthusiastic about it as I was. She took on the same expression she'd shown before the jeweler's window when I'd shuffled my feet. "Go," she said.

"I'll get set up and then I'll come back for you," I said. "Or you can join me. Either way. We'll start a life in Washington!"

I was convincing myself. It didn't cost anything. I could picture us both driving around Washington, taking in the Lincoln Memorial, seeing the cherry blossoms fall, speaking French. She looked sympathetic or with resignation or just plain sad, it was hard to tell. She had done all she could do, she said with her eyes.

"Let me go, honey, please," I said. "It'll be fine. It won't take long. It's a chance to move forward. Let me take it."

"Do it," she said. "You have to. But let's spend a night together in a real bed first."

I then saw myself finding a motel where we would never be spotted, signing a bogus name, and going further than we ever had before. "Sure," I said. "Let's."

I said goodbye to the Welcoming Center. I shook Curt, my boss's hand and he said I might be making a mistake. "There's opportunities galore in East Tennessee. There's everything they've got elsewhere, and you can't beat the weather." He couldn't help taking the Welcoming Center line, even to me.

My one small suitcase packed, car gassed up—Sunny using the cover of visiting a girlfriend in Knoxville—we stayed in a motel cabin by a stream. On the way she took off her blouse and that little white bra and put on one of my T-shirts. I wore a shirt she had given me. In our room with pine boarding we listened to music, we took showers together, we heard party noises nearby. We hardly slept. We examined each other's bodies. We told jokes. We confessed secrets. She tried out a nightgown I could see through. The bedsprings creaked but we paid no attention. I lost track after twelve times because I didn't believe anyone could do it that many. This was once again a dream. If you could be this happy in a motel cabin by a stream, with one woman, then you could go out and conquer the world.

I drove her to the bus station for her trip back to town. I was going to drive off alone. "I'll wait for you forever," she said. "I'll never love anyone else."

"I love you. There will never be anyone else but you."

I drove away, up a curvy, narrow mountain road, out of Tennessee, leaving Sunny Dale behind.

the return of the native

After so many summers dies the swan, and I return. It is not the same town, but then it is no other place either. The train station is still there, but it looks grimier, if that's possible and fewer people are in the waiting rooms—one that used to be for whites, the other for "colored," though neither designated as such now. The drinking fountains are not designated either, but are out of service. I walk past the Welcoming Center in the Andrew Jackson Hotel, where I used to put in one boring hour after another and pray for release. Now released, I glance through the plate glass and see a new beaming face behind my old desk. I see people moving around normally inside, my absence not making any difference. No one notices me outside. I feel like Emily in *Our Town*, returning from the dead.

I go to the old poolroom, and it smells of chalk and stale smoke and spilled beer as always. A smiling fellow I had gone to high school with, a man now, corners me. "Want to chalk up for some nine ball?"

"No, I'm just looking around."

I'd been gone for a few years, but he didn't ask where I'd been. He hadn't missed me. I didn't have to ask what had happened to him because I could tell nothing had. He thought he could still beat me in pool, and I'm sure he could. I walk down Main Street and up Market Street. The mannequins behind plate glass in Auburon's

Men's Shop still wear vanilla-colored windbreakers, dark tuxes, and gray flannel trousers but, the window has become fly-specked, whereas it gleamed before. The mimeographed menu pasted on the front window of the Roxy Grill, where Sunny and I had eaten spaghetti and meatballs on festive nights out, still lists the dish. It has gone up fifty cents. At home, where I have now crashed, I sit by the bay window and read, and look out, and brood. My parents don't know what to make of me and neither do I.

My car still runs although it leaks oil and needs an overhaul, which I can't afford. With heart pounding, I drive past Sunny's old home on the other side of town at around three miles an hour in the afternoon. I see her mother hanging laundry in the backyard and her father drive into the back garage. It is as if everything is back to normal, as if nothing has happened or changed there. I speed up if I think they may be looking my way. At night, when the sun goes down, I drive past the second-story apartment where Sunny now resides. The shades are drawn and that leaves me to imagine what is going on behind them. No shadows move beyond them. I have to see her in the flesh, have to, have to hear her voice once again. The thought leaves me weak and trembling as stage fright once did when I had to speak before an audience.

I spend a good half hour combing my hair and adjusting my clothes before the mirror and then I walk in the dress shop where she still works part-time. It's the same old dress shop, although not with as many customers as it used to have. She is in back. I spot her, my first glimpse of her since I left. I look over some gauze-thin scarves on the front counter. I hold up a red and purple one to the light, and feel the faintly perfumed fabric as if I might buy something in a women's dress shop. She sees me. Our eyes connect. She smiles in the old way, and I watch her stride toward me—the same walk, but with what I take to be a new confident air. She is before me. The beauty spot is there beside her eye. She is calm, a studied calm. I try to be nonchalant, try to remember one of the witty greetings that have been careening around in my head. My mind goes blank and my heart pumps in my chest. "Hello," I say.

"Hello," she says. She still has the girlish trill. But like the town, she is not the same.

*   *   *

After I had left her standing that hot summer's day some time before, I had driven straight to DC where, a hand on the wheel and eyes darting for signs, I sought to get my bearings. There were cut-offs, construction, masses of cars. This was not Tennessee anymore. This was big time. I drove across wide Memorial Bridge and was welcomed by an array of gray marble against a blue sky. It was grander than grand. I went dizzyingly around circles with fountains or statues in the center, down shaded, tree-lined streets, no more sure where I was than if I'd been in Paris. In my head I was writing to Sunny about all this and then I saw a space for parking that miraculously didn't have a fireplug beside it. I careened in, gabbed my fake alligator suitcase, and knocked on the first door I came to with a "room for rent" sign.

It was a fleabag a block away from the red brick Presbyterian church where J. Edgar Hoover prayed. I took a room. It was on the top floor and occupied a space the size of a large closet back home. The rooming house was filled, from top to bottom, with the remains of those going to a different drummer. Leading off was our landlady, an ex-showgirl, who dyed her hair and painted her lips bright red and was in love with J. Edgar Hoover. Two aging veterans of some past war or wars took up space in the attic, their choice of drink, Thunderbird. Later, on a holiday, I tried being a Good Samaritan and gave them a bottle of Chivas Regal. They mumbled thanks, squinted at the label, and that was it. A month later, when I chanced by their attic room, I discovered the bottle of scotch still unopened among the glittering array of empty wine bottles.

Two hard-bitten women were on a lower floor. One was slightly prettier and better built than the other, if that was saying much, and they got into horrific, hair-pulling melees at least once a week. "She fucked my fellow," the less pretty one explained to any who would listen the morning after a screaming, glass-shattering evening. Adding a slight note of dignity to the surroundings, however, was a rather stiff and utterly silent man who occupied the house's most spacious room, one that faced the street and got a breeze. He came and went without a word or nod to anyone. His wore a dark suit and tie and carried a cracked, expensive-looking briefcase. He received a great deal of respect because he supposedly held a substantial position in government. How anyone in a high government position could end up in this ruin of yesterday was anyone's guess. No one ever came to call for him. But I thought I understood. We might share a common trait. He was a loner, and I was now one too. You were free but you had to pay for it. It was a bargain you made with fate, and it was a predicament. One morning he was found sitting by himself on the stairs, tie askew, shoes off, blasted. He was glassy-eyed, mouth open, unable or unwilling to speak or hear. He was also unable to get to work.

"Are you OK? Do you need help?"

Even the half-loaded winos were concerned. We got him to his room which was, strangely enough, not in disorder but as neat as a West Point cadet's. He lay rigid on his narrow bed, eyes open, and we tiptoed out, closing the door softly behind.

The dignified man was free to get poleaxed, to get fired, to be heaved on the street. I could relate. For whatever the reason, there was nothing like the freedom I felt now in Washington, DC and out of Tennessee. I could walk to Georgetown over the "P" Street Bridge anytime I wanted. I could order a stack of pancakes, sausage on the side, in the Copper Skillet on Connecticut at one in the morning. I could see an Alec Guinness comedy. If I took the wrong turn and got lost for two hours in some no-man's-land, I didn't have to hear anyone scream at me. I didn't have to check in with anyone. *A rolling stone gathers no moss!*

There was one thing, though: I had to pay the rent and pay for the pancakes. I came by the first job that would have me, one that didn't require a suit and tie and that could be left as easily as a movie, and that job was as a concessionaire on a tour boat that went up and down the Potomac. *Oh, how free! How little required!* I showed up at noon, donned apron and white jacket, and got behind the counter while the ship's motor vibrated beneath me. I immediately wolfed down a hot dog or two on the house, and then I served passengers. Afternoons we chugged to Mt. Vernon and back; at night we took on passengers for an excursion to an amusement park where carousel music rended the air and evoked the ending of *Strangers on a Train*. It was cool onboard, tropical on land. The sun blazed or the moon shone on water or it rained. Nothing to do but serve weenies, hamburgers, and drinks and watch the landscape come into view and then disappear. It paid little, but all I needed. When summer ended, I became a ticket taker in a movie house where I had recently seen, and been awed by, Rossellini's *Open City*. A perfect job: you were out of the weather and you didn't have to speak. And I knew I would return to Tennessee, but not yet. Not yet. *Free!*

We wrote, Sunny and I. Every time I came into the musty rooming house, my heart leapt when I saw on the battered hall table where our scant mail lay an envelope with her neat handwriting in blue. I would climb the flights, secure my door behind me, and run my hand over the usually thick envelope for awhile before opening it: "My love . . . my darling boy . . . I visited Granddad and lots of cousins in the mountains last weekend . . . I went to a movie with some girlfriends last night . . . It wasn't the same without you . . . Tell me about everything that you're doing . . . I can't hear enough! When do you want me to come up?"

Under the glare of a dangling unshaded bulb, sitting on the edge of my bed, I wrote, "We'll be back together soon . . . I picture us now together, where we will be, what we'll do . . . but bear with me until I get firmly established. It's taking more time than I thought. I've left being a trainee for riverboat management and now—guess what!—I've just landed something in the movie business. It's down the ladder, but it's the movies and it's only up from here. I'm learning the ropes. Soon we'll be back together. Soon!"

"The movies!" the reply shot back, scarcely a minute after I put my letter in the slot. "I walk around waving your letter at the ceiling. I nearly shout so Granddad can hear me in the mountains . . . Tell me all . . . Are they making a movie in DC like *Mr. Smith Goes to Washington* or *Advise and Consent*? . . . I can't wait to see you . . ."

"Soon," I wrote.

I didn't get past imagining her walking into this domicile, little blue suitcase in hand, a nifty hat on her head. Would the two women screaming behind closed doors shatter her equilibrium? Might the clinically depressed government worker be seated on the stairs, head between his legs, zonked? Would the two winos be talking about Pancho Villa and Chesty Puller? "Soon," I wrote, but drifted. Outside my room, Washington was like a Rockefeller preserve to a man on the loose. You could walk through Dumbarton Oaks as if it were the Tuileries. You could step in the small Phillips Gallery off Dupont Circle, no questions asked, and find a Degas or Whistler waiting in a reverential light and hush. You could catch Dean Acheson in a homburg, strolling from Georgetown down to Foggy Bottom. A man alone could drift around and stumble on nearly anything. I drifted into a restaurant up Connecticut Avenue where foreign students, gadflies, and ex-pats of all stripes had drifted and congealed. You heard French, you heard German, you heard stories and told them that would never be allowed in Tennessee. You could nurse a beer and stay till closing. What would Sunny think? Would she be bored and dismissive? How would she fit in?

"Soon," I wrote. Soon I'll be coming back. But I kept drifting. And "soon" began extending itself.

The weather changed, the leaves fell. There came that envelope that day on the hall table with her distinctive handwriting: thinner than usual and that was a sign. I climbed to my room, turned it over and over in my hands, then ripped it open. "I have waited. And waited. I still love you, you understand, but I have started dating again. I just wanted you to know . . ."

I looked out the grimy window, looked down at my unmade bed and the piles of the *Washington Post* beside it. I pictured her stepping into a Cadillac convertible . . . where . . . I stopped right then and there and went to the communal hall phone. A pad lay next to it, there to list all long-distance calls. I had been the principal long-distance caller since I arrived, in fact the only one, calling from afar to her—invariably when I was high and delirious. Now I wasn't. I took the receiver from its cradle and held it to my ear, and here came the familiar buzz. Do something. But then the landlady took that moment to explode through the front door and waddle toward me. "Guess who I just saw coming out of Harvey's Steak House, young man? You'll never guess."

"J. Edgar Hoover," I said, putting the receiver back.

Such are chances lost, decisions postponed, fates sealed. The landlady was going on about the camel hair coat and snap-brim hat and the G-Men around him, and I was backing my way outside. I walked down Connecticut and everything seemed strange, dream-like. How could people walk normally, have life go on while Sunny was stepping into a car someplace, scooting beside some handsome, smooth-talking dude? The pain was exquisite. I didn't call that day. Why, why didn't I? I tore tickets in half that night. I didn't call the next day. It was as if I was outside my body, watching myself act—or not act, in this case. I had made a mess and I didn't know how to get out of it. Why'd I have to fall in love? Why'd I have to hook up with this perfect woman at this time? Why'd I have to choose now between Sunny and freedom? I wouldn't think about it, that's what I'd do. I would be free for a little longer that way. Everything would remain the same for just a little longer. I would see how long I could last. As long as I didn't call, things would remain the same. Her foot would still be poised to step in a stranger's car and my hand would still be holding the receiver.

A month later she called. One of the women below flew to get me. "Some girl's on the phone for you," she bellowed.

"Who?" I said, although I knew.

"Oh, just some girl. She didn't say."

How could anyone call Sunny "just some girl"?

Sunny's voice had that trill I knew so well, but it was immediately serious. "I'm coming up to Washington," she said.

"When do you want to do that?"

"I can fly up tomorrow. I've checked plane schedules."

"But that'll cost you a lot of money. Oh, honey!"

The image of her coming through the squeaking front door, met by the overpowering stench of a fleabag was more than I could bear. I looked around at the hallway's cracked, yellowing wallpaper and the frayed, dusty carpet on the stairs. I pictured the women screaming on the lower floor, the wino fumes increasing as you climbed the stairs, the government official lying flat and catatonic so that she had to step over him to get to the door of my dank, sour room. It wasn't Tennessee in the springtime. "No, wait," I said. "I'm coming back. I've been planning to. I just haven't told you. We'll talk. We'll be together as always. We'll work it out. Because . . . because I love you, I do."

"I love you," she said.

"Oh, I love you," I said.

I didn't ask about the dating scene or about the faceless mass of eager men that might be pulling up before her home. There could be no competition. How could there be? Not after what we had been through and how she said "I love you." I loved her. By God, I was going to pack up and go back! I knocked on the landlady's door to give notice and heard the answer of a soft, delicate snore inside. That was enough to let me stall just a little longer. I went to the movie theater to tear tickets and give notice and found out, oh, my sweet Jesus, that a French film festival was on tap for the following week. Gerard Philipe and Micheline Presle led off in *Le Diable au Corps*. I couldn't check out right now. I would never have this chance down in Tennessee. What did a few weeks' delay matter? If I was returning to Sunny for an eternity together, what was the hurry? The festival lasted a month and a half and the last film was *The Sheep Has Five Legs* with Fernandel. It was a comedy.

A postcard came on the hall table, an unusual sight. Usually postcards went the other way, out in droves from DC. It showed Main Street of from the place I had left, shot from up on a hill, all in bright colors as if every day was bright and lovely there. The card had to be for me. I turned it over. There was one sentence. In strong black ink as if by a paintbrush it read, *You are a bad person!* Not even with a signature! Jesus, God, Christ. It was like being in a terrible highway wreck that I didn't see coming, with blood all over the place. I stood paralyzed before it. What to do? What terrible accident had I caused? It was like I was a drunk driver who had caused it all and would soon be justifiably hauled into court. I didn't tear tickets that night. I walked and walked and walked. I walked through the deepest heart of a black ghetto a stone's throw from the Capitol's dome. Not all of Washington is Dumbarton Oaks and the Phillips Gallery. This was like going up a jungle river, looking for Kurtz. Only the faces that met me were not solemn and unfathomable. Many giggled. Some pointed and giggled. Others widened their eyes, wary, on guard, prepared to take offense and possibly attack. Come on, I thought, I can take it. I deserve it. Kill me. As I stepped past the boundary near Constitution, where presidents roll down, a gruff voice called out, "What you think you are, boy? A nigger? Stay outta here!"

I knew I should have called Sunny right after she wrote that she was going out with others. I should have gone back definitely when I got the postcard. What was in me that made me brood and hesitate? Was the call of freedom so powerful? Deep down did I sense that if I gave up ship at this moment that all was lost? I would become a Rotarian, I would never break free. I knew deep down, though, that I would never love anyone like I loved this girl from Tennessee. How could I? In any case I had waited too long. All good things do not necessarily come to those who stand and wait.

An envelope came that didn't have Sunny's handwriting. It was from my mother, and didn't require going to my room to open, to be private. Maybe I should have waited and sat down. I tore it open and inside was a wedding picture from the hometown paper: Sunny in a long white wedding gown. She had married someone else.

I had not been gone that long in calendar time, but it felt like an eternity of separation. Tennessee had said to her, Get married, raise a family. To me, it had said, Get out of here. I would be gone, but I would return.

* * *

When I did return, she was everywhere in town. She was in the traffic that passed; in the smoke of the poolroom; in every image and situation of every dippy movie I watched alone; in the strong sunshine of a Sunday afternoon. It took easing into the dress shop to catch her in the flesh. And there she stood before me, calmly smiling up, a foot shorter as always. Her calmness, her lack of any grudge, her steady, beneficent gaze, threw me. Where had her anger gone? Was I going to miss her anger now? I noted that she wore a glossy pair of new black shoes. She wore a pink blouse. Her hair was longer. I tried not to look at the two rings on her finger, a diamond shining.

"Yeah, hi, hello," I said, all witticisms out the window. At that moment, I noticed Timber Ted passing on the street talking to himself. He had grown enormously fat. I was going to have to get adjusted to that, too. "Say, how's your family doing? Are they OK?"

"Oh, fine. Dad's slowing down, may retire. Emily got married. She married a dentist from church. I couldn't have picked out a better man for her. They have this great house on the lake."

Has this woman forgotten that once we lay buck naked atop each other, our starving mouths at each other's middles, going at it like maniacs? Has she forgotten that I've seen her from the bottom up and I never saw a more lovely sight? Does she not know that I have gazed straight ahead at her asshole—and a pretty little thing it was, too—and that that fact should mean something. Has she forgotten that everything I learned about lovemaking and love I learned from her—and, let's hope, vice versa? Does she not know that everything I learned about a woman I learned from her? She was my first and only love. Can she stand there now in her new black shoes and pink blouse and not remember K-Y Jelly? Has she forgotten the Jell-O? Can she not remember how just before we began to go at it in the car I'd always go take a leak and she would call out from the window, "Be sure and shake it." Has she forgotten we used to call it "the kid?" Has she forgotten it all?

"I've been traveling around," I said. "I've been out on the West Coast and up to Lake Tahoe. Wish I could have made it to Alaska."

"I'm sure you've seen a lot of sights."

"Listen, Sunny," I suddenly blurted out. "What I really wish is that I could have had two lives, one of which would have stayed right here in town with you where I belonged."

She gave me a sympathetic look, one a mother might give a child who has received a bad report card. "Everything has worked out for the best, I think," she said in her new confident voice. "I'm certain of it."

"Yeah, I guess so."

"And I do hope everything turns out well for you."

Who was she talking to, a stranger?

"Aw, I'm doing OK," I said. I did not want pity. It was worse than censure. I was getting angry. "And Sunny, I don't think I'm a bad person."

"Oh, I know you're not." And there came that flash in her eye. "I really never thought so. Even when I was the maddest at you, deep down I was proud of you for sticking to your guns and striking out. No one else in town would ever have had the guts to do that." She suddenly smiled that old Sunny smile. "Hey, I left a woman waiting in the fitting room. I better scoot. Take care!"

She flipped up her hand, as if just saying so long, and made her way toward the fitting room without looking back. I tried to be just as cavalier, turned, took a step, and knocked an old lady off her balance. My lips went dry and I had trouble focusing. For sure I couldn't return to that dress shop. I had my dignity and if I kept popping up I might face a restraining order. She did have a role in a Little Theater production, directed by Kiki Polk, and I got to see her there. I saw her new married name on the playbill and my heart sunk. *That's not her name!* I sat far back in the orchestra. She came out for curtain call and there she was—the legs, the flashing amused eyes, bowing to the audience from the waist. I wouldn't be picking her up later and driving to a cow pasture.

I was back home again. My father spent his time mostly in an overstuffed easy chair, six feet from a huge picture screen, sound blasting. These were his golden years. My mother, more perky, saw to it that that things got done in the house, but she held on tightly to the banister going up and down the creaking stairs. My father labored up the stairs more slowly and painstakingly. I watched them. Their marriage had undoubtedly had its turbulence, its unresolved conflicts, but somehow had managed to reach a goodnight kiss from my father to my mother every night. Tremors had undoubtedly registered on the seismograph, but nothing major, nothing to cause an earthquake.

* * *

I had returned, a prodigal, no longer a boy. My brother Harold had long since left, was married and a paterfamilias in a nearby town, going gray and stoop-shouldered by the minute. He was no longer the Trickshot I had once known and sought to emulate. In a reversal, he sought out my company, which was flattering at first, but a drag after awhile. Later, much later, his hair would become thin wisps and his weight would drop below one hundred. I would carry him to the bathroom the way my mother used to carry me when I was a child. As he lay on a hospital bed that day in the future he motioned me over. I leaned close. He whispered, "Remember those ducks? Think Doc Powell ate them?" We laughed, what you might call a laugh. He paused, as he had to do, marshalling his thoughts. "June Lunt," he said, and pointed.

I touched his hand.

* * *

Settling down in town was out of the question. I had blown it. I had torn off suit and tie, donned Levi's, and had thrown away any privileges. The Bible calls it "birthright." I had taken off and thrown away my birthright. It was as if I was now in the South Seas, in a Maugham or Conrad story, where a Brit one day decides not to dress for dinner and is banished. I was now Trevor Howard in *Outcasts of the Islands*. I loved that movie.

I had been trained at the university to join the state's hierarchy in one form or another, but I had hit the open road. I had made my choice. But I loved the town, or, more accurately, the memory of it.

Every time I thought of the place I was reminded of George Bernard Shaw—or was it Oscar Wilde?—who said, "The Irish will do anything for their country except live in it." I was now back, but it was no more my old hometown than Sunny was still my girl. Now at night I lay in bed and listened to trucks and cars roar past on the street. Used to be I knew every car that passed by the sound of its motor. Now I had to dial a number on the hall phone, where before an operator would say, in her country accent, "Number, please," back when I called Sunny incessantly. Used to be I knew every policeman in town. Things change. Yet my tires still bounced the way I remembered every time I crossed the railroad tracks.

I circled Sunny's apartment like an Indian. I occasionally peeked in the dress shop. I endured god-awful, interminable Little Theater productions for just the sight of her at curtain call. I could only think of her—little things, like the scar on her wrist, the beauty mark on her cheek, her green eyes. I made up stories in my mind, as I had made up stories in my mind in an earlier guise about how I won a state championship basketball game with a last-second shot from mid-court as the stands erupted. I dreamed of her at night. She's come back! We're together again! Then I would wake up and the stories in my mind would begin. If waking hours were a symphony, Sunny was the leitmotiv. She was always there. Stories became my refuge where I could rearrange things. There became stories within stories. One story had us back together where we laughed over the stories. The reality was, though, that next to loving her was the sickening grief over losing her. I was going crazy. And crazy doesn't listen to reason.

I picked up the phone and dialed her number. I just did. It surprised me that I was doing it. But I had presence of mind enough to keep my finger poised over the cut-off bar. I wasn't that crazy. "Hello," a whiney male voice answered. My finger came down. A night or two later I tried again. Same thing.

Our phone rang at night as I sat in exhaustion and reverie, wishing I had some sassafras tea to calm my nerves. "Hello." No one on the other end. I could hear breathing. I was not going to hang up. "Hello, hello, *hello,*" I went. I heard, or thought I heard, a baby gurgling in the background. I said, "Sunny." That was all. The line went dead on the other end. *She still loves me!*

* * *

Gilmore came back from some mysterious stay in San Francisco. He came back not in Levi's but wearing an honest-to-God ascot; his Air Force uniform had long since been put in moth balls. He came back to stay after his father's funeral. G.W., the once-whirlwind Dr. Polk with the surgeon's focused eye and the unquenchable thirst, had gone from one of the most alive men I ever met to wheelchair and then to the grave. Death just blotted him out. Occasionally a colorful story about him would crop up, but in an abbreviated way and lacking the ginger and humor of before. He was dead now, so what were you going to do? Other people took his place—Gilmore for one. Gilmore had inherited a bundle, a real bundle, and what he did with it became the talk of the town.

Gilmore opened an "office" down on Main Street. What he did there was anyone's guess, but you could find him there during the working day if you cared to. The place was piled high with thick tomes, loose manuscripts, a roller deck, and a globe as big as the one in *The Great Dictator*. He confided in me—*but don't tell anyone!*—that he was compiling the definitive study of East Tennessee. "Jackson riding into Jonesborough on horseback. A duel or two. Lincoln passing through. The brief, highly overlooked State of Franklin. And of course James K. Polk, our former president. It'll be bigger than *Gone with the Wind*."

"That's great," I said, looking out his second-story window at Main Street traffic that had much less bustle than when we were growing up. I was thinking, Yeah, *The Key to All Mythologies*. Go for it.

Gilmore took his place beside me at the window. He held his hands behind his back in a Winston Churchill pose. "I have a surprise for you. You'll never guess. It'll shock you, I'm sure."

"What?" I feared what might come next. Was he going to let the cat out of the bag at last? It would be a relief to not have to skirt the issue.

"I'm getting married."

"You what?"

"Married. I'm financially able now. And I must do it quick before she changes her mind. No church stuff."

"My God. Who?"

"You'll meet her. *Elle est très formidable.* Big in all departments. Strong appetites. And you know what she likes about me?"

"What?"

"She likes my bod."

"Your what?"

"My body. She's crazy about my body. When a woman falls for your body you must surrender. You have no choice. Remember that."

Gilmore got married. He married a woman named Stokely, the widow of a man who, in the prime of his life, had been killed by a speeding motorist while stopping to help someone change a tire. Fate seemed to throw curves at Stokely. She and Gilmore snuck off to Gatlinburg to tie the knot. They returned like regular newlyweds except for a few touches. Stokely towered over Gilmore and she did the hugging and kissing. "This is the sweetest old thang," she said in an exaggerated drawl. She had grown up further south, down in New Orleans.

Gilmore's swagger increased and he took Stokely's embraces and flattery as his due. He told his war stories, although everyone knew he'd never been near a battle, and he sniffed and savored the ceremonial dollop of wine before allowing Stokely's, or anyone else's, glass to be filled. They took a duplex in one of the new fancy developments going up. I was often invited for dinner but made excuses after a few trips. Stokely was fine at the beginning, but if more than a couple of bottles were uncorked, a scene would surely follow. She drank. She had a drinking problem. One evening started off well with Stokely encouraging Gilmore to tell more of his experiences in the 82nd. It got off the tracks after two after-dinner cognacs. Stokely said, words slurred, "You did hand-to-hand in the 82nd, didn't you, sweetheart?"

"No, that was in ranger training at Bragg."

"Show me. Come on. Show me how you take somebody down."

Gilmore laughed it off, but Stokely persisted. I'd had more than one cognac myself—they didn't come along every day—and had trouble following, and not stopping, what happened next. They both stood facing each other, Gilmore saying, "Please, please, Stokely. Cut it out. I don't want to hurt you."

"Come on, sugar. Try. You won't hurt me."

In a flash, as if I were watching a car wreck, Gilmore was flipped over flat on his back and Stokely was astride his chest and pinning his arms to the floor. We had just had *coq au vin!* I had to lift her off. Stokely was laughing her whisky laugh and I was smelling her whisky breath and Gilmore was red in the face and sputtering. Finally, he was laughing, too. "I slipped," he said.

"Sure, sweetheart. Let's try her again."

"No," I said. "Come on, you two."

Whatever they were up to, whatever their marriage, whatever it was, it worked. I was no stranger to the ironic, but here was a real humdinger. Here was my old pal Gilmore who had never dated a female for real, as far as I knew, had never expressed crazed interest in their flesh, here he was bonded in matrimony. Here I was, someone who had always had little cunts running around in his brain, like the TB bacilli that came poring out of Tom Wolfe's brain when they cracked it open, here I was unmarried, alone and miserable. Was marriage, like the priesthood, a refuge from fucking?

* * *

I continued my sly drives by Sunny's apartment. She was a low-grade fever that never went away. Nothing cured it, no matter the antidote. Then it went dark there. Then the shades went up in the day and it looked as if everything had been moved out. She's left town! She's doing what I had done originally! But, no, her husband was still in town. It was Timber Ted, wouldn't you know it, who introduced me to him. I was standing by Leggett's magazine rack where I had first met Sunny and was thinking of that day when Timber Ted waddled over gleefully. He seemed to have gained a hundred pounds. Fast food chains had now hit town.

"Hey, there's someone I want you to meet. It's a shame you two haven't met already. Let me bring him over." He was off before I could stop him and ask who it was, although I knew immediately who it was. "Here, I'd like you two fellows to meet," he said, bringing Sunny's husband over. "You two have something in common."

If called on later, I couldn't have picked him out of a police lineup. I was left with no idea what he looked like or what he said. I went numb. Later I tried to conjure up an image and all I got was someone in wire-rim glasses who had the wide hips of a potential fat man, someone to keep Timber Ted company. He wasn't a matinee idol, I was assured of that, and that freed me from past fantasies of deadly good looks. That was all the meeting had done except to introduce a new thought in my head—*what does she see in him?* I could have asked where he and Sunny now lived, but of course I didn't. I drove round and round town, hoping I'd find out on my own. I would have called Information but feared unreasonably that I would be nailed as a stalker—which I guess I was. Then I forgot about the phone. I was driving by Gilmore's duplex and saw some panties on a wash line that looked mighty familiar. They could hardly belong to Stokely, Gilmore's new bride. Much too small. Could it be? Could wild chance have put Sunny's panties hanging to dry by the duplex of Mr. and Mrs. Gilmore Polk?

* * *

I dropped by their place well before the sun had passed the yardarm, well before Stokely broke out the bottle. Yes, I found out, Sunny and her husband had moved into the duplex next door. They had a new baby. *Yes, yes, I knew, I knew she had a baby, but I kept repressing it. It didn't matter, it didn't matter. Nobody could take away what we had had together!* Sunny and her husband were moving up in the world, up into the solid middle-class and establishment of the town. The news came from Stokely. Gilmore paced around, trying to change the subject. "Oh, she's a great gal," Stokely said. "I liked her right away. One of the funniest gals I've ever met in this town." *My Sunny?* "You know her, do you?"

Gilmore groaned from the corner. "Why don't we have some iced tea?"

"Yes, I know her," I said. "I'd love to see her again."

"Well, doggone it, shoot fire, she might just be home. I'll tell her you're here and would like to see her."

"Don't do that, Stokely," Gilmore said. "It's not right. They used to be—"

"Oh, sugar plum, just this once. What harm is it going to do?"

She sailed out and Gilmore said, "A mistake. This is not good. You've got to forget her and go on. This is crazy."

I wasn't listening. I was picturing her walking in. I was preparing myself to be jolly. To be smiling. To talk about all the wonders I had seen on the road. To be entertaining. I pictured how wonderful she would look in a home setting. I would hold her and hug her and speak into her ear about how much I would always love her. Stokely came back. In her arms she carried a bundle. A baby.

"Sunny can't come. But I got to bring this sweet thing down for you to see. Have you ever in all your life seen such a wonderful little critter?" And she went into baby talk while Gilmore cringed and looked to the ceiling. Sunny wasn't coming. "Here, hold her for a while. Smell her. You'll never smell anything as sweet in all your life."

I took the baby and cradled her. It was then that a guillotine came down and separated my head from my heart. I was going to have to learn how to move on. Here was *finis*. Here I was holding it in my arms. Sunny was gone.

Stokely, of all people, gauged my expression. A woman's intuition? "You're out of here, aren't you?" she said tenderly, reaching to take the baby.

I looked into the baby's eyes. They were Sunny's flashing green. I was moving on. Yes, I nodded, I was out of there. I was really out of there this time.